DAVID ROBERT BASTABLE

WHILE THE CAT'S AWAY

ISBN: 979-8-6795-5454-2

Cover design by Sarra Burton
Contributing Editors: Joel Mark Harris and Candice Neveu

Find out more about this author visit
www.davidbastable.com

For our girls Ella & Monroe

CHAPTER 1

The senior students in the auditorium at Russell High School were the first to hear the gunshots. They were rehearsing for their final performance of Grease, which was to take place later that evening, when the initial shots were fired. Mrs. Hernandez cut the music, and the song *'You're The One That I Want'* came to abrupt stop. The distinct popping of a firearm echoed throughout the hallway, growing increasingly louder, as it approached the auditorium. Before anyone had a chance to digest what was happening out in the hall, Mr. Reed, the school's Science teacher, barged through the auditorium doors, shouting.

"He's got a gun!"

"Quick everyone, get down behind the stage, hurry, hurry!" Mrs. Hernandez said shakily. For an elderly woman, the heavy set, robust drama teacher moved quickly. Her chubby faced, dimpled smile had disappeared, as she and Mr. Reed quietly herded all but two of her students to take cover. They began huddling frantically together behind the stage, settling only seconds before the auditorium door swung open again. The crack of gunfire pierced the air as the gunman entered the room.

The two stranded students, Dennis, the stage manager, and his classmate Eric, had been operating the spotlights in the glass sound booth at the back of the auditorium, before the Science teacher had first burst through the doors. They were not able to reach the rest of their classmates and had taken refuge behind the last rows of chairs located just in front of the sound booth, near the back of the large auditorium. The only thing separating them from the gunman were the thirty rows of metal chairs.

"Fuck, is he in here?" Eric whimpered, trying to peek over the chair in front of him.

"I don't know. Keep your head down," Dennis whispered hastily, while searching down toward the stage through the arms of the chairs.

Only moments earlier the front six row of seats had been bubbling with lively, chattering students, as they enjoyed some of their fellow classmates rehearse on stage, and now the seats were empty, and the room was eerily quiet. Dennis followed the gunman's silhouette as he moved slowly across the front of the stage. The only sound was the clomping of boots, until a startling bang echoed throughout the theatre as the automatic delayed doors slammed shut.

"What was that? Can you see him?" Eric sputtered in a shaky whisper.

"Yeah, sort of," Dennis replied.

"Who is it?"

"I don't know, I can't really see his face." His hands trembled while he continued to spy through the gap in the chairs. "It looks like he's wearing some sort of body armor and combat boots. He's got a few guns on him too. Oh shit ..."

"What?" Eric gasped.

"He's coming up the stairs," he sputtered, while reluctantly keeping watch as the dark figure thumped up the steps in their direction. Around halfway, at about the fifteenth row of chairs, Dennis could not bear to watch any longer and planted his face down to the carpet.

They silently counted the remaining fourteen steps. Upon hearing the shooter's labored breathing, Eric let out a desperate whimper, before quickly covering his mouth. Dennis reached over with one hand and pressed it squarely on top of Eric's quivering fingers, while both bodies braced for the inevitable.

Suddenly a female's shriek echoed throughout the auditorium, which was instantly followed by muffled chaos, as students crawled about behind the stage, attempting to quiet other mouths and restore their safety. The army boots paused at the 29th count. The boys' adrenaline filled bodies, vibrated uncontrollably, as they were certain that their demise was merely seconds away. Everybody sat in complete silence for a few seconds, which felt like hours, until more rustling and muffled sobbing, broke the cover for the students behind the stage.

Dennis, with one hand still gripping Eric's mouth, braced himself with his other hand on the back of the chair, while pressing his sweaty face against the cool metal seat in front of him. He dared to glance down to his right and saw that the heavy leather boots were now pointing in his direction, only a few steps away. He felt a hot rush and was sure a heavy breath had landed on his shoulder. He squeezed his hand tighter on Eric's mouth to muffle his whimpering, while continuing to focus on the boots, as they slowly turned and pointed in the opposite direction.

A warm sensation flooded down, soaking the legs of his jeans. As the familiar odor of urine began to sting his nostrils, Dennis knew that one or maybe both of them had pissed their pants. He continued to keep an eye on the retreating boots while silently praying that the predator had not caught the strong urine scent. To his relief, the boots began to clomp back down the stairs of the auditorium. Seeing the gunman reach the stage, he motioned to Eric with his finger against his own lips with one hand, while releasing the tight grip on this friend's white lips. They sat in silence while watching through the row of chairs as the gunman made his way around the back of the stage.

"Oh no," whispered Dennis, as the man disappeared behind the stage.

A young girl screamed before several repetitive blasts echoed throughout the auditorium. Silence followed as the two boys continued to peer through the slots in the chairs. The shooter reappeared from behind the stage and Eric quickly lowered his head back to the carpet. Dennis watched as the shooter methodically tromped through the auditorium while repeatedly

4

whistling a taunting tune that sounded like "you who", before exiting through the auditorium doors and out into the hallway. The doors slammed shut behind him and the room remained silent for a few moments. The boys shuddered at the thought of the bloody massacre that must be waiting for them behind the stage.

"Quick, someone block the door!" pleaded a familiar struggling voice from behind the stage.

Smoke billowed above the stage as the two boys approached. The pungent odor of gunpowder engulfed them as they maneuvered around the bullet casings scattered across the floor. They gazed in shock and horror at the carnage. Bullet holes punctured blood-spattered walls, as dark red pools oozed across the hardwood floor, joining to form one large bloody puddle below the several motionless bodies that were slumped together.

Dennis helped his struggling drama teacher to her feet, and onto a nearby chair, as Mr. Reed lay motionless, face down in a pool of blood. A few of the students, who had escaped being shot, sat stupefied, staring, as Eric stood frozen, gawking helplessly back at them. The gruesome scene was now filled with various sounds ranging from whimpers to wails. More gun blasts and screams sounded in the distance. Only this time they were single pops of what sounded like a handgun. The shots were sporadic and seemed targeted, rather than the more random rapid firing of the automatic weapon that had been used in the auditorium.

"The door … quickly!" urged Mrs. Hernandez before Dennis scurried over toward the doorway.

"Eric, come give me a hand," Dennis barked, glancing down at the boy's urine-soaked pants.

"Sorry for almost getting us killed," Eric mumbled, while the two boys wrestled with an upright vintage piano, wheeling it against the auditorium doors. Looking down at the yellow stain on his pants he continued, "And sorry about this."

"Don't worry about it," Dennis said. "When I first smelled it, I thought I had done it." They smirked at each other sheepishly, before stepping back to ensure the door was blocked. The boys returned to the stage to discover that their Science teacher had moved.

"Did you guys see who the shooter was?" Mr. Reed asked, as he kneeled, wiping blood from his head with his tie. "Wow, heads can really bleed a lot." He sat bewildered, staring beside him at the pool of his own blood. Relieved that their teacher was still alive, they both shook their heads, assessing his grazed scalp. Mr. Reed looked around to absorb the situation. "My god," he gasped, realizing his surroundings, as tears began to run down his bloody face. Wiping the blood and tears with his sleeve, he turned back to the boys and continued, "Do you think you guys could make it to the sound room? There is another door over there that connects to the machine shop. We need to block that too, so there's no other way in for this fucking maniac!"

Even with the chaos that had just ensued, the boys were taken aback by their respected teacher's slip of the tongue. With slight hesitation, they turned and began running back up the stairs to the sound booth.

"Be careful boys," groaned Mrs. Hernandez as she struggled, dizzily, to keep herself upright in the chair.

The boys quickly reached the doors to the sound room. It had been a couple minutes since they had last heard any gunshots, so the shooter's location was unknown. Eric reluctantly followed his friend through the glass door. Their hearts raced as they made their way over to the heavy metal door that connected to the machine shop. Making sure it was closed, they sat together with their backs pressed up against it, while taking a minute to catch their breath.

"This is fucking crazy," Eric said, while gasping for air.

"I know. I don't know why anyone would do something like this," Dennis replied, reaching for the doorknob.

"Dennis, wait!" Eric said while grabbing his friend's arm. "What if he's in there? Let's just block the door with something."

"The machine shop has some stuff we could use to protect ourselves in case this bastard comes back," Dennis argued.

"But if we just block the door, he can't get in. Let's just do what Mr. Reed told us to do."

"What if the police take too long to get here? If he gets in here, we're all sitting ducks. Let's grab some tools from in there, just in case this fucking prick comes back."

"Ok fine, let's go," Eric conceded.

Opening the door just wide enough to squeeze through, they entered the room. Even though the door was connected to the sound room, neither of them, like most of the other drama students, had ever been in the reputed machine shop which they called the 'hood'. Typically, only the students who had taken shops as an elective, who usually had mullets and looked tough in their black leather, hung out in the shop, while intimidating the more academic students. The unfamiliar room was dark, appeared to have no windows, and they were not even sure what they were supposed to be looking for.

Turning on the lights was too risky, so they just crept through, relying on the dim red glow from up high in one corner to guide them. As Dennis noisily knocked over some tools, the boys froze momentarily, then proceeded further toward the red glow.

"Hey look, an emergency exit! It must lead outside. Let's get the hell out of here!" Eric pleaded.

"And what about the others? We can't just leave them. Let's just grab some shit and then block the door. Once we've done that, we can go help everyone and then decide what to do next. The cops should be here any second, I'm sure."

"Ok, sounds like a plan," Eric complied.

Moments later the boys arrived back through the doorway to the sound room, where they sat and surveyed the inventory of items that they had collected.

"What are you going to do with that? Tie him up?" Dennis scoffed, pointing to the coiled rope Eric had retrieved.

"I don't know, I just grabbed what I could. Maybe I'll lasso the fucker!" Eric boasted as his cheeks reddened. He jumped to his feet and headed bravely back into the dark room.

"Where are you going?"

"I'm going to grab an axe I saw in there. My hands were too full to grab it and it might come in handy," Eric replied.

"Too risky! Come on! Let's just go back."

"I'll just be two seconds," he responded before turning and disappearing into the darkness, leaving Dennis alone outside the door.

After nervously taking a seat with his back against the door, Dennis perused the cache they had collected. The inventory included two hammers, a hacksaw, a three-foot ruler, a staple gun, and the rope.

"What are we going to do with a staple gun?" Dennis muttered.

Waiting anxiously, he realized it had been quite some time since he had last heard any gunshots and wondered if the police had possibly arrived. Maybe they had shown up and already taken down the assailant. With any luck, the shooter had killed himself and the nightmare was soon to be over. As he continued to think of other possible scenarios, a bright light shone in from underneath the door. Dennis hopped to his feet, pulled open the door to what he expected to be police, and was instantly blinded, forcing him to shield his eyes from a burst of brilliant light that exposed the once darkened room.

"No don't! Please, don't do it!" Eric screamed.

Seconds later, deafening blasts of gunfire echoed through the machine shop.

CHAPTER 2

The piercing wail of the telephone's ring was not far off that of a speeding ambulance's siren. Alec Jenkins thought for a moment that he'd had a heart attack and was on route to a hospital, when he was so abruptly woken. It wouldn't have surprised him as the fifty-year-old was a prime candidate for a cerebrovascular accident. He had been smoking a pack a day since he could remember and his stressful career also factored in, as it involved regularly making million-dollar decisions for his clients. Although taking on the presidency at Woodward Financial loaded extra stress, he was compensated very well; his nearly half million-dollar income made him the highest earning employee in the history of the company.

He had fallen asleep with the television blaring once again. With his eyes still half closed, he reached to answer the call, while his other hand systematically grabbed the remote from beside him on the bed and turned down the volume. On this early Monday morning the CNN panel was already overly animated as they discussed President Trump's tweets from the previous evening. After nearly muting the volume, he glanced at the tweets.

"How is this idiot our fucking President?" he muttered, picking up the telephone. "Hello?"

"Good morning Mr. Jenkins. This is your 6 a.m. wakeup call!" Alec pushed the receiver away from his ear as the woman's boisterous voice was too much for his pounding headache.

"It's six already?" he grumbled.

"It's actually twenty past six. Sorry for the tardiness, but it was a little hectic down here this morning." She paused and then quietly continued, "I'll make it up to you later if you're up for it." He cringed, and after he had not responded, she continued. "We have a car waiting out front to take you to the airport, whenever you're ready. Have a good trip Alec, I'll see you when you get back!"

Even though the tall blonde was less than half his age, Tanya had developed a serious crush on him. A few days earlier, he had nearly drowned himself at his regular watering hole after having yet another rough day at the office. Afterwards, as he stumbled through the front doors of his building, Tanya helped him get up to his apartment door. The next thing he remembered was waking up to find her lying beside him. Although she was very attractive, he was embarrassed and did not want the others in the building to find out. It was unprofessional and something he never would have done sober, but like many times before, the bottle had skewed his judgement. Ever since that regretful evening, he had tried to avoid her as much as possible.

With one hand hanging up the receiver, the other frantically scrambled to open a fresh pack of cigarettes. As he inhaled the toxins, he groaned at the thought of yet another trip. With his lit cigarette hanging from his bottom lip, he reached for the half-empty bottle of whiskey, twisted off its lid, and took a few large swigs.

After a bizarre telephone conversation with his sister a few days earlier, he had decided that he would visit her in their hometown for his so-called vacation. Although Russell, Manitoba was at the bottom of his list of places to go during his time off, he had not been able to get that conversation out of his head, and so the decision was made. He was anxious to see his sister to find out what the hell was going on. The siblings had drifted apart over the years, only keeping in touch with the occasional telephone call. They had not seen each other in over twenty-five years since their parents' untimely funeral.

Alec rubbed his eyes while selecting items from the large collection of expensive suits hanging in his closet. With respect to Armani et al, he butted his cigarette into the overfilled ashtray on the nightstand. Numerous burn holes dotted the carpet beside the nightstand, as he had a habit of falling asleep with a lit cigarette still in his hand. Dirty dishes filled the kitchen sink and overflowed onto the countertops. Although he had hired a cleaning lady soon after moving into the condo, lately, he had been cancelling her services. He was too embarrassed to let her see how filthy he had let it become and figured it would not be fair to have anyone clean up his mess, even if it was her job.

Alec forced himself up and made his way over to the shower, while stepping over several empty bottles of the Jack Daniels strewn on the floor throughout the apartment. His greasy slicked back salt and pepper hair was in much need of a wash and cut. His once bright blue eyes, which his old hockey buddies once referred to as 'chick magnets', now floated within a jaundice-yellow film. Heavy dark bags drooped below, as deep crow's feet stretched across from each corner to his slightly uneven sideburns. The tight muscular arms and buff chest, he had once boasted, were now soft and saggy. It was not quite a dad bod, as he had no children, at least none of which he was aware. The man who once worked out at least two hours daily, had lost all desire. He had replaced his time at the gym with the bottle, and it showed.

After drying off, he kicked a pile of dirty clothes into the closet, and then got dressed. As per his routine he had put on a suit, and for a moment pondered changing into jeans and a t-shirt. It seemed more appropriate for the occasion, but reeked of effort, so he resolved to removing his tie and undoing the top button of his shirt.

Stepping out of the apartment, he felt like a new man with his freshly shaven face and slicked back hair now tucked behind his ears. Although his life was on a downward spiral, Alec managed to keep up with his professional appearance, when necessary. While exiting the elevator, he noticed Tanya at the desk, engaged in a conversation. Looking down to avoid any potential eye contact, he quickly slipped out the front door, unscathed. The limousine driver watched as Alec approached the vehicle.

"Off to Canada eh, Mr. Jenkins?"

"You got it."

Clive had become used to Alec's wafting whiskey cologne, but this morning's boozy draft was more potent than usual. In his first month working for Woodward Financial, the large overweight driver had made a good impression within the company. His outgoing personality and friendly demeanor made him instantly popular with upper management. If his passengers were not chuckling at his cheesy jokes, they were surely enjoying the driver's self-deprecating humor. Clive had a real knack for using his obesity to entertain people.

A sober Alec enjoyed the jovial man's company, but as per usual of late, Alec was too hungover and irritable to want to converse with Clive. He mistakenly locked eyes with his driver, briefly, in the rearview mirror, before averting his eyes downward and grabbing for the bottle of water that was conveniently situated in the cup holder beside him.

15

"Did you hear how they came up with the name for their country up there, Mr. Jenkins?" Clive asked, trying to disguise his upcoming attempt of a joke. After receiving no acknowledgement, he continued anyway, "They had all the Indian Chiefs from each tribe get together and they drew letters out of a hat. One chief pulled them out, one at a time. He pulled out the letter c and said, 'c eh'. Then he pulled out the letter n and said, 'n eh'. Then he pulled out …" but before he could finish, Alec interjected.

"I get it Clive, very funny." He glared out the window while gulping down half the bottle of warm water. "Ugh, warm again?" He muttered angrily while slamming the bottle back into its holder.

"My apologies sir, I'll be sure to stock some ice next time."

"Thanks," Alec replied while feeling like a pompous jerk.

"Sorry Clive, I've just got a pounding headache this morning and didn't mean to take it out on you."

"No worries sir," Clive replied, while smiling back at him through the rearview mirror.

Clive had been a driver for the firm long before Alec had started. At first, he typically just drove around most of the company's top executives, but soon after Alec was promoted to President, he was chosen to be Alec's personal driver. Mostly Alec chose Clive because he was the most punctual and attentive

16

of all the drivers, but he also genuinely liked the man and normally enjoyed his company.

Over the years, he witnessed his obese driver consume several Big Macs, and envisioned the man's heart exploding while being behind the wheel, catastrophically sending them both into oncoming traffic. Alec watched through the rearview mirror as the buttons of the man's dress shirt held on for dear life, and he wondered, cynically, if today would be the day. The odds were higher than most, as Clive was well into his eighties, and surely his cholesterol must have been through the roof. Alec was saddened thinking Clive's days were surely numbered, before coming to the realization that his own days may be running short as well. He had now entered his fifties and with all damage he had done to his body with the stress, booze, and cigarettes undoubtably shortened his lifespan.

As the limo rolled towards the airport, Alec wondered if he was making a mistake heading to his hometown. As the distance increased between himself and his condo, so too did his anxiety. He thought of another time he had felt this way; it was shortly after his high school graduation, while being on a bus to the Winnipeg airport, where he would catch a flight to Vancouver, to live with his Uncle Perry.

His uncle was a very successful businessman and idol to Alec, and he would live with his uncle while attending university. Alec had known for years that the small lumber town he had grown up in was not a place for him. If he were to become a successful businessman, he would need to get out of that town, so when his uncle offered him a place to stay, he did not hesitate.

As Clive pulled into the airport departures lane, Alec wiped his sweaty palms along the tops of his pants before taking another swig of the warm water. The anxiety of the upcoming trip had made his mouth dry and hands clammy. Clive stopped at the curb before opening Alec's door.

"Here you are sir. Have a good trip."

"Thanks Clive," Alec replied before turning and making his way to the entrance to the San Francisco International Airport.

Upon reaching the Delta Airlines check-in desk, he was swiftly greeted by one of their employees.

"Where to sir?" the woman asked without moving her eyes from the computer screen in front of her.

"Winnipeg, Canada" Alec replied, handing over his ticket.

"Sorry to hear that," she said with a chuckle, before glancing up at him.

"Yeah me too," he replied, smiling back, as she passed back his ticket.

After having to endure a long line at security, Alec was finally able to board the plane, where he took his window seat and rested his head upon the back of his chair. To his immediate left, a mother barked at her young son and daughter who were fighting over an iPad. They continued to reach and flail across the aisle to each other, while their father wanted nothing to do with disciplining them, as he continued to read a magazine, leaving his wife trying to manage the situation. They were clearly going to be an annoyance to Alec and everyone else on the flight. Alec eyed the father, and wondered what the man, wearing a beautiful three-piece suit, who could afford four tickets in first class, did for a living. If he were to hazard a guess, Alec assumed he was either a physician or a dentist, and his wife, with her frazzled appearance and behavior, was surely a stay at home mother who was emotionally hanging on by a thread. As he watched the woman continue to struggle with her menacing children, he felt badly for her, while at the same time feeling a personal sense of relief for choosing a successful career over having a family.

Although there was no way his parents would have ever flown their whole family anywhere, due to his mother's fear of flying, Alec could not help thinking of how his parents would have handled this drama. He recalled a similar experience where he and Chelsea had briefly argued at the movie theatre, and his mother had threatened to get up and leave. Like the man in the three-piece suit, Mr. Jenkins had not taken his eyes off the movie screen and left the 'woman's work' to Mrs. Jenkins to handle bratty children. Alec had accepted the dated excuse that it's just how things were back then, but it wouldn't fly now, not these days. Both the mother and father were supposed to be hands on with their kids, yet this man in the three-piece suit sat in his own world and did nothing.

Alec watched the two young men out the window as they struggled loading the luggage into the underbelly of the plane and wondered what he and his sister had been arguing about that day. His thoughts then shifted to the recent, strange conversation, which had led him to this trip.

"Alec, you work too hard and the time off will probably do you some good. Why don't you come home for a visit?" Chelsea asked.

"To Russell?"

"Yes, why not? You haven't been back since Mom and Dad's funeral."

"For good reason," he muttered.

"Oh yeah, that's right, you're too good for this town. I think you should come here for your vacation. Maybe a visit with your big sister is just what you need. You can stay at my place!"

"Maybe. But, if I do, I'm not going to stay at your place. I'll just book a hotel; I don't want to impose on you and the kids."

"Kids?"

"Yeah, your kids."

"Kids? What kids?"

"What are you talking about? Your kids, Jason and Kendra. Also, I'm sure Ron wouldn't want me hanging around the house either."

"Jason and Kendra? What in god's name are you talking about? You know I don't have any children. And who the hell is Ron?"

"Chelsea, you're freaking me out. I am talking about your children. The ones I've spoken with on the phone several times. The ones you can't stop talking about."

"Alec, you're scaring me. Please come home."

After that conversation, Alec had decided he had better go see his sister, as she had clearly suffered some sort of mental breakdown. He had booked a one-way ticket, as he wasn't sure how long he'd be staying, but he hoped to also go somewhere else during his vacation time. He had never been to Fiji, which may be too hot in summer, but figured if he still had time, he would book that trip after sorting out what was happening to his sister. As the runway disappeared, he began thinking of Russell, Manitoba, a place where he had spent the first eighteen years of his life, but oddly, for some strange reason, had very few memories.

CHAPTER 3

Watching from the tiny window of the Boeing 737, as the plane made its final descent toward the patchwork quilt of landscape below, Alec remembered the endless, colorful squares of farmland crops. He missed the ocean already as he followed the narrow, winding blue trail of the river's oxbows. He had forgotten the monotonous flatness of the prairie's terrain and grown accustomed to navigating his way through the undulating streets of San Francisco for the past twenty-five years. He wondered if his dislike for his hometown would be as predominant as it had been when he was a younger, restless man.

He had not thought much about the town of Russell since he had moved to San Francisco. After a short apprenticeship with Woodward Financial he was offered a full-time position with the company. Alec was a good fit for Woodward Financial, as most of their employees were young, ambitious, and driven to succeed. He liked the hard work and excessive work hours that the competitive company expected of him. He especially liked working for Mr. Rhodes, who was the President of Woodward Financial when Alec had first started working there.

Harold Rhodes was seen by most as a successful, crotchety, old man whose main two loves in life were his career and his golden retrievers. The old man thrived on burning the midnight oil, often sleeping in his office overnight, making a quick dash home in the morning to walk the dogs. His employees would often joke, around the office water cooler, about who would take over walking the retrievers after the old guy's stress induced, massive heart attack. Alec, on the other hand, remained respectful, and always admired his boss for his dogged determination, and superior work ethic. This did not go unnoticed by Harold, and the feeling was reciprocated. It was well understood, early in Alec's career at Woodward, that he was next in line for the title of President. In staff meetings, Mr. Rhodes would often speak highly of Alec and his achievements. He had coined the phrase 'What would AJ do?', much to the envy and annoyance of co-workers.

The jealousy he received being Rhodes' protege did not bother Alec one bit. In fact, he thoroughly enjoyed it because he was not there to make friends; he was there as a competitor, to make his way to the top. It was a common sight at the company parties, while others were drinking and frolicking about, to see Alec and Harold in a back corner, discussing company strategies. Harold Rhodes was indeed a workaholic, and his employees' predictions were correct, as he died after a massive heart attack, during the first week of his retirement. Alec could not shed a tear at his own parents' funeral, however at Harold's, he sobbed like a baby.

Unlike most of Alec's previous business flights, this one was surprisingly enjoyable. The fighting siblings calmed down a few minutes after takeoff, allowing him to enjoy one of the in-flight movies, starring one of his favorite actors, Denzel Washington. He had always been a huge fan of Denzel's, but it had been years since he had seen one of his movies. As the airplane began its final descent, he vowed to watch more movies in the future.

With Winnipeg being a little over three hours from Russell, Alec's secretary, Ellen, had lined up a car service for him a few days prior. Usually Alec would choose a Cadillac or some other overpriced rental, but with the town of Russell being so small he figured he would just walk everywhere, so the car service made more sense. Chelsea had offered to pick him up, but he declined, as that would have entailed a three-hour debate as to why he was not staying at her place. He would spend time with her, as he was worried about her current state of mind, but not too much time.

The airport was much larger and newer than he had anticipated. As he made his way through the terminal, he was more impressed with each new section he passed. As Winnipeg is one of Canada's main hubs, the government had recently injected a twenty-seven million-dollar renovation into its airport,

24

and it was now more than three times the size, since the last time he had been through.

Searching for the car service desk, he pulled out his cell phone and switched off airplane mode, when he suddenly collided with a very tall man, knocking Alec to the floor.

"Oh geez, I'm so sorry sir," the man apologized, while helping Alec to his feet. The sun piercing through the massive skylight, reflected off the balding man's head, momentarily whiting out his entire face.

"Not your fault. I wasn't watching where I was going," Alec replied, squinting, trying to get a better look at him.

"Oh no, is this your phone?" asked the man, picking up Alec's broken cell phone and handing it to him.

"Oh shit," Alec replied, while examining its shattered screen. "Yeah, looks like it's completely toast; can't even turn it on now."

"That sucks. Hey wait a minute … Alec? Alec Jenkins?"

He had not even left the airport and he had already had his first encounter with someone from his past. It had been so long he had forgotten how common it was to run into people you knew within the confines of the K-shaped Manitoba border. The normal six degrees of separation was more like two degrees here, he surmised. One of the things he first appreciated upon moving to a larger city, like Vancouver, was the privacy and anonymity provided within a much larger, less friendly population.

"Uh, yes that's me. I'm sorry, do I know you?" he asked looking up at the taller man, while still attempting to turn on his cell phone.

"It's me Tim … Tim Byrd." Alec stared blankly at the man's large hawkish nose and bulging Adam's apple, as it forged up and down while he spoke. "Don't you remember me? We went to high school together."

"Byrd? I'm sorry, but I can't say I do."

"We were in the same drama class in high school. Remember those crazy musicals with Mrs. Hernandez?"

"Oh, that's right! Wow, it has been a long time. What's it been, over thirty years?"

"Yes, I think so. What are you doing in town?"

Alec still had no recollection of this man but was astounded at how Tim could remember who he was after all the years. Not only astounded, but annoyed that he was going to have a discussion with some guy about things that he would not recall that had happened over thirty years ago. One of his biggest pet peeves was small talk, especially small talk with people he did not know, or care to know. His Uncle Perry had explained several times the importance of remembering faces and names, because not remembering showed a lack of interest and incompetence, which was not good in the business world.

"Just here for a quick visit with my sister," Alec replied. After finally conceding that his cell was completely useless, he dropped it into his shirt pocket then studied the man's face, hoping to jog his memory. "How's your family doing?"

"They're doing well, thanks for asking. My youngest is about to graduate from high school. Crazy how fast time flies as we get older, isn't it?" Alec nodded while continuing to search for the sign for the car service desk. "Sorry, but did you say you were here to visit your sister?"

"Yeah, it's been quite a long time since we've seen each other," Alec replied.

"Oh, I thought she uh .... well," Tim sputtered appearing somewhat confused.

"Thought what?" Alec questioned, now giving the man his undivided attention.

Tim looked at his watch, completely ignoring the question. "Listen Alec, it was nice to run into you, literally, but I've got to run, otherwise I'm going to be late for my flight," he said before turning and scurrying off in the opposite direction.

"Wait! What were you going to say about Chelsea?" Alec shouted, to no avail, as his old classmate vanished around the corner.

Alec looked around until he noticed a sign that read GROUND TRANSPORTATION, so he headed towards the desk below. Upon his arrival, he was greeted by a man in a suit and tie, standing behind the desk.

"Hello sir. How can I help you today?"

27

"I believe my secretary made a reservation for me."

"Your name?"

"Alec Jenkins."

"Let me take a look, Mr. Jenkins," the man said before hitting some buttons on his keyboard. After a few clicks on the mouse he continued, "Jenkins ... hmm, where are you hiding Mr. Jenkins?" His eyes continued to search the computer screen in front of him while Alec waited patiently. "Ah yes, there it is," he said before looking up at his customer. "Ok, I'll just need your signature on a couple forms and then my man Denzel will drive you."

"Denzel?"

The man took his hands off the keyboard and laid them out, Vanna White style, and presented the tall black man, who was suddenly standing beside him. Denzel's resemblance to Denzel Washington was uncanny, but just as he was about to mention it, he thought of the reporter who was once mocked for mistaking Samuel L. Jackson for Laurence Fishburne, so Alec decided he'd better not risk embarrassment.

As he and Denzel made their way into the airport's parking lot, Alec could not help but notice that the driver also walked liked the famous actor. Denzel Washington had a very distinct swagger, as did this double. People must have told him several times how he resembled the great actor, but after hopping into the backseat of the car, Alec decided he would stay with his decision to not bring it up.

As Denzel's eyes checked on him in the rearview mirror, he thought back to the odd conversation he had just had with his old classmate. He wondered what Tim was eluding to, regarding his sister, and he would spend most of the ride contemplating the possibilities.

His driver clearly did not attempt to smell like the great Denzel Washington, and it was not long before the car was filled with his bad body odor and cheap cologne. Although Alec did not know the actor Denzel, he assumed the man had a wonderful aroma. Surely a man of such class and prestige, would practice good hygiene, and could afford a good cologne. Although the resemblance was uncanny, the odor most certainly was not. Smelly Denzel, looking in the mirror, had caught his passenger watching him, and for the first time Alec heard him speak.

"Where to sir?" Smelly Denzel also did not sound anything like the famous Denzel.

"Russell please," he gasped, before lowering his window for some much-needed fresh air.

"Yes sir," retorted Denzel, with a scowl, before muttering something inaudible. After exchanging a brief glance in the mirror, as Alec leaned toward the open window, he realized the driver was offended. As the car pulled away from the airport he continued, "You know Russell is over three hours away eh?"

"Yes, I know," Alec chortled, as he was reminded of Clive's joke with the 'eh' reference. They exchanged another look in the mirror.

"You're going to need to close that window once we get on the highway … or you'll be eatin' lotsa bugs out here," the driver smirked.

"That's fine," he sighed. "Please stop at the cemetery on the way into town first. It'll be the one just off the main street, just before Russell."

Alec had not been to his parents' burial site since the day of their funeral. He was not looking forward to the visit, but figured they would be going right past, so he felt obliged. He peered out the car window at the flat horizon as they sped along the highway, trying to recall any memories of Tim Byrd. Although he had no recollection of the man, he did remember his high school drama teacher.

The aging, jolly teacher, who had a real passion for teaching, had left a lasting impression on almost all her students. The lady had no control of her overworked sweat glands, and her clothes were always damp, clinging to her roundish form. Alec never anticipated liking her class, but Mrs. Hernandez's dimpled smile and twinkly enthusiasm was contagious, and she had a real knack for getting her students to buy into the program. It certainly helped that the woman was funny as hell. She would scuttle around the auditorium, dabbing her forehead with a handkerchief she'd kept tucked away in her support bra, gleefully shouting inspirational quotes to her "future academy award winners", determined to keep them motivated.

Mrs. Hernandez was not like any of his other high school teachers. She was compassionate and generally concerned for the wellbeing of her students, and by the end of the twelfth grade, she had become more of a friend than a teacher to Alec. When his troubles at home started, he confided in his teacher, as she always took the time to listen to his problems and offer good advice when needed. With his head pressed between the back of his seat and the car's window, he drifted off to sleep thinking of dear old Mrs. Hernandez.

He was abruptly awoken as his head bounced off the vehicle's closed window. Denzel's feeble attempt to avoid the large potholes at the cemetery entrance failed miserably, and they both bounced around the car's interior like propelled pin balls.

"Just up here on the right," Alec barked, massaging the side of his head. As the car pulled to a stop and he reached for the door handle, and noticed his palms were sweaty again. "I won't be long," he said, before closing the car door.

He was startled to see a young couple sitting at, what appeared to be, his parents' gravesite. Along with their gravestones, Chelsea had insisted on adding an expensive granite bench, upon which the young couple was perched. He had not noticed them while pulling up, so their sudden appearance was startling. As he approached, he wondered why two people he didn't know, would be sitting at his parents' gravesite. The snapping twigs beneath Alec's feet seemed to scare them off, as they quickly got to their feet and retreated in the opposite direction.

"Excuse me! Excuse me! Hey, where are you guys going?" Alec shouted while running after them. The man began to run, pulling the woman reluctantly behind him. Alec's legs felt like concrete, as he had trouble keeping pace. Within seconds, the couple seemed to vanish right before his eyes. With his hands down on his knees, he took a moment to catch his breath, before returning to his parents' graves. Flopping onto the bench, he looked around to see if he would find the couple, but they were nowhere in sight.

A sense of nostalgia came over him as he thought back to his parents' funeral, before realizing that it was at this very spot where he had last been with his sister. He was holding her in his arms while she sobbed, lamenting that it was not fair for them to die. Their tragic bus accident was hard for many, but especially devastating for Chelsea. Before their deaths, she had conversed with them daily, and visited with them on a regular basis. Their parents had always been afraid to fly so they would take the bus or train whenever possible. Alec thought it was a perfect excuse for them not to visit him while he was attending university, as the trip by bus was a taxing forty hours.

He remembered that moment vividly. While holding his sister, he had stared at their parents' headstone, which read:

SUSAN JENKINS & GERALD JENKINS
BELOVED MOTHER & FATHER TO
CHELSEA & ALEC JENKINS
THERE ARE NO BUSSES IN HEAVEN

He thought it was a ridiculous epitaph and had fought with Chelsea when she initially told him of her plans to write the cause of death on their headstone, but as usual she had got her way. He also remembered being annoyed that she had put her name in front of his, but this was not a surprise. While his sister suffered in anguish that day, he had been mostly angry. He was mostly angry that his parents had allowed their relationship to sour. He was also angry that Chelsea contributed to the souring relationship, by being the perfect child, at least, he thought, in their parents' eyes.

He suddenly craved a cigarette and a stiff whiskey. Rising to his feet, a hot rush and heavy wave of nausea came over him, and he suddenly felt lightheaded. Fearing that he may faint, he reached for the back of the bench to brace himself, then sat right back down. He kept his face in his hands until the nausea began to drift away. Feeling the blood rush back to his head, he slowly got back to his feet. While wiping his mouth with his sleeve, he noticed the fresh lilies sitting on top of the headstone and wondered if the couple he had just seen there, had left them. He glanced down at the gravestone again and utter confusion smacked his mind like a ton of bricks. He stared, in complete disbelief, while once again reading his parents' headstone.

SUSAN JENKINS & GERALD JENKINS
BELOVED MOTHER & FATHER TO
CHELSEA & ALEC JENKINS
FLYING TOGETHER IN HEAVEN

Flying together in heaven? He wondered why their headstone would have been changed. Surely his sister had orchestrated the change, but it did not make any sense as to why. As he stumbled back to the car, he wondered why Chelsea had never mentioned the change. His sister would have a lot of explaining to do.

After a few minutes' drive from the cemetery, they entered the town of Russell. Alec groaned while passing an old rusted sign which read, *Welcome to Russell! We're all down to Earth but if gravity goes, we all go!* Even as a young boy he had always hated that sign. He thought it was cheesy and although it was now badly weathered, he was amazed that it was still standing after all these years. As they rolled past the sign, he looked back at it and noticed someone had spray painted in large black letters *NEVER FORGET* with the number 620 circled underneath.

"Where are you staying sir?" Denzel asked, looking into his rearview mirror.

"The Marby Hotel. Do you know where that is?"

"The Marby? Oh yes," he chuckled.

As Denzel maneuvered the car through the pothole-filled parking lot of the Marby Hotel, it was just after three o'clock in the afternoon. Alec shoved the car door open before it had come to a complete stop, as he could not wait to get out. The stifling body odor was now taking a hold of him and permeating his belongings. He feared that one more minute in that car would require a lot of bleach, and potentially having to burn all the clothes he was wearing.

The Marby Hotel had been there since he could remember, long before his parents had moved to the town. It was a real dive, even back when he was a child, and appeared to be in even worse shape now, with exception of the brand-new sign. It had always been, and still was the only hotel in town, so visitors had no other option. Back in junior high school days, he and his classmates would often skip class to play in the hotel's lounge as it had arcades and pool tables. Because the lounge was licensed, it was restricted to anyone under the age of eighteen, but nobody from the establishment had ever enforced the rules, so Alec and his friends loved going there.

After making his way through the lobby and past a woman asleep at a slot machine and two drunk men arguing over who was going to take her home, Alec approached the front desk. Upon hitting the call bell beside the sign that read 'hit me hard if you want service', he was promptly greeted by the front desk clerk.

"Can I help you?"

"Yes, I'm checking in."

"And what name would it be under?"

"Jenkins."

"Hmm, I don't see …" he said as his brow furrowed, while he navigated the mouse, struggling to find the reservation.

"My secretary would have booked it a few days ago," Alec grunted.

"Ah yes, here it is. Sometimes you just need to be a little patient," he muttered while still focusing on the computer screen.

"I'd prefer a room that offers the most privacy," Alec said while looking back at the riffraff behind him.

"Guys! Knock it off!" shouted the young desk clerk at the two men who had begun shoving one another. "Take it outside," he barked, while rolling his eyes, before diverting his attention back to Alec. "Sorry about that; these guys just get so wound up when they see a prize woman like Anita drunk and vulnerable. You know one time ..."

"I just need the room please," Alec interrupted.

"Alrighty then," the man replied. "Ok, let me see here," he said, while turning to look at the keys on the wall behind him. "Ah yes, you're in luck. Our penthouse suite is available, although I must let you know there is a prime rate for this room of a whopping fifty-five dollars per night."

"Yes, that's fine," Alec replied, growing more impatient.

"I'm sorry sir, but have I done something to annoy you?"

"No, not at all," Alec sputtered, realizing he had been rude to a young guy he had just met, who was simply trying to do his job. "Sorry Edgar," he said while focusing on the man's badge, "I've just had a long day."

"No problem at all, I get it," he replied with a grin. "Just a couple more things and we'll get you on your way Mr. Jenkins.

How long will you be staying us?" The clerk's professionalism and politeness only increased Alec's level of embarrassment.

"I guess that'll depend on how long Anita will be staying," Alec smirked, trying to lighten the mood. The two shared a smile before Alec continued, "Probably just a couple of days."

"Ok, I'll just need a credit card for the incidentals." After taking down the credit card information, he passed the card back to Alec along with a key to his room. "Oh, I almost forgot to mention, the central air for the hotel has been on the fritz lately. We are working on it. Let me know if you need anything while you're here."

"Thanks Edgar, I appreciate it. Actually, can you tell me where the closest liquor store is?"

"Right across the street," he said, pointing at the small building adjacent to the hotel.

"Oh perfect. Mind if I leave my luggage here for a few minutes?"

"No, not at all. I can actually have someone take it up to your room if you'd like."

"That'd be great. Again, my apologies for being an ass earlier," Alec said, before turning to make his way out the door.

After returning from the liquor store, he gave Edgar a saluting nod while holding his purchase up in the air. They exchanged a smile before Alec entered the elevator and pushed the number six, then watched as the doors creaked to a close. For a few moments he thought he was stuck, as nothing happened, but then with a boom and a rattle, the elevator begrudgingly began to make its way to the top floor, screeching along the way. After jerking to an abrupt stop, the doors opened to present a dated fuzzy runway of dirty orange carpet, which aligned the hallway, complementing walls of peeling, faded wallpaper, and scuffed, shit coloured doors. The pungent stench of urine mixed with burnt popcorn assaulted his nostrils, as he proceeded down the hallway. "Just wonderful," he muttered aloud.

While squeezing the paper bag containing the prized bottle of Jack Daniels in one armpit, he opened the door to room 620. Surprisingly, the room was large and clean. Even though the furniture was old and tired, it had a newer looking, mid-sized, flat screen television. For fifty-five dollars the Marby Hotel offered a surprisingly decent room, as well as a pool hall and a part-time strip club on the main floor. A hotel like this in a big city like San Francisco would cost at least two hundred dollars.

After unzipping his luggage, he unpacked, then stretched out on the large, firm bed. It was just past noon, and he could already hear the music thumping from the strip club below. The bass from Def Leppard's *Pour Some Sugar on Me* bellowed through the ventilation all the way up from the six floors below. He lay motionless, fixing his gaze at a yellow stain on the ceiling above and smirked, picturing what was surely a woman covered in tattoos, with thick black mascara and a backcombed mullet, working hard on the dance floor.

He thought about Chelsea and wondered why she would have changed their parents' headstone, but no reasonable explanation came to mind. He remembered being shocked upon hearing that his parents were going to come out to see him as they had never visited him during his four years of living in Vancouver. It was not until his uncle called to let them know that Alec was about to graduate at the top of his class, that they would plan to visit. His relationship with his parents had soured, but upon hearing the news of their intended visit, Alec had felt a glimmer of hope that they would be able to reconcile. Hearing the shocking news of their tragic deaths from his Uncle Perry that early morning, would prove to be most unsettling.

The bus had been hit by an avalanche and was pushed over the side of a mountain in the middle of the night, just past the town of Jasper, Alberta. Memories of that morning haunted him for years. The whiskey had helped dull the pain over the years, but as he lay on the hotel bed, the pain and anguish overcame him. He sat up, picked up the receiver, and dialed his sister's number. As it rang, he eyed the bottle of whiskey.

"Hello?"

"Hey Chelsea, it's me." The bottle he had just purchased was out of reach, but he remembered his bag on the nightstand contained his flask that still held a few ounces. He reached over and opened the bag, digging until he found the flask, then screwed off its lid and took a swig.

"Hi Alec! How are you?"

"Just a bit tired from the flight, but besides that, I'm fine. How are you doing?"

"I'm … ok. You just get in?"

"Yes, I actually just checked into the hotel a few minutes ago."

"Why are you staying in that dump when I've got plenty of room here?"

"It's fine Chelsea. I told you I did not want to put you out. You've got a full house over there with those kids."

"Kids?"

"Yes, Jason and Kendra," he replied, frustrated. "Also, I'm sure Ron wouldn't want me hanging around the house either."

"Again, with the children talk? You know I don't have any children. And who the hell is Ron?"

A chill ran up the back of his neck as his concern for his sister's welfare grew more intense. Neither alcohol nor drugs could have been the issue as his sister never touched the stuff. Even with a headache, she would always refuse to take a

Tylenol. He had heard of early onset dementia and wondered if perhaps that may be happening with her.

"Chelsea, I have pictures of Jason and Kendra on my fridge at home! You sent them to me for god's sake!"

"Alec, have you been drinking again? Are you drunk right now?" Her voice had become shaky.

"No, I'm not drunk," he replied angrily.

"Alec, I need to see you. What time are you coming over?"

"I'll be by your place in a bit."

"In a bit?" she pleaded.

"Yes, sorry. I need to do a couple of things, and then I'll head on over. You do still live on Bonny Street, right?"

"Yes, of course. What things? You just got here."

"Work things, Chelsea."

"Ok fine. I'll see you soon. Don't take too long. We need to talk."

He was not sure, but it sounded like she had started crying by the end of the conversation and Alec found himself fighting off the tears. Something was clearly terribly wrong with her. The most recent photo that Alec had received from his sister, was of her oldest child, Jason, standing with the championship baseball team he coached. Chelsea was a very proud mother and every year without fail, she would send her little brother photos of her children. Alec had searched for that last team photo, after she had first mentioned she had no children, but could not find it. He had also searched for the several other photos she had sent but was unable to find them as well. He seemed to have misplaced the box that he had kept them all in, over the many years.

With their brief phone calls, she would still manage to find time to complain about her deadbeat husband. It was usually towards the end of the conversation, at which point he had already tuned her out, but he did recall, on several occasions, her whining about Ron not being supportive enough and that he was drinking all the time. His own conversations with the brother in law were brief and usually only because he had been the one who answered the phone.

He was exhausted from the shortage of sleep from the previous night, compounded with the early flight, so he just wanted to relax for a bit before finding some energy, and making his way over to his sister's place. Although he was anxious to see her, he was dreading what he might find. If he was being completely honest with himself, he needed to have a few more drinks before seeing Chelsea. As per usual, the bottle had taken priority. After swigging the remains in the flask, he grabbed a glass from the minibar and the bottle of Jack Daniels.

Like he had done so many times before, he promised himself he would tackle his drinking problem soon, but for now he needed just a few to take the edge off. After propping up a pillow behind his head, he stretched out on the bed and turned the television to see it was on the CNN channel. It appeared the same panel was having yet another conversation about more ridiculous tweets from President Trump. The guilt from avoiding his sister quelled with each slurp, while he searched through the channels. After several ounces of whiskey and two reruns of Friends and Seinfeld, he was finally lights out.

CHAPTER 4

The sun, at nine o'clock on the Tuesday morning, beamed through the old rickety windows landing directly on his forehead. The penthouse suite would be too bright for anyone, let alone a man with Alec's hangover. He would have drawn the blinds and slept even longer, but unfortunately the Marby did not come equipped with any, so he was forced out of bed.

As he splashed his face in the bathroom sink, an all too familiar feeling of shameful disappointment consumed him. He was supposed to be in Russell to help his sister, yet he selfishly let his drinking problem get in the way. Jack Daniels was as fierce as Mike Tyson in the mid-eighties and Alec was as vulnerable as any of those guys Mike beat up those days. Lately, he was not much of a fight for his competitor and yesterday's match was a knockout. The dark eye sockets and ashen complexion looking back at him in the bathroom mirror appeared as the loser at a post-fight press conference. He knew he needed to be stronger and planned on doing so.

After Chelsea did not answer his phone call, he got dressed. He choked down some of the room's stale coffee while getting caught up on a few last-minute work emails on his laptop. He had forgotten to set up his work email before leaving town, so he quickly made the change. Now all future emails would be forwarded to his secretary, Ellen. Surely the board members would be happy now knowing Alec Jenkins was officially and literally 'currently out of office'.

Stepping into the elevator, he saw his reflection. The bags under his eyes now seemed slightly less obvious than the day before. He could not believe that he had slept for as long as he had but was happy as he felt somewhat rejuvenated and only slightly hungover. The long rest, even if it was mostly alcohol induced, was needed. The stress he had been under, while trying to balance the bottle and his job, was exhausting. After finding out that the board was enforcing his time off, he realized he had failed miserably.

Riding the slow elevator down, he again became infuriated, imagining what must have transpired at that board meeting, which they held behind his back. Disappointment weighed heavy, as he knew they were right with their decision. With a thud the elevator had finally reached the main floor and as the doors opened, he was immediately greeted by Edgar.

"Good morning Mr. Jenkins! I hope you had a good sleep." The sarcasm in his voice was blatant.

"Just marvelous," Alec replied sarcastically. "I take it there's no continental breakfast offered by the hotel."

"No sorry, there is not," Edgar replied chuckling, as Alec made his way out the lobby door.

He hoped the long walk to his sister's place would air out his alcohol-filled pores, as Alec knew Chelsea would not approve of his abuse on his body. As he walked, he could not help but notice how the homes in the town had deteriorated. Growing up, he recalled how the young vibrant prosperous town was full of brand-new beautiful homes and now, over a quarter of a century later, the town appeared to be bruised and battered. Most of the homes now had peeling paint, missing shingles, dented siding, and sagging eavestroughs. Several of the homes had boarded up windows. The last he had heard, the lumber mill was suffering, but Alec was aware of how dire it must have been. Most of the town's residents worked there and apparently, most were now struggling to make ends meet. Even though he had not lived there as an adult, or even thought of the town since he had left, Alec felt sadness for the town and its residents.

The streets were empty with no signs of any children or activity. Back when he was young, those streets were full of children playing. Now the only sign of life came from behind a closing curtain in a home he had just walked past. After turning the corner, he saw his old high school up ahead on the right side of the road, and a burst of nostalgia came overcame him. As he neared the school, he decided to take a quick detour to go inside. If anyone had told him that the trip home would bring on feelings of nostalgia he would have laughed, but to his surprise, so far it had.

Stepping into the building, he saw the famous bench where he and several students would hang out most breaks and lunchtimes. Before he had attended the high school, he had heard of the bench and how all the cool kids would hang out there. Because of Alec's popularity on the hockey team, he was accepted by the older cool kids who hung out there during his freshman year. Initials filled the bench from all the students throughout the years and to his surprise his *AJ* was still there.

After entering grade eleven, he did not spend much time at the bench with the popular crew. While they focused more on partying and popularity, Alec began to focus more on his academics and his plans for getting out of Russell. Most of the jocks hung out by the gym and although Alec was one of the best players on the school's hockey team, he chose not to spend much time with the jocks either. By his senior year, he became quite the loner. He typically would just show up to school as the first bell rang, signaling the start of class and would leave immediately after his last class ended.

Looking around, Alec could see the school was nearly empty and wondered if the students and teachers were already on their summer break. He could not recall the exact date, but as it was late June, he assumed that was why no one was around. The empty halls may have also been because of exam week, a week that he recalled being very stressed in his senior year. The pressure he had put on himself that week was immense. Even though he was top of his class, plans were already in place and he wanted no hiccups with getting into university in Vancouver.

His squeaky shoes echoed throughout the empty hallways as he made his way around the school. Russell High School is a large building that holds hundreds of students, as families from all the surrounding towns sent their kids to the school by bus. The main floor holds several classrooms, a state-of-the-art auditorium, a very large cafeteria offering a wide variety to its students, and a massive gymnasium. The gym's high ceiling has given Russell the privilege of hosting the nation's annual high school volleyball tournament for several decades. The second floor holds a massive swimming pool, where year after year Russell's elite water polo team holds their games.

Alec slowed as he approached one of the classrooms where some of the heinous shooting had occurred. His palms became sweaty and his heart raced, and he realized he had nearly blocked

49

out the event completely from his mind. He peered through the small door window leading to the classroom where the shooting had started. Although the room had been painted and contained different furniture, its layout was as he remembered. Above the entrance to the room was a memorial plaque with names of students who were in the room the day of the horrific event. While walking away, he glanced at the plaque and heard what sounded like someone waxing floors in the distance.

As he walked through the long narrow hallway, he checked out the large cafeteria on his left which was opposite several rows of lockers. His locker all throughout his tenure there was in the last bay, directly across from the entrance to the cafeteria. While entering the last bay, he looked at the locker numbers. He continued to scan them while approaching his, which was the last one on the left-hand side. 617, 618, 619, and then he found his, locker number 620. He stood back a moment, realizing the coincidence of it being the same number as his hotel room, then pulled back on the door and was surprised to find it was not locked. In his freshman year he had signed the bottom of his locker with his initials in big black letters and was amazed to see it was still there after all these years.

"Can I help you?" barked a voice from behind. Alec startled, whirled around to see a tall elderly man standing in the entrance to the bay of lockers.

"No, that's ok, thanks. I was just passing by and thought I'd check out my old school."

The unimpressed man raised one bushy eyebrow at him, while holding the waxing machine tightly in both hands. His unlit cigarette dangling from his mouth while he replied, "Oh really?" He scoffed while looking Alec up and down. He pushed a button, and the floor polisher began to hum. "Well don't be scuffing any of my floors son. I've been doing this for forty years, and I'm getting pretty tired of it. I don't need you making me work any harder than I have to."

"Forty something years? Wait, are you Mr. Hope?"

"Sure am," he replied while continuing to wax the floors.

"Oh wow! You once saved me from getting my ass kicked!"

In Alec's first day of high school, some senior students had begun bullying him and his friends, shoving them into lockers as they walked past. Mr. Hope had come to their rescue by grabbing one of the bullies by his throat and threatening him. Throughout the rest of his high school days, Alec always had a special place in his heart for Mr. Hope. Now that he knew it was him, he wondered how he had not recognized the man. He had not changed much; in fact, he had not changed at all, even after all those years.

"Oh yeah?" he said, unenthused, while continuing to wax.

"You probably don't remember me, but I'm Alec Jenkins."

The janitor stopped and growled, "Jenkins? Yeah, you're right, I don't. So now if you don't mind, I need to finish these floors."

Taken aback, Alec slid past the man, then headed towards the exit. Looking back, he watched as the agitated man lit his cigarette, while staring back at him, before Alec made his way around the corner. Upon reaching the front doors, he took one last look back, figuring it would probably be the last time he would ever see the place.

Exiting the school, he gathered his whereabouts and headed south down Darcy Street towards Chelsea's home. Noticing a corner store on his walk he got the strong desire for a cigarette, so he went inside. Alec tried making small talk with the two people working inside, but neither appeared to have any interest in speaking with him.

Leaving the store, he popped a cigarette in his mouth and realized it would be the first smoke he'd had since arriving. Going a couple hours without a cigarette was rare to Alec – never mind going more than a day. He thought of the oddity while he continued his way down the street, lighting the cigarette.

Twenty minutes later, Alec had walked nearly the length of the town and reached the top of his sister's street. Looking up, he saw the street signs which read Darcy Street and Bonny Avenue, then began making his way down Bonny Avenue, where his childhood home sat at the end of the road in the cul-de-sac. He smiled upon seeing a few kids out playing street hockey, something he had done for most of his childhood years on that very same street. The children argued over the legalities of the goal that had just been scored as he walked past. As they whined at each other he could not help but smile again, recalling the very similar arguments he and his childhood friends had forty years earlier.

He stood in the middle of the cul-de-sac, looking around. To the left of his childhood home was the Hamilton home. The much older Hamilton kids did not hang around Alec and his friends very often, but they would spy on them when they would have parties while Mr. and Mrs. Hamilton were out of town. It was at one of those parties where Alec had seen people having sex for the first time. The older Hamilton brother had caught a glimpse of Alec watching through the fence and later threatened to hurt him if he told anyone. The threat worked as Alec never told a soul.

To the right was the Richardson's home with a family of three younger girls. Because the Richardson kids were younger, he also did not play with them much, but did rely on the girls to fill in when their street hockey games were short a couple players. At some point during his days in junior high school, the Richardson family moved away, and an elderly couple moved in.

Directly across the street lived the Spencer family and his best friend, Grayson Spencer. In elementary school the two boys were inseparable. They spent most of their childhood playing street hockey or riding their bikes all around town. Their mothers also became friends and spent a lot of time together. Grayson had a stay-at-home mother and his father worked at the local mill.

Looking over at the Spencer's home, Alec noticed the massive dents on the garage door. Surely those were the same dents the two boys had made over thirty years earlier by shooting pucks at it while working on their slap shots. Like many others in the town, the Spencers had not done much to fix the wear and tear on their home. Reminiscing over the dents, he noticed, out of the corner of his eye, that someone was looking at him out the front window to the home. The curtains closed and Alec wondered if the Spencers still occupied the home.

Turning his back to the dented garage door, he saw his old childhood home across the cul-de-sac. In the eighties, the large, brown, two-story house was one of the most beautiful on the street. Mr. and Mrs. Jenkins took great pride in the upkeep of their home. On most summer weekends the couple would be seen working in their several gardens. Elm trees lined the perimeter of the yard while a black chain link fence kept their pets from escaping the backyard. From what he could see, the gardens were completely gone and only a neglected lawn remained. The once smoothly paved walkway, which led to the front door of the home, was now cracked and concave with several weeds defiantly forcing their way through.

Stepping over the weeds, he realized someone had been watching him again, as the curtains swung from side to side as he approached. Without thinking, and perhaps feeling a little nostalgic, he knocked on the front door to see if the home's current owner was home. This spontaneous move, he instantly regretted. If someone had opened the door, he did not know what he would have said, but luckily nobody answered.

The sound of a train whistle reverberated from behind the home bringing him another sense of nostalgia. Bonny Avenue was the last street on the south side of the town and only a short distance behind it was the lumber mill. A small field with a marsh and three sets of train tracks were the only thing that that stood between Alec's childhood home and the log mill. The three sets of tracks were used to transport the wood in and out of the mill and the sound of the train's whistle was a regular occurrence, so the locals had grown accustomed to hearing it. He walked away from the home recalling how much he had enjoyed hearing that whistle from his bedroom while dreaming of getting away.

As he turned and headed back up the street towards Chelsea's home, he noticed the curtain from the Spencer's home was pulled back again. Walking away, Alec knew he was being watched.

He was not sure why, but when he was living in Vancouver, it annoyed him that Chelsea had lived so close to their parents. Thinking back now he was probably just jealous of her and their parents' relationship. Chelsea had moved out of their parents' place while Alec was young. She had saved every penny she had made working at the local grocery store and used it for the down payment on a house, just a few blocks up the street, and she had lived in that home ever since. Although she never admitted it, Alec was pretty sure that their parents had chipped in on the down payment. He remembered, during his university years thinking that there was no way they would have done the same for him. This, he confirmed to himself, was just more blatant proof of their favoritism toward the golden child.

Upon reaching his sister's door he rang the buzzer and waited a few moments. As nobody answered, he leaned on the buzzer a few more times, but still no one came. After laying a good thumping on the front door, a woman finally appeared. At first, Alec did not recognize the woman with the long greasy hair and dark bags under her eyes, but then as she smiled, he realized it was Chelsea. Anyone who did not know the woman would think she was well into her seventies, but she was not yet into her sixties.

"Hey stranger!" she cheered, reaching out to him with her arms wide open. A wave of immense guilt rushed through him, as her skinny arms wrapped around him.

"Hey Chelsea, how are you doing?" he asked, squeezing her tightly in his arms. Even though he was still overwhelmed with guilt, he was very happy to see her. As they embraced, he could not recall the last time he had felt this loved.

"I'm doing well," she replied, but he could tell she was lying. "Come on in! Sorry about the mess, things have been a little crazy around here lately, and I just haven't had the time to clean up."

"Don't worry about it, Chelsea. Hey, sorry about yesterday; I think I was coming down with something because I ended up falling asleep pretty early."

"Oh gosh, no worries. I'm just so happy to see my baby brother!"

Alec took off his shoes and entered the living room. The place was almost exactly as he had pictured it, old fashioned and very clean. If she thought her place was a mess she would've been disgusted by the current condition of his place. As she rambled on asking questions of his trip and other small talk, he eyed her place, looking for any evidence of Ron or her kids. Not only were there no pictures of any them, it was quite evident that she lived alone in the home. There was no dining room table, only a small kitchen table, one only a person living on their own would use to eat at. He wondered if Ron had left her and taken the kids with him.

"Okay Chelsea, now that I'm here, can you tell me what happened?"

"What happened with what?"

"Your kids and Ron. Where are they?"

"Again with the kids talk? Seriously Alec, are you okay?" she asked, wide-eyed, before walking over to the small kitchen table where her brother was now sitting. After pulling up a chair beside him, she placed her hand on his knee and continued, "Have you been taking drugs?"

He stared right back at her wondering the same of her, as Chelsea's appearance was not far from the crack addicts he had seen in Tenderloin, an area where you would find many of the homeless from San Francisco. The siblings were at a bit of a standoff, both thinking the other had lost their mind. Although he had been drinking quite excessively lately and was probably having some sort of mental break down, the conversations he'd had with Chelsea about her kids were still very clear in his head. He had been certain that those conversations had happened, but with all that had happened recently, he was beginning to wonder.

"Chelsea, I'm doing just fine. Are you trying to tell me you don't know who Jason and Kendra are?"

"That's exactly what I'm saying. I have never had children and you know that! You know that I've always wanted children, but you kind of need to have a man around to make that happen," she replied angrily as her eyes began to water. "Jesus Alec, you've been here for five minutes and you're already upsetting me?"

"What about Ron?"

"Ron? Who the fuck is Ron? Seriously Alec, you're freaking me out here."

"Can you grab me a glass of water please?" He had suddenly begun to feel hot and lightheaded. His mind raced, thinking of all the strange things that had been occurring since the moment he had landed in Winnipeg. She hustled over to him with a glass of ice-cold water and he chugged it back and then gathered himself. "Do you mean to say that you've never been married, and you've never had any children?"

"Yes Alec, that's exactly what I'm telling you. Why in god's name would you think that?"

"Because I've spoken with them on the phone," he blurted in frustration. "Jason, your son, who loves baseball and Kendra, your daughter, who loves to paint!" He stared at her, hoping something would click and she would have answers.

"Alec I'm only saying this because I love you, I think we need to get you some professional help," Chelsea said, wiping the tears from her eyes. Then they both just sat there looking at each for a moment. "Listen, you're my brother and I would never lie to you. I've never had children, nor have I ever been married. Trust me, I think I would know." With nothing left to say, she rose from the table and poured two cups of coffee.

"What do you take in yours?" she asked, before blowing her nose into a tissue she had pulled out of under her bra. He sat motionless while staring at the wall. "Alec?"

"Oh, just a little milk please." She placed the cup in front of him while Alec continued to stare blankly at the wall in front of him, wondering which of them was losing their mind. With so many bizarre things happening on this trip, it was feeling like an old episode of the Twilight Zone. He took a sip of his coffee and began thinking of all the strange things that had occurred, including the headstone. "Hey Chelsea, have you gone to visit mom and dad lately?"

"Yes, I visit them almost every weekend. I bring mom fresh lilies from the garden out back. Remember how much she loved them?"

"Yes of course, how could I not remember? She had them all over the house."

60

"Are you going to go see them while you're here?" Chelsea asked as she began washing dishes, gazing out the kitchen window.

"I already did, that's why I'm asking. What happened to their head stones?"

"Oh no. Don't tell me their headstone were destroyed again," she sighed, keeping her eyes at something out the window.

"Destroyed? No, but ..."

"Thank god. Last year some punks did a lot of damage in the cemetery and they destroyed mom and dad's headstone. I had to get it redone, remember I told you about it when it happened." Alec watched her while she continued looking out the window.

"No, I don't remember that. Why did you change what was written on their headstone?"

Turning to face him, she snarled, "What are you talking about? I got them redone with the same epitaph. It cost me a lot of money you know, and it would've been nice if you had chipped in for that."

"Well I don't ever recall you telling me about this, nor do I remember you asking me for money. If you had I would have obviously given you some," he replied hastily.

She had always been the queen of guilt, another trait passed down to her from their mother. She turned her back to him and started back with the dishes. "Oh, that's right, I forgot the city

61

slicker has lots of money. I left you several messages about it, but you never called me back."

"I don't recall any messages about a damaged headstone," he said quietly. The truth was she probably had left him those messages and he had most likely deleted them without ever listening to what she had to say. "Well how much was it? I'll give you the money right now."

"Just forget it. I can't even remember how much it was."

"I'm not going to just forget it. They were our parents, so I'm just as responsible for their headstone. I just don't get why you'd put that crap about flying together in heaven."

"I'm not going to fight with you Alec. We agreed upon that the first time we had gotten them done, so I don't understand why you're bringing this up again. You're the one that insisted on that flying together in heaven bullshit."

Alec sat back in his chair and looked at his sister with disbelief. "Chelsea tell me, how did our parents die?"

"Stop it!" she shouted, slamming the cupboard. "That was a long time ago Alec. Why do you want to drag all this shit up again?" Tears began to run down the side of her cheeks. "Oh great, I'm crying. Are you happy now?"

He knew the right thing to do was to console her, but instead he just sat there staring at her while she buried her face in her hands. Things had become awkward, and he did not know what else to say. He sat silent for a few moments, listening to her cry, before rising to his feet.

"Listen Chelsea, I've got to run."

"You just got here and now you're leaving already?"

"Sorry, I have to get back to the hotel," he said, turning and making his way to the front door. "Things have been pretty crazy at work lately and there are still some things I have to take care of before I can fully enjoy this time off."

He knew she probably did not believe a word of what he had just said but he needed to get out of there. The walls felt like they were closing in on him and the lightheadedness had returned. The headstone had been changed and why his sister was lying about it did not make any sense to him, but the panic attack was taking over, and he needed to leave.

"You're always running away," she said, before blowing her nose again.

"Listen Chelsea, everything is going to be ok," he said, patting her on her shoulder. "I'll give you a call tomorrow after I get all caught up at work and we'll talk some more then, ok?"

"Yes fine, but are you ok? You don't look so good," she replied looking concerned.

"Yes, I'm fine. I'll call you tomorrow," he said, pulling her into his arms.

Hugging Chelsea, he was suddenly reminded of the awful photographs the local newspaper had shown of their parents' bus accident, and the anger he felt towards them for publishing them. The fact that his mother had devoted much of her life to that very same newspaper, should have stopped them from showing such a gruesome scene.

He pulled away and saw the mascara running down Chelsea's face. She looked like shit and was now talking about things that never happened. He did not like seeing her like this and wanted to help her, but his anxiety had now turned into a full-on panic attack. He felt paralyzed and weak. He twisted the door handle and pushed open the front door.

"You know they loved you very much Alec," she said quietly. "They were just upset that you left us all behind." Her voice cracked and more tears rolled down her cheeks. Alec stopped and stood with his back to her, waiting for her to finish. "They blamed each other for why you'd never visit or answer their calls. I know you think they pushed you away, but it was you who pushed them away. They always loved you Alec, even after you left."

"If you say so," he said before the door swung closed behind him.

He had been hoping to clear up a few things during his visit with his sister, but now he was even more confused. Where were the kids? Even if Ron had left her and taken the kids, surely there would have been some trace of them left behind. Maybe it was too hard for her and she had tossed everything out in hopes of blocking them from her memory, but that seemed unlikely. The stress of seeing his sister in shambles created an insatiable urge, so he picked up another bottle of Jack Daniels from the corner liquor store. He promised himself just a couple drinks to calm the nerves.

As he walked through the front doors of the old hotel, he could see Edgar engaged in a conversation with a couple that appeared to be checking into the hotel. Edgar glanced over and the two exchanged a nod before Edgar seemingly gave a disapproving look when seeing the bottle in his hand. "Mind your own business Edgar," Alec muttered to himself while waiting for the elevator to arrive. He held the bottle close to his leg trying to hide it while anxiously waiting for the elevator doors to open.

Riding up, he tried to fight the urge, but failed, and took two large swigs of the whiskey before the elevator reached the top floor. As he walked through the door to his room, he headed over to the minibar to grab a glass. Taking a seat on the edge of the bed, he filled the glass to the top then took a large swig. His hand trembled and he wondered if it was because it had been too long since his last sip of alcohol or if his sister's breakdown was getting to him.

After finishing the glass, he filled it again, while continuing to go over his conversation with Chelsea. Even if he were able to help her, how would he begin, after all he did not know anything about mental breakdowns or depression, which was clearly happening to his poor sister. She needed professional help and he knew of only one person that might be able to help her. Perhaps his sister would speak with someone she knew – someone she was once close with.

He grabbed his laptop out of his bag, then returned to the edge of the bed, before opening the Facebook website. Several red alerts lit the top of his home page as the site reminded him that although he spent little to no time on the site, he still had 188 friend requests, 44 unread messages, and 620 notifications. Under the search bar he typed in her name and three matches came up. After further review, he determined none of them were who he was looking for as none of the images could have been a match.

After spending another fifteen minutes googling her name and finding it had hundreds of matches, he was unable to track her down. He stared at the phone on the nightstand before calling the front desk.

"Hello Mr. Jenkins. How can I help you?" Edgar's voice bellowed through the other end of the receiver.

"Hi Edgar. I am trying to find a phone number ..." Alec hesitated, having second thoughts.

66

"Oh, no problem sir," Edgar responded, seemingly eager to help. "I can find what you're looking for here. Are you looking for a number to a restaurant?"

"No, I'm actually looking for a residential number."

"Oh ok. What's the last name?" Alec contemplated hanging up while taking another sip from his glass. "Mr. Jenkins?"

"Sorry, it's Edwards ... Sarah Edwards."

"Ok, give me one second," Edgar said. Alec could hear him punching the keys on the computer while he muttered the name of what he was searching. Alec sipped the remnants of his second pour, as he reached for the bottle of whiskey.

"You know what Edgar; she probably doesn't live here anymore, so don't worry about it," he said with the phone squeezing between his right shoulder and cheek, using his left hand to pour himself a third glass.

"Ah, here it is!" Edgar cheered. "Have you got a pen?"

"Um ... one sec," Alec replied, scouring through the drawers. "Ok, go ahead".

"Ok, it's 7-7-4-2-1-2-0."

"Great, thanks!" Alec replied while jotting down the number.

"You know if you're ..."

"Thanks Edgar," Alec interrupted, before abruptly hanging up the phone. He sat on the bed, contemplating whether or not to make the call. His hands continued trembling as he tried to think of someone else to call for advice. After not being able to think of anyone else, he picked up the phone and dialed the number.

"Hello," answered the sweet soft voice. Alec froze, and after a few seconds the woman's voice came through the receiver a second time, "Hello?"

"Hello, is this Sarah?"

"Yes, this is she. And you are?"

"Sarah Edwards?" Alec asked, but already knew it was her. She had a unique childlike voice, and although he had not heard it in decades, he had never forgotten it.

"Yes, the one and only. Who is this?"

"It's Alec … Alec Jenkins." After receiving no immediate response, he continued, "I'm in town and thought maybe we could get together."

After a few moments of awkward silence her voice came through the other end, "Alec? Is it really you?"

"Yes, it's me," he laughed awkwardly.

"Jesus," she replied quietly. A few moments passed and Alec began to think he should say something, but then Sarah's voice came through again. "Well this is … I mean … wow, it's been a long time."

"Yes, it has," he said, fiddling with the pen in his hand, frantically trying to think of what to say next.

"What are you doing in town?"

"Just in for a visit. I got some holiday time so thought maybe I'd come check out my old stomping grounds."

"Oh really?" she asked, sounding skeptical.

"Yes, I figured this time of year would be better than coming back in the winter when it's freezing out."

"Oh, I see," she replied. A few more moments of awkward silence before Alec thought of what to say next. Just coming right out and asking her for help with his sister after all these years did not seem appropriate.

"I actually wasn't sure if you'd be in town," he managed to squeeze out.

"Why wouldn't I be?"

"I just meant I wasn't sure if you still lived here."

"Oh. Yup, I'm still here."

"Well, I'd love to get together for a coffee or something. Are you free tomorrow?"

"Um …" she said as the sound of a doorbell rang.

"Yes, I guess so. Hey, I've got to get going. There's someone at my door, but I've got some time around noon tomorrow, if that works for you."

"Yes, that'd be great. I haven't been here in years. Where is a good place to get a coffee?"

"How about Barny's?" Sarah asked.

"Barny's is still around?"

"Yup. It's the heart and soul of this town," she replied sarcastically.

"Barny's would be good. Meet there at noon?"

"Sure," she replied as her doorbell rang a second time. "Ok, I've got to go!"

"Perfect. Looking forward to ..." he began before she hung up ending the conversation abruptly.

Taking in Sarah's apparent lack of enthusiasm, he reached for the bottle and twisted off the lid, but then restrained from pouring another glass. As he put the cap back on, he lay back on the bed thinking of the good times they'd had together.

They began dating early in their freshman year and dated throughout high school. Alec lost his virginity to her on the evening of their graduation. Less than two months later, he moved to the West coast and their relationship quickly dissolved as the distance proved to be too difficult. At first, Sarah made most of the effort to keep them together. She visited him a few times in Vancouver, but Alec pulled further away as his focus on his career consumed him. During his third year in university the two went their separate ways and he never heard from Sarah again.

She was a great girl, and he was disappointed that he had let her go. He often wondered how different his life would be if they had stayed together and gotten married. If they had, he most likely would not have ended up in the deep rut that he found himself in now. Over the years, he had thought of Sarah from time to time, and wondered if she had ever gotten hitched. One of the things that attracted him to her, besides her stunning looks, was her charming personality. Sarah was well-balanced; she was brilliant and focused but could also be laid back and goofy.

Rolling onto his side, he faced the nightstand and for the next several minutes battled the urge to take another drink. He knew it was just a matter of time before he would give in, so he stood up and sighed, grabbing the bottle. He poured the golden-brown liquid until it nearly filled the glass. The allure of its wafting sweet perfume reached his nose as he lifted the glass to take a swig. The heavy weight champion, Mike Tyson, would win yet again. Maybe one day he would be able to take down the champ, but not today.

A bright white light suddenly filled the room, forcing Alec to let go of the bottle, while attempting to shield his eyes. The bottle hit the floor, propelling the golden liquid across the vintage carpet, as the challenger's head bounced off the floor.

CHAPTER 5

"Remember, dinner is at five o'clock sharp Alec!" shouted Mrs. Jenkins.

"Mom, it's the playoffs and the Habs are on the tube tonight. Can't I just have dinner at Grayson's house?" Alec shouted back while crossing the street.

"Why don't you boys just watch the game here?"

"Because we're playing hockey too and dad is going to be watching the Oilers game anyway."

Alec's father was also a huge hockey fan and like most other Boston Bruins fans hated the Montreal Canadiens. This year he had become a big fan of the league's newest team, the Edmonton Oilers. Although this 1979-1980 season was only their first in the National Hockey League, they showed great promise with some excellent young talent. They had finished with a below five hundred record, but their bright new gifted player, who went by the name of Wayne Gretzky, had tallied an incredible 137 points in only his rookie year. Heading into the playoffs, they were in tough, as they were the sixteenth seed and they were matched up against the league's best, Philadelphia Flyers.

"Ok fine," Mrs. Jenkins sighed. "Just don't be late."

This was a regular conversation between the ten-year-old and his mother, but each time the boy would still come home past his eight o'clock curfew. When the neighborhood kids got together, they would become enthralled in whatever game they were playing, and no schedule could ever be followed. Mrs. Jenkins was a great cook and Alec preferred her cooking, but Grayson's mother allowed them to watch the hockey game on the couch while they ate.

Across the street from the Jenkins' house, Alec entered through the side door to the Spencer home. He was over there so often that knocking was not required. Their house was like his second home, and Mrs. Spencer treated him like her own son.

"Hi Alec!" she said, with a smile before opening the door to the basement. "Grayson, come on upstairs, Alec is here to see you." While the two stood waiting she turned to him and asked, "Would you like something to drink before you head outside, sweetheart?"

"No, thank you."

"Coming! I'll be right there," the pubescent boy's voice shrieked from the bottom of the stairs. Moments later, Grayson appeared fully dressed in goalie equipment, and the two of them headed out onto the driveway to play hockey for endless hours.

"Hey, it's my turn to play net!" Alec whined.

"No, it's not. You were in net last time," Grayson snarled back.

"I was?"

"Yeah, don't you remember? Then after I destroyed you, we watched the Stars light up your Habs!"

"No pucks boys, tennis balls only! You're destroying my garage door!" shouted Mr. Spencer from his living room chair. The man rarely left his seat from in front of the television; from the moment he returned home until the moment he went to bed.

"Yeah, whatever dad," muttered Grayson.

It was late spring, which meant one thing to the boys, the NHL playoffs had begun. It seemed like every year their favorite teams met up in the playoffs, and this year was no different as the Montreal Canadiens were again playing host to the Minnesota North Stars. The two teams had developed quite the rivalry and so had the two boys playing outside on the driveway. After a couple of hours, Grayson's mother beckoned the boys to come inside.

"Boys, the game is starting!"

As usual, the two bolted for the couch in the living room to see the beginning of Hockey Night in Canada. After the first period the boys were right back out on the driveway for some more one-on-one hockey. After the intermission ended, the boys were back in their seats to catch the start of the second period. It was game six of the Stanley Cup finals and the Montreal Canadiens held three games to two lead. And after watching the Canadiens score in overtime, to win hockey's most prominent prize, the Lord Stanley Cup, the boys were right back at it on the driveway.

"Better luck next year buddy," Alec snickered.

"Shut up, you little bitch," Grayson fired back. Alec teed up a slap shot which missed the net and the garage behind it. "Nice shot asshole."

The boys laughed while Alec ran to retrieve the ball. With the long narrow driveway, the boys placed the net in front of the garage sitting at the end of the driveway. Grayson's father was constantly telling the boys to move the net elsewhere because they were ruining his garage door, but each time his mother would defend the boys. When Alec returned from retrieving the ball, he noticed the car pulling up the driveway.

"Oh, come on," Grayson whined.

"Who is that?" Alec asked.

"It's my weirdo cousin."

"Shit, you never told me Eddy was coming over."

"Sorry, I didn't know," Grayson replied. "Now my mom is going to make us hang out with the little piece of shit."

Eddy and his mother stepped out of the car that was now parked in the middle of the driveway blocking where the boys had been playing. The odd-looking boy waved to the two older boys, but they did not wave back. Giving him a warm welcome might give him the idea that they actually wanted to play with him.

Eddy had an extremely rare chromosomal disorder called Cat Eye Syndrome or CES for short. The disorder came with a variety of side effects with its most distinguishing facial feature of eyes that appear to be those of a feline. The man who discovered the disorder fittingly named it Cat Eye Syndrome. The condition also causes growth delays, so Eddy was much shorter than a regular eight-year-old child. His odd eyes, stunted growth, cleft lip, pointy ears, and albino looking skin were all symptoms of CES and made him a prime target for bullying at school. His jet-black hair and odd demeanor also did not help his cause.

No one bullied the poor child more than his own cousin. Grayson had a real dark side and hunger for destruction, and he acted upon it often with his much smaller and younger cousin. Still, each time Eddy would learn of a trip to visit his cousin, he would become overjoyed. The smile on Eddy's face was quickly extinguished as the boys turned their backs on him. The boys' mothers hugged then began to make their way into the house.

"Alright boys, be sure to let Eddy play too," ordered Mrs. Spencer.

"Aww mom, come on! Do we have to?" Grayson whined.

"It's either that, or you go straight to your room," she replied with her hands on her hips. "What's it going to be, Grayson?"

Eddy's mother interjected, "Eddy, can just come inside and hang out with us and watch television."

"Not a chance. These boys are just fine playing with him, isn't that right boys?"

"Yes Mrs. Spencer," Alec replied.

"Fine," Grayson grumbled.

The sisters then disappeared into the house to gossip about today's happenings on the Oprah show. Grayson and Alec continued to play while ignoring the young boy.

"Last warning," blustered Mrs. Spencer, peering out the kitchen window.

"Here Eddy," Alec said, passing him a hockey stick which was much too large for the short boy.

He was not very athletic and struggled with the stick, but they were not going to help him. Eddy did not care; he was just happy to be around the older boys. He stood holding the stick awkwardly, while watching the older boys as they continued to shoot the ball around.

After another yell from the kitchen window, the boys decided it would be best to go play elsewhere. They headed towards the large marsh behind the houses in the cul-de-sac. They would often go there to catch frogs and get into mischief, like lighting off firecrackers or throwing rocks at the trains on the tracks behind the marsh.

"Does he ever talk?" Alec asked as they walked along behind the homes.

"Not much, I think he might be retarded or something," replied Grayson.

"He doesn't really look like any retarded person I've seen before. He is weird looking though. Those eyes are freaky, man."

"I know, the little fucker is so weird. My mom says that he's got magical powers, but I think she says that because she feels bad for him."

"Magical powers?"

"Yeah, apparently the midget can see the future or some shit."

"Like a psychic?"

"Yeah, well that's what my mom says, but if you ask me, he's just a loser."

The pack mentality had kicked in, as the older boys continued the cruel talk. Racing on towards the marsh, Eddy struggled to keep the pace, but heard every word.

CHAPTER 6

The intense ring of the telephone, from somewhere above his head, woke Alec abruptly. The right side of his now bruised face throbbed from the blow it had received on last evening's face dive. The floor in room 620 could really pack a punch, and after he peeled himself up to his knees, assessing the damage, he massaged his cheek while stretching his jaw. The last thing he remembered was the room becoming engulfed in a flash of white light.

He groaned while rising to his feet, then maneuvered his way over to the blaring phone, side-stepping the broken glass around his bare feet. He wondered if he had fainted from standing up too quickly, or if it was the result of the liquor, he had consumed the previous night. As he picked up the phone, he searched for the ringer's volume button to turn it down but was unsuccessful finding one.

"Good morning Alec, Richard Goldman here," chirped an equally annoying voice.

Although they had worked together for several years, Richard insisted on saying his full name every time he called. This was just one of the Vice President's several idiosyncrasies that annoyed his boss. The man was a dead ringer for a younger version of Woody Allen. His small stature, dark black curly hair, combined with beady eyes behind black thick-rimmed coke bottle glasses that were topped by thick bushy eyebrows, was the reason his coworkers called him by the name of his doppelganger. This was something that the proud, smaller Jewish man preferred, and he would encourage fellow employees to do, which is why Alec refused to play along.

"Hello Richard, what can I do for you?" he asked, eyeing the clock radio. He was shocked that it was already nearly noon. Had he really been out cold that long? He quickly calculated that he must have been laying on the floor for around fifteen hours, which would explain why his back was so sore.

"I just wanted to see how you were doing," Richard responded. He wanted Alec's position so badly and Alec was certain that Richard was the driving force behind the company's decision to enforce his time off. Richard wanted his boss as far away from the company as possible so he could wedge his way in, but Alec was not going to go easily. He planned on getting his shit together and getting back to the successful man he once was. Once that happened, he would, without hesitation, fire Richard.

"I'm doing great. I've settled in and have been catching up with some family and old friends."

"Ah, that's good to hear," replied the pompous ass. "I also wanted to let you know that you don't need to worry about things back here. I've got everything under control while you're gone."

"That's great, thank you," he replied while pointing his middle finger at the receiver. "Listen Richard, I appreciate the call, but I really must get going. I've got an old friend that I'm supposed to meet up with right away."

"Sounds good Alec; we'll talk soon. Oh, and don't hesitate to call if you need to ..." but before he could finish, Alec had hung up.

The man's bullshit was so thick he wondered if he had any dignity left in his bones. Alec hopped into the shower, then stood under the steaming hot water for several minutes until his anger finally subsided. Richard knew how to get under his skin, but he would never let him know that it did. After rinsing off the lathered soap, he tried to stretch his back by twisting then trying to touch his toes. His back loosened, but his jaw was still quite sore, so he continued to rub it while trying to make sense of how he ended up on the floor.

While getting dressed, his thoughts turned to Sarah. The butterflies in his stomach began doing their thing while his hands became shaky. They had shaken before, but that was normally due to a hangover, or withdrawal, or combination of both, but this time it was something else. He could not recall the last time he had ever been this excited to see a woman.

Approaching the front steps to Barny's Restaurant, he remembered their family tradition of Sunday night dinners there. In the lobby, he noticed the restaurant had not changed in the slightest. While looking at the daily special of a meatloaf sandwich and fries for $6.20, written in chalk on the front of the hostess stand, he requested a back table, and then had a sudden uneasy feeling he was being watched. He glanced around the restaurant and noticed a young boy with odd-looking eyes staring at him. He recognized the eyes, simultaneously recalling seeing them in his dream from the previous night. They were the very same eyes as Eddy Sutton.

"Alec?"

He whipped around to see a beautiful smiling woman looking back at him, with her long red waterfall of hair draped to one side over one shoulder.

"Jesus you scared me!" Alec snorted, clutching his chest.

"Wow, it really is you," Sarah replied. She was just as gorgeous as he had remembered. Only a few fine lines had started tiny crow's feet from the outer edges of her large brown, nurturing eyes. He was shocked to see how well she had aged and was quickly embarrassed, realizing that she probably found the opposite in him. He looked back over his shoulder towards the table where the odd young boy had been staring, only to find the same child returning his gaze with normal brown eyes.

"Sorry, I didn't mean to scare you," Sarah said, while also looking at his subject of distraction.

"No, it's ok," he replied before returning his attention to Sarah. "Sorry, I'm just a little jumpy today."

"Recognize someone over there?"

"No, I mean … I thought …" he looked back at the child again, then turned back to Sarah. "Never mind," he said dismissively. "Wow, you look amazing. I mean really great!"

Taking her hands in his, he stepped back, smiling, and checking her up and down, while becoming self-conscious of his own appearance. He sucked in his belly and craned his neck to avoid exposing a developing double chin. He tried to look cool and composed, but his ear-to-ear grin gave him away.

"Come on, this way. I saved us a table." As they made their way over, several patrons gawked at them, muttering quietly to each other. "Oh, just ignore them," Sarah grumbled, while not breaking stride toward the back corner of the restaurant. "They don't see many new faces these days."

"Is this our old table?" Alec asked, sliding into the booth.

"Well, I guess it is. I'm surprised you remembered," Sarah smirked.

"How could I forget? We spent a lot of time at this table, probably weeks of our lives." Alec chuckled.

"Coffee for you as well?" fired the waitress, extending a pot of coffee from one arm and clutching several menus in the other.

"Oh, yes please," Alec replied, watching the steam rise from Sarah's cup.

The busy waitress quickly filled his cup and asked, "Need menus?"

"No thank you," Sarah replied. "Just having a quick coffee."

"Actually, could I ..." Alec started before noticing the waitress had already moved on to the next table. "Geez, you've got to be quick here. I see the service here hasn't changed."

"Nope," Sarah replied. "Not much around here has."

"I think she's the only waitress working right now," Alec said while looking at her puffy ankles and old sneakers. "Poor lady," he continued. Turning back, he caught Sarah gazing intently at him and then quickly looking down at her cup. The two watched the scene as the waitress scooted from table to table, flipping her order pad, and barking back and forth at the other patrons. They sat a bit awkwardly, looking around the restaurant. "So, how's Sarah?"

"Sarah is fine ... I guess," she replied. "And how about Alec?"

"Oh, no complaints ... I guess," he replied with a smile. "So, when did you move back to Russell?"

"Believe it or not, I never left actually," she replied. "I know it's embarrassing," she chuckled. "I'm one of those lifers we said we'd never end up becoming."

"Hey, I'm not judging," Alec said, somewhat relieved, as she had finally cracked a smile.

"Oh, I'm sure you are. If the shoe was on the other foot, I'm sure I would."

"So, I hear you fulfilled your dreams and became a psychiatrist."

"Yes, that's right. Were you keeping tabs on me?"

"Something like that," Alec smirked before taking a sip of his coffee. "So, you're a real 'Russelltin' huh?"

"Russelltin!" she said laughing. "My god, I haven't heard that in ages. Yes, I guess I am." Back in their high school days, they had assigned that term to all the locals who they predicted would forever be a resident of the town.

"Whatever happened to Australia?" Alec asked.

"Australia?"

"Yeah, you were going to move there."

"Oh right, Australia. I may have just said that because you were moving to the States. Anyways after my mom got sick, I couldn't really go anywhere."

"I'm so sorry about your mom, Sarah. I know you two were very close".

"Thank you."

"So, after she passed, you just ended up staying?"

"Yeah, well, after she died, I had to deal with her estate and everything. The whole thing just happened so fast and she hadn't

85

really prepared much. I was going to put her house up for sale, but the market was so bad at the time that I just could not bring myself to sell it. I wouldn't be able to get nearly half of what the place is worth."

"Fair enough. That must've been difficult."

"It was," she replied.

"How do you like working out of your home?"

"It's got its pros and cons, but for the most part I must say I do enjoy it. What about you? Still the big businessman?" she asked facetiously.

"Oh well, you know …"

"Sorry Alec, that was rude of me."

"No, that's quite alright," he replied. They sat awkwardly for a moment. Sarah stared out the window, seemingly distracted, while he struggled to carry the conversation. "So, who's the lucky guy?" He asked after noticing the ring on her finger.

"Lucky guy?"

"Husband," he replied, focusing on the band on her left ring finger.

"Oh this," she said, laughing and twisting it around her finger. "This was actually my mom's wedding ring. Someone told me years ago I should wear it to keep the creeps away at the gym."

"So, you're not married?"

"Nope, never been." She sipped her coffee, appearing to be in deep thought. Alec wondered if she was thinking of a man from her past, perhaps someone she had been close to marrying. "How about you Alec, ever tied the knot?"

Alec shook his head, then replied, "Nope, me neither."

"I must say, I'm not surprised," she said with a hint of bitterness. "Let me guess, you put everything you've got into your work?"

"Yeah, pretty much," he replied, lowering his head. Being a workaholic seemed suddenly not to be such an admirable quality.

"Oh god. I'm sorry."

"It's ok," Alec replied while lifting his head up. "You're entitled to your resentful feelings toward me. I get it. I just thought maybe after all the years ..."

"What?"

"Oh, I don't know."

"Did you think you'd just roll back into town and everything would just be hunky dory between us?" Sarah's demeanor had suddenly become more formal.

"Well not exactly. To tell you the truth, I didn't know what to expect." He awkwardly sipped his coffee and watched as Sarah did the same. "We were just kids. It was a lifetime ago."

Sarah then smiled and sighed, "Yes it was, but we had such a good thing going. Then you just totally shut me out."

"I know; I was young and an idiot."

She focused on her coffee briefly before looking back out the window. "You know, I did resent you for so many years after you left. I mean I totally got why you left, but never understood why you just totally cut me off." He watched her intently, as she continued gazing out the window. It was not until she turned back to face him that he realized her eyes had welled up. "My god, we were just kids."

"I know," Alec agreed quietly.

"Seriously, it was like what, thirty years ago?"

"It may have been a long time ago, but we were really in love," he admitted quietly, before reaching over tenderly patting, and squeezing her free hand.

"Ugh, I'm sorry. I am so embarrassed. I don't know where this is coming from," she blubbered, blowing her nose into a tissue, making a loud honking sound.

Alec flapped his elbows, jokingly, for comic relief, "Oh, I see you're still doing that honking thing, hey?" She tried to fight cracking a smile but could not resist as they both burst into laughter. Alec noticed several of the other customers being entertained by them.

"It's hereditary, unfortunately. A family trait if you will." Sarah finished wiping her nose, looking up proudly, and tossing her head. "My mom passed down my fabulous red hair and it came with a side of goose call."

"Yeah but don't forget, she also passed down that wit and beautiful skin," Alec replied with a warm smile. "You know I

88

never loved anyone else? You were my first and last," Alec confessed quietly.

"Really? I was in love a few times and almost got married a couple times."

"Really?"

"God no," she chortled. "Slim pickings here in Russell, let me tell you. Remember our first date?"

"Hmm … I think it was here, wasn't it?"

"No, I think we came here on our second date though. Our first date was at Tipsy's."

"Oh god, that's right," he laughed.

"You remember?"

"Yes of course. The Tipsy Cow pool hall. Is that place still around?"

"No, it burnt down years ago."

"Ah, that's too bad."

"I think it was hit by lightning or something," she replied before taking a sip. "I can't believe you forgot our first date!"

"Hey, that was like thirty-five years ago!" He smiled, realizing that the chip on Sarah's shoulder had finally started to crumble.

"I remembered," she said with a coy grin. After a refill, while reaching for some sugar, their hands collided, and they playfully wrestled over the packet. He felt a rush, and his cheeks reddened. "Feels like our first date all over again," she said smiling.

"You know what I do remember?" he asked, smirking.

"What's that?"

"I remember the end of that first date."

"Is that so? And what happened?"

"I remember walking you to your house at the end of the night. I was so nervous because the whole date I'd been trying to build up enough courage to kiss you and I was running out of time. I thought I had to kiss you, or I was done."

"Done?"

"Yeah, my dad told me before I left the house to make sure I kissed you on the very first date. Otherwise, I'd fall into the friend's zone."

"Oh my goodness, that's hilarious. Your dad actually said that?" After taking a sip of his coffee Alec nodded, then snorted in laughter spewing coffee from his mouth. Without breaking her stride, the waitress slapped a stack of napkins on the table on her way past. They looked at each other and burst into laughter again. Alec dabbed the coffee from his face while Sarah wiped down the table, as the other patrons continued to peer over. "What else do you remember?" Sarah asked, pushing her coffee to the side making room to perch her elbows, then cupping her chin in her hands.

"Hmm, well … we kissed. I remember you telling me that I should use less tongue!"

A woman in the next booth scowled in audible disapproval, as Sarah burst into laughter. She quickly covered her mouth to muffle the outburst. As the coffee continued to flow, so did the laughter and stories from their mutual past. Her laugh was infectious, and Alec did not want the conversation to end.

"More coffee you two?" asked the waitress nicely, clearly working on a potential tip, as the restaurant began to empty.

"Oh wow, I guess the lunch rush is over," Alec replied, noticing they were the only table left in the restaurant. "I'm ok for coffee, how about you Sarah?"

"I've had way too much, she replied, holding up a vibrating hand. That's enough for me, thanks." They watched as the waitress disappeared through the swinging kitchen door. "You know there's a place not far from here that has pool tables," she said, raising an eyebrow, bashfully.

"Oh really?"

"Yes really. It's actually just around the corner."

"Let's go," he said, sliding out of the booth, and placing a twenty-dollar bill on the table.

"Twenty bucks for two coffees?" She said, sliding out of the booth.

"Well we were probably here for five hours," Alec replied, glancing back over his shoulder as they exited the restaurant. "Besides, that smooth napkin maneuver of hers was priceless."

Sarah edged past the barricaded sidewalk, which was about to be repaved, then began tiptoeing along the curb to the street. With her arms extended to her sides, she placed one foot in front of the other, as though walking a tight rope. "I have smooth moves of my own," she bragged, while Alec followed closely behind. He was reminded of the many times years ago; he had seen her do that same thing.

"Always the ballerina," he snickered, after losing his footing and stumbling onto the road.

"You know it," she replied, fixing her eyes forward. He continued to follow before noticing a truck full of kids weaving carelessly towards them.

"You'd better get back off the road," Alec cautioned, as he jumped over to the sidewalk. Ignoring him, she continued to prance along the curb, in dance land, while the truck neared, swerving from side to side. Alec quickly grabbed her by the waist and pulled her off the curb towards him, as the truck passed closely, producing a big wave of muddy water, which splashed up from the puddle.

"Assholes!" Sarah shouted.

"I had a feeling they were going to do that. Are you ok?" He asked, while shaking his fist at the disappearing truckload of hysterically laughing teenagers.

"Yes, I'm fine. Thanks, you totally saved me from getting soaked!"

Once entering the pub, they made their way over to the pool tables. Along the way, they were greeted with a familiar reception, of more gawking and whispering from the locals who filled the pub. Sarah pulled Alec by the hand, towards the pool tables.

"Just ignore them, Alec. People in this town don't see many city folk."

Alec was not sure, but could have sworn, one of them mouthed the words *'fuck you'* as they walked past. He did a double take at the grubby looking, toothless man, before being pulled away by the fast-moving redhead. She plopped her purse down on a high-top bar table, then headed towards the bar.

"I'll get us some drinks while you rack them up," she said, taking charge.

Alec wanted to avoid consuming hard liquor around her, as he wanted to impress, and maintain some self-control. He did not want Sarah to see how low he could go when he has too many whiskeys. He was relieved when she returned with two drafts in her hands as he could handle the weaker brew much better.

"Do you want to break?" Alec asked.

"No, the guest should break," she said, before sipping her beer. He envisioned kissing her as he watched the foam float against her luscious lips.

Alec wiped the foam from her upper lip then licked his finger. He turned away and faced the table but knew she was smiling behind him. He sank two balls off the break, then continued to sink several solid balls until missing his final shot on the eight ball. After missing her only attempt, Alec banked the eight ball into the corner pocket and tossed his cue onto the table. Without looking back, he walked over to the bar and ordered two more pints. The balls were wracked upon his return where Sarah stood with a grin.

"Ok Vincent, your break again."

"Vincent? Is that a Color of Money reference?"

"You got it," she replied.

After all these years, it felt like they were picking up right where they had left off. Movie quotes were always a part of their repertoire. He was no longer nervous being around her, instead he was more excited as he remembered how much he enjoyed her company. Sarah now appeared to be seriously focused on the game. As he continued to admire her elegant struggle to put just one ball in a pocket, he kicked himself again for not having asked her to join him in San Francisco. She would have loved an exciting life in a metropolitan setting, especially because she was too worldly and sophisticated for the simple life in a small town.

She, and her profession in psychiatric medicine, were wasted on a small town like Russell, and although Sarah said she was only still staying there by default because of commitments, he felt like he had abandoned her.

After losing badly again in the second game, Sarah said, "Care to make the next game more interesting?"

"You got someone else for me to play?"

"You're such an asshole," she rebutted.

"I'm your Huckleberry. What did you have in mind?"

"Well Doc Holliday, how about a wager?"

"Ok sure. What's the wager?"

"You tell me what you want first," she replied with a smirk, then took a sip of her beer.

He stared into her eyes trying to get a read, then just blurted out, "How about a kiss?"

"A kiss? I don't think so," she replied giggling.

"Well, what do you want if you win?"

"Good question." She perched on a stool and rubbed her chin, pondering. "Oh, I know, but first you have to agree that if we do make this wager, I will get some sort of handicap. You're clearly much better than I am, so how about we play three games and I just have to win one of them?"

"Ok that sounds fair. Now, what do you want if you win then?"

"A fabulous foot rub," she said, studying the pool table.

"Ok, but if I win, I get the foot rub."

"Ok fine," Sarah sighed, grabbing her cue stick in one hand and the blue chalk in the other. Standing the butt of the cue on the floor, she placed the chalk onto the tip of the cue and twirled the cue with her bare foot.

"What the hell was that, Sarah?"

"Didn't I mention that I was in a pool league in university?"

"No, you didn't. So, you're telling me you're going to shark me now? Now who's the Vincent?"

She winked at him, then proceeded to run the table clear all the way down to the number nine ball. After banking the nine ball into the side pocket she said, "By the way, Vincent was Tom Cruise's character, and he was the one that got sharked. Don't you remember, the real shark was Paul Newman's character, Fast Eddie."

Alec reached for his beer and before downing the rest, he replied, "Well, what can I say besides, I'm impressed? I guess I owe you a foot massage."

"Yes, you do. And it'd better be a fabulous one." They briefly locked eyes across the table, before Sarah's phone vibrated in her purse.

"Another beer?" asked the waitress as she approached.

"Um … no thanks," Sarah replied, checking her phone. "I've actually got to get going." Alec had high hopes of their day together continuing and his disappointment did not go unnoticed.

"Sorry Alec, but I really should get going. I have to deal with this," she said, reading the text on her phone.

"That's ok," he said, attempting to mask his disappointment. He wondered who had sent the disruptive text, and what could be so urgent that she had to leave. She quickly gathered her things and stood up from the table.

"To be continued?"

"Absolutely!" he replied, trying not to sound discontented. As she reached into her purse he quickly interjected, "No Sarah, this one is on me. Vincent lost, so he's got this tab."

She laughed, then leaned in and gave him a hug. "Ok fine, but lunch is on me tomorrow. Meet you at Barny's at noon?"

"Sounds good!" He continued to smile as she disappeared out the front door. Sitting alone at the table, feeling like a spectacle in his dress clothes among the locals, he made his way out of the pub.

Walking down the street, he caught a whiff of Sarah's perfume from his shirtsleeve, and caught a wide silly grin in his reflection, as he headed over to Chelsea's place.

Knocking on her front door, he prepared himself for another difficult discussion. But after several loud knocks, he assumed she was not home, and gave up, planning on giving her a call later that evening. Walking up to the darkened front entrance of the Marby, he realized that the sunset was almost fully buried in the horizon. They had spent nearly the whole day together, yet it had merely felt like a couple hours. He could not wait for another date with Sarah. Pulling open the lobby door to the Marby hotel, Alec was overwhelmed with a blinding white light. The silent white blast was so intense that it dropped him to his knees. A deafening ringing in his ears diminished momentarily as he heard Edgar calling for him.

"Mr. Jenkins! Mr. Jenkins, are you ok?"

Edgar's voice faded as the ringing increased, and Alec felt himself losing consciousness. As the room went black, he heard a voice hiss a name into his ear.

"Eddy."

CHAPTER 7

Alec felt a little guilty as he watched the little guy struggling to keep up, but at the same time, he was still irritated that Eddy had ruined their hockey game. If he and Grayson had to hang out with the little weirdo, he was going to have to earn it. Eddy's thick jet-black hair reminded him of the hair on his Lego men, as it did not waver in the blowing wind. His ghostly white cheeks bulged and caved with each labored step. His animalistic eyes bulged while they focused on the boy's forging ahead.

"Is your dad going to be bummed when the Bruins get knocked out of the playoffs again?" Grayson puffed, as they raced along.

"They only lost the first game. I doubt the Penguins will beat them. Anyway, I think the Oilers are his team now," Alec replied.

"The Oilers?"

"Yeah, he likes that Gretzky guy."

"Oh yeah, he's good, but there's no way they're going to beat the Flyers," Grayson said, picking up some rocks along the way.

"Yeah, I agree."

After crossing over some railroad tracks, the older boys reached the marsh and began skipping rocks across its shallow water. Several lily pads floated atop the green algae. The boys scanned the marsh searching for frogs. A few moments later Eddy finally arrived at the marsh, breathlessly panting. He studied the boys as they skipped rocks across the surface of the water. After the eight-year-old attempted and failed miserably at even one bounce, plunging and plopping his stones, Grayson laughed mercilessly.

"Granny can throw better than you Eddy. You're such a pathetic runt," he heckled.

Although he felt bad for him, Alec was under the watchful eye of his mean friend. Feeling the peer pressure, he too chimed in, "Did your momma teach you how to throw Eddy?"

The boys continued to tease and laugh at the odd-looking boy as he pathetically continued, unsuccessfully. Eddy's strange eyes filled with tears, but he kept on trying, until eventually one managed to skip once before sinking.

"Good one Eddy!" Alec cheered, before seeing Grayson's look of disapproval.

"Big deal, he got one bounce," Grayson sneered. "Eddy, are you an albino or what? Why is your skin so white?"

"I think he's a vampire," Alec offered quietly, hoping only Grayson had heard him.

Eddy turned and glared at Alec with his sinister eyes. The boy's eerie appearance and ominous aura sent a chill up Alec's spine, halting any further comments. Grayson, who was completely unaffected by his cousin's ghoulish ambience, continued tossing rocks into the marsh. Alec stood quietly as the boy's catlike predatory eyes remained fixated on him.

"Holy shit, check out that huge frog!" Grayson shouted, before darting off in its direction. The diversion released Alec from Eddy's paralyzing stare as they both turned to see Grayson splashing through the water.

"Grab him Grayson," Alec blurted, still feeling uneasy.

"Got him! Now it's time to have some fun with this bastard," Grayson said with a sinister grin.

The boys would often catch frogs and put a lit firecracker into their mouths and watch it explode, sending its arms and legs flying. This was something Alec knew his parents would disapprove of, but felt obliged to participate, and a part of him enjoyed it in a sick, curious way. He wondered if those feline eyes were still upon him but could not bear to look, as he made his way over to Grayson, where he was squatting, while squeezing the helpless frog between his hands. As Alec approached, Grayson rose to his feet and held out his hands to show him the frog when it suddenly lurched and bounced in Eddy's direction.

"Grab him Eddy!" Grayson shouted. Eddy hesitantly took his eyes off Alec and turned his attention to the escapee, as it hopped past him and into the water. "What are you waiting for?" Grayson shouted. "Get in there, you little bitch!"

The older boys stood and watched as Eddy reluctantly rolled up his pants, then waded into the water. It was unlikely the eight-year-old would be able to find the frog now, but his older cousin had left him no choice. As he begrudgingly made his way through the marsh, the knee-high water continued to rise up his legs until it reached his rolled-up pants. He turned to make his way back to shore before his older cousin started to toss rocks in his direction.

"Hey, be careful Grayson," Alec cautioned, as he thought of the several warnings from his parents of the things that could poke his eye out.

"Don't be such a pussy," his riled pal replied, continuing to throw. "The little fucker just needs some motivation." Eddy shielded his head from the rocks, then turned and retreated out into the deeper water. "See, there he goes."

"If you hit him, he's going to go crying to momma and then we'll be in deep shit," Alec protested.

"You lost him, you idiot! Fuck, you're such a pathetic loser," Grayson shouted before bending over to reload. "Come on Alec. Time for the little shit to learn his lesson."

"Wait, there's another one!" Alec shouted, trying to divert the focus onto an alternative target. Not only did he feel worried for him, he did not want to mess around teasing the supposedly clairvoyant boy, especially after seeing that menacing look.

Grayson ignored him and continued to throw rocks in Eddy's direction, chortling hysterically.

"Come on man, don't be such a baby," Grayson whined, then leaned over and whispered, "Dude if we scare him a little, maybe he'll leave us alone."

To appease his bullying buddy, and avoid becoming a target himself, Alec picked a few of the smallest pebbles he could find and began pitching them, underhand, at the boy's feet. Eddy cupped his hands over his head, attempting to shield himself from the missiles. Suddenly a distinct dull thud silenced the marsh, as a jagged rock bounced off the top of Eddy's black head. The moment of silence was shattered as Eddy let out a high-pitched, crow-like shriek, then began to howl uncontrollably like a beaten dog.

"Oh shit," Grayson said before looking over at Alec.

"Eddy, are you ok?" Alec gasped. "Eddy?" he shouted, after getting only more howling in response.

Eddy's wails grew louder while he staggered out of the water. The older boys stood frozen in shock, helplessly wondering what to do, and as blood oozed between Eddy's fingers, he suddenly became dead quiet. He paused, glaring at the two older boys, while blood gushed down the side of his head, over his ear and onto his neck, then turned and disappeared through the willows along the bank. Alec and Grayson looked at each other in panic, then chased after him. As they began to narrow the gap, Eddy disappeared silently past the trees ahead, leaving a trail of blood drops on the path behind.

"Eddy, come back!" Alec shouted. "We didn't mean to do it!"

"Oh no, we're in so much trouble Alec. My mom is going to kill me!"

"Mine too. Where do you think he went?"

"Probably to his mommy. Fuck, we're so screwed," Grayson whimpered, trying to maintain his tough exterior.

As the boys scrambled for their next move, a loud bang sounded from the direction of the clearing, past the trees, where Eddy had been headed. The usually, all too familiar racket of metal on metal had startled the boys at first, but they soon recognized it as the impact of two resting locomotive cars returning to life, as they connected car to car. A second impact sent a loud echo down the tracks and a row of reluctant cars jerked backward and forward, as they linked and were lugged away. The boys were aware of the danger that occurred daily in their neighborhood, but their fear of getting into trouble was quickly replaced by worry for the naive visiting cousin's safety and wellbeing, as the danger escalated. They picked up the pace while running towards the tracks.

CHAPTER 8

"Mr. Jenkins? Sir, are you ok?"

Alec opened his eyes to find Edgar standing over him. Laying on the floor of the hotel lobby, Alec wondered if he had fainted. He rubbed his head as he sat up, trying to collect himself.

"Edgar, what happened?"

"It was the strangest thing. You came through the lobby door then immediately fell flat on your face. You were totally out cold."

"Where did the bright light come from?"

"Light?"

"Yes, there was a light, a blinding light. It's the last thing I remember."

"Well, I didn't see any light," Edgar replied, moving his arm beneath Alec's to help lift him. "Let's get you to your room." The two struggled onto the elevator and made their way to the top floor. "Which room are you in again?" he asked, practically dragging his guest along the hall.

"620," Alec replied. After struggling to open the door they entered the room where Edgar led him to the edge of the bed before helping him to sit. "Thanks Edgar. I'm so sorry. I'm really embarrassed. What time is it?"

"Nothing to be embarrassed about sir. It's half past eight," Edgar replied, looking at the clock on the nightstand. "Can I get you anything?"

"No, I'll be fine. Thank you for your help. I think I'm just going to call it an early night."

"Are you sure you don't need anything while I'm here?"

"Yes, I'm sure. Thanks again Edgar."

After the door closed behind the hotel clerk, Alec took a couple Tylenol then laid his head back onto the pillow. He turned on the television and wondered if his throbbing headache may be a migraine. He had never had one before but had heard the pain was excruciating. His brain felt as though it had been battered with baseball bats. The only thing that seemed to lessen the pain was when he closed his eyes, so he kept them closed while listening to the television.

From the vintage voices he could tell it was a rerun of an older hockey game, as the legendary Bob Cole and Harry Neale's commentating bellowed from the television. Peering over his toes, he noticed the men skating wore the jerseys of the Montreal Canadiens and the Minnesota North Stars and he recalled seeing this game when he was a kid. It occurred during the early eighties and he remembered Montreal going on to win the game in overtime.

He continued to lay his head back on his pillow, taking in the scratching skate sounds and tweeting whistles of the game. A few fond memories from his childhood came flooding in. He remembered the hockey games on the driveway with his old friend Grayson. But the good memories took a sudden turn that dreadful day at the marsh, and after all these years, Alec still felt guilty for tossing rocks at that poor little boy. His sad memory was triggered by the realization that it had all started with he and Grayson watching this very game.

He wondered what Grayson had ended up doing with his life. Through elementary school the two boys were nearly attached at the hip, but once they entered junior high school, they began to drift apart. Alec's interest in sports had him surrounded by new friends with the same interests. He was surprised when Grayson did not try out for the school's hockey team, but after hearing that his parents had split up, Alec understood. Grayson seemed to lose all interest in playing sports and Alec did not see him around much after that. During their freshman year in junior high, the moving truck loaded up all of Mr. Spencer's belongings while his son sat on the front steps bewildered and sobbing uncontrollably.

"He shoots, he scores!" Bob Cole's voice roared throughout the hotel room, as the Canadiens had taken the lead. Alec then reminisced over the times he had ribbed Grayson whenever the Canadiens beat the North Stars.

Guilt crept in, as he thought of the time some of his new jock friends teased his old friend in the hallway of the junior high school. He should have defended Grayson, but instead just uncomfortably witnessed and then laughed along with them. They had been such good friends for so many years, but that event put the final nail in the coffin. By the time high school rolled around, the two boys would only nod while passing one another in the hallways. After graduation, he completely lost touch with Grayson and after his parents' passing, the only person from Russell Alec kept in touch with was his sister Chelsea.

He had been in town for only a few days and the memories had started seeping in. He was not sure if he would like the other memories this trip had in store. The fainting and white light incidents had also become a growing concern. After the first episode, he'd just written it off to having too many drinks, but now that it had happened again, he became more unsettled. His focus was still on his sister, and he needed to figure out what was going on with her before anything else. He picked up the phone and dialed her number.

"Hello?"

"Hey Chelsea, it's Alec."

"Hi Alec."

"How are you doing?"

"I'm good. So, what happened?"

"What happened with what? What do you mean?"

"I thought you were coming to Russell?"

"Huh?"

"I knew you'd bail," Chelsea said with an irritated tone.

"What are you talking about? I am here."

"You're in town?"

"Yes Chelsea. What are you talking about? I just saw you yesterday."

"Yesterday? I think I would have remembered seeing my baby brother. Seriously, stop messing around. When are you coming to town?"

"Chelsea, I am in town."

"Oh ok," she replied sounding confused. "Well, why don't you come by tomorrow for lunch?"

"Ok sure."

"I'm so excited to see my baby brother!"

"Yes, I'm looking forward to it," Alec replied. They sat in silence for a few moments while he tried to digest what was happening. Any discussion of her family, or lack thereof, and her declining health, would be navigated carefully, because the last time it left them both upset and confused. For now, he just wanted to reunite with his sister and would leave her problems to a professional. "Hey, guess who I ran into," Alec said, trying to change the conversation.

"Who?"

"Sarah."

"Sarah Edwards?" Chelsea asked.

"Yes."

"I always liked that girl. How's she doing?"

"She's good!"

"Is she still doing the psychiatrist thing?"

"Yeah, she told me she's helped several people," he replied. "She actually said she's worked with many locals suffering from depression." After no response he continued, "It was so weird seeing her. I mean it was great, but it was like we had not missed a day. She also looks half her age. Do you ever run into her?"

"No, haven't seen her in years. Well, I don't get out much these days. She had both the brains and the beauty. Never understood why you let that one get away, little brother."

He could not have agreed more. His mind quickly veered to the possibilities of what might have happened if they had stayed together. Sarah Edwards probably would not put up with the current Alec Jenkins, at least not for long. She would have soon realized that the once-promising young businessman had pissed away his career, and she would lose all interest in him soon enough.

"Yeah, you're probably right," Alec sighed. "Anyways, I should get going. See you tomorrow Chelsea."

"Looking forward to it. Love you," Chelsea replied, before hanging up.

Bob Cole's voice continued to fill the room, while Alec tried to put together a plan to help his sister. In the morning, he would head over to Chelsea's again and maybe, after they had another conversation, things would become a little clearer. For now, he decided to call it an early night as his head was pounding. The stress of his sister's diminishing health, along with his blackouts, was exhausting. Before falling asleep, he promised to consult a doctor if his blackouts continued.

CHAPTER 9

Thursday morning, he awoke to a loud thump in the hallway. A variety of noises in the Marby Hotel were becoming expected, and Alec was beginning to get used to them. He would amuse himself in a game to identify the source, but when this one jolted him upright, he was not pleased. While making a complaint call down to the front desk, he was surprised at the time, noticing it was already nearly half-past eleven in the morning. After hanging up he had a quick shower.

First, he had planned to meet up with Chelsea at her place, and then he would rendezvous with Sarah afterwards, for lunch. By the time he put himself together, he opted to just have a quick visit with Chelsea and then go directly for his lunch date with Sarah as he was already late. While hustling through the lobby and before leaving the hotel, he noticed some strange looks from the staff that were working the front desk, and assumed it was due to his recent complaint, but then wondered if perhaps word had gone around about his fainting episode.

With no taxi in sight, he dashed over to his sister's place. A little perturbed after determining she was not home, Alec wondered where she could have possibly gone. After all, she seemingly did not have any friends and had mentioned she rarely left the house. As it was half past noon, he sprinted over to the restaurant to hopefully catch Sarah before it was too late.

Feeling that he must be a sweaty mess as he entered the restaurant, he grabbed some napkins at the doorway and discretely dabbed his reddened face and regained his composure. Turning back around, he was relieved to spot the gorgeous redhead sitting at their booth. They smiled at one another, while he made his way over. The scent of her perfume grew stronger as he approached, and he could not hide his excitement to see her.

"Good afternoon! I'm so sorry I'm late," he said, approaching the table.

"That's ok," she assured him, as she tapped playfully on the seat in the booth beside her. He had always thought it corny when he saw couples sitting side by side in restaurants, but not today.

"How are you doing today?"

"I'm good. How are you?" he asked, sliding in beside her. He actually felt like shit and was still a little freaked out about fainting the night before, but he was not about to reveal his weakness.

"You were always a shitty liar," she replied, studying his face. "So, are you going to tell me what's wrong?"

"Well, there's been some weird stuff going on lately," he conceded.

"Care to share?"

"Not right now Sarah. You have to deal with this crap all day long with your job and I'm sure it's the last thing you want to talk about."

"Seriously Alec, you can talk to me. I really don't mind."

"Maybe another time, but not today," Alec replied. "Thank you though, I appreciate it." He could tell by the look in her eyes that she was sincere, but he did not want to unload his sister's problems on her just yet. He desperately wanted to help Chelsea, but felt the timing was not appropriate as they had just reconnected. He also had not anticipated such strong feelings for her and did not want to ruin the moment by starting the date discussing his serious family medical problems.

"Coffee folks?" asked the waitress, standing at their booth holding two empty cups and a pot of coffee.

"You again," Alec chuckled.

"Huh?"

"We were in here yesterday and you served us."

"You're mistaken. I wasn't working yesterday. Anyway, would you like some coffee?"

"Yes please," Sarah replied before looking over at Alec with confusion.

"Oh sure," he replied.

"You folks need any menus?"

"No, we're ok. Just the coffee, thank you," Sarah responded. The waitress walked away muttering something under her breath. "She wasn't our waitress yesterday."

"Yes, she absolutely was our waitress," he argued quietly.

"No, she wasn't," she whispered back. "Do you think she's lying then?"

"Yes, she is lying. And now, so are you. Why?"

"You're wrong."

"I'm not wrong."

"Still stubborn I see," she replied, turning her attention to something outside the window.

"I'm only stubborn when I know I'm right," he replied with a coy grin. He did not know what sort of game Sarah and the waitress had conspired to play, but he quickly decided to just let it go.

"You mean when you think you're right," she snapped back playfully, and Alec smiled sheepishly in return.

"The town has deteriorated and become pretty rough since I left," Alec said, watching her gaze out the window.

"How so?" she asked, turning back to him.

"There just don't seem to be many people out and about like years ago. I saw quite a few derelict houses with boarded up windows ... not to mention the people," he said quietly, raising a brow toward the other patrons.

115

"Oh yes, I guess it has changed a lot since you left," she replied quietly, perusing the others. "People keep to themselves now, not like in the old days where everybody knew each other's business. Things really went south after the shooting." They sipped their coffees, shifting their eyes downward, in a moment of thought, as the waitress sauntered past their table. After seeing she was out of earshot, Sarah leaned in and whispered, "Hey, speaking of that, do you remember the Booths?"

"The older couple that lived down the street from you?"

"Yeah," she responded, seemingly surprised that he had remembered them.

"I used to cut through their yard on the way to your house. He was a cop, wasn't he?"

"Yeah, that's right. Well a few years ago Mr. Booth shot his wife, and then himself."

"What? Are you serious?" Alec blurted. Seeing the other patrons staring over, he whispered, "Does anyone know why?"

He thought back to the last time he had seen the Booths. He was cutting through their yard and was startled when Mr. Booth shouted at him. At first, he thought he was yelling at him for cutting through his yard but realized, when seeing the man smiling with his arm up in the air, he was just saying hello. The neighbor and his wife were deeply focused playing Scrabble and drinking a pot of tea on their patio. Each time he had seen them, he recalled their overly friendly appearance, and he now wondered what possible motive could result in him doing something so horrific.

"I heard he may have had some post-traumatic stress disorder after retiring from the police department. He was one of the police officers first one the scene at the high school shootings, you know. His neighbors said he'd started acting strange following the incident."

"Oh my god, that's awful." Nausea came over him as he pictured Mrs. Booth begging for her life, before her beloved husband shot and killed her.

"Mr. Booth wasn't the only one who went crazy. Do you remember Mrs. Hernandez?" she continued.

"Yes, of course. She was my favorite teacher, why?" Alec quizzed, leaning in closer as he noticed others gaining interest in their conversation.

"Well, a couple years ago she was stabbed to death by one of her students."

"Jesus Christ!" he gasped. "By who?"

"I can't remember the kid's name. I'd never heard of him until then, but I think it was an Eric, or Eldon, or something like that. Actually, I'm pretty sure it was Eric."

"Wait, Mrs. Hernandez was still teaching a couple years ago? She must've been ninety years old." Alec momentarily had an odd duplicity of feeling both horror and guilt for ever skipping her class.

117

"I think she was over ninety, actually, but they kept her on in some capacity, as she was apparently still as passionate as ever. At least that is what the article in the newspaper said. She was my favorite teacher too. Remember when she made you wear that dress for Shakespeare?" she asked, giggling.

"Oh god, yes. She told me she'd fail me if I didn't!" They shared a laugh, as the waitress methodically refilled their coffees. "You know the only reason I took that class was because you were in it?"

"Really? That's so sweet," she said, then squeezed his hand in hers. "Wait a minute, you always skipped that class though!" They laughed again, then sat quietly as Alec envisioned the jolly woman dabbing her sweaty forehead with the towel from her bra.

Sarah continued to fill him in on a few of the town's other strange occurrences of the past thirty years. Alec was unaware of any other murders in Russell that occurred after he had left. The school shooting in his senior year had evidentially triggered a rippling effect, sparking several other tragedies, as there had been a total of six murders in Russell, in recent years, which was unusual for any small Canadian town.

As they chatted, Alec continued to feel the attention of the other patrons. He surmised it was probably due to his well-groomed, executive appearance. His stylish crisp blue dress shirt, black wool dress pants, and Berluti loafers, sharply contrasted the grungy muscle shirts, saggy old torn jeans, and hygiene deficit of these particular locals. A couple sitting two tables over, on closer inspection, wore plaid flannel pajama bottoms. Alec wondered if they felt intimidated, being upstaged by his fancy attire. Although Sarah was a local, her stylish attire was more subtle, and understated, as her profession made her more sensitive to the plight of others. Outside of her workplace, Sarah, had always been, and would always shine as a very likeable person. Alec felt that he could have benefited from more years around her diplomatic influence.

"So, how is it even possible that such a good catch like Sarah Edwards has never been married?" Alec asked, glancing at her dainty hand resting atop his.

She laughed while pulling it away, then replied, "Well you know, Russell didn't exactly raise a lot of Brad Pitts!" He smiled as she eyed the man at the next table, as he dug some food out of his beard. "I thought I had found Mr. Right, but then he took the wrong turn and left."

"Sarah, I wanted ..."

"Alec, you don't need to explain yourself. What is in the past has passed. Let's just move on." She put down her cold coffee while he studied her face, struggling with what to say next. As the awkward silence loomed, Sarah laughed, continuing, "I guess the sex just wasn't good enough!"

"Yeah right! I bet I was quite the stallion back then," he replied sarcastically. Sarah was smiling, but he could tell there was still some hurt and resentment behind that smile. "You were my first, you know?" he confessed.

"Really? You never told me that. Maybe if I had known, I wouldn't have made you wait so long," she said chuckling.

"We were just babies, weren't we?"

"Yes, we really were," she replied.

"I was such an idiot. I should have asked you to come to Vancouver. Would you have actually come with me if I had asked?"

"Maybe," she replied, shrugging her shoulders. "But I would have ended up having to move back here anyway, with my mom getting sick and all. It just wasn't meant to be, I guess."

"Sarah, I'm so sorry that I wasn't there for you when your mom got sick."

"Well thanks for apologizing Alec, but you really don't need to," she said, trying to hold back the tears.

"You ever worry you'll get it?"

"What, breast cancer? Yes, all the time." She took a sip of her cold coffee and gazed out the window. "My doctor probably thinks I just like him touching my boobs because of my frequent elective checkups," she divulged, scoffing nervously.

Alec laughed along, examining his empty mug. "So besides you and I, you've never had a serious relationship?"

"Well, I wouldn't say that."

"Oh really? Please, do tell!" The thought of her being with another man was surprisingly unsettling and it took him a little off guard.

"I did date someone named Grayson, but I guess we were only a little serious."

"Don't tell me it was Grayson Spencer?" he said loudly, while emphatically smacking his hand down on the table.

"Yes, did you know him?"

"Yes, we were best friends in elementary school!"

"Really?" she asked in disbelief. "I don't remember you ever mentioning him."

"I probably never did. We stopped hanging out well before high school. That's so weird you mentioned him because I've actually been thinking about him since coming back here. So, you guys actually dated?"

"Yes, but only for a few months. That was years ago though." As she looked back out the window, he got the feeling she did not want to talk about it anymore, but curiosity got the best of him.

"I was actually …" he started to respond when something vibrated on the bench beside Sarah. As she dug into her purse Alec continued, "… thinking of tracking him down while I was out here. How's he doing?"

"Grayson actually died," she said, pulling her phone out of her purse. "He was…" she paused, before reading the text on her cell. "Oh shit! I'm sorry Alec, but I've really got to get going. I totally forgot about this appointment and now he's at my place!" she said, sliding hurriedly out of the booth.

"Wait, Grayson is dead?"

"Yes," she replied, before pressing the phone to her ear. "Hey, sorry, I'm just running behind, but I'm on route. I'll be there in five minutes." She hung up, then turned to Alec and said, "Sorry Alec, but I really need to get going. Talk later?"

"Yes, for sure. I've got some stuff to do anyway."

She reached into her purse, but Alec swatted her hand away while pulling out his own wallet. She smiled, leaned in, kissed him on the cheek, and returned to her call before heading towards the exit.

Alec did not actually have any other plans as he had hoped to spend more of the day with Sarah. With her suddenly being busy, and Chelsea apparently not at home, he figured he would check the local movie theatre to see if there was a matinee.

As he approached the theatre, he noticed a sign indicating there was a matinee, and it was a double feature, starring none other than Denzel Washington. Alec hadn't seen either movie and had no other plans, so figured he may as well stay for both. "What are the odds," he muttered out loud, while walking through the front doors past the two posters promoting each Denzel film.

Stale popcorn permeated the lobby walls and nostalgia hit him as he stood alone at the cashier. Roman J Israel would be the first film, and he had heard good things. The Equalizer 2 was the second film and although he had not seen the original Equalizer, he figured it must be good because Denzel never made a bad movie. Sitting through back-to-back films in a movie theatre was something he had once enjoyed doing regularly in his teens, but his current schedule allowed no such indulgence.

Eagerly waiting for the cashier to appear, he checked out the old posters high up on the wall. There must have been a hundred of them and most were of movies from the eighties and nineties. He wondered if they were the same posters that he had seen there back in his youth. He peered through the dirty cracked glass window to see if there was someone working on the other side but did not see anyone. The matinee was supposed to start in twenty minutes so he wondered if he may have arrived too early. He hit the service bell and shortly after could hear some rustling from the back room, followed by silence. After a minute, he hit the bell again. An elderly, hunched woman with thick glasses and greasy grey hair appeared from the back room.

"Yeah, I heard you. I'm coming, hold onto your horses," she grumbled, making her way to the glass. "For how many?" she asked, continuing to chew from the tuna sandwich in her hand.

The smell of the tuna combined with the woman's body odor seeped through the slot in the glass and assaulted his nostrils.

"Just one please," Alec sighed, as though in lonely despair, in a futile attempt to force back the fumes.

"That'll be eight dollars and fifty cents."

After flashing the woman his bank card, she rolled her eyes while pointing her hooked yellow fingernail to the handwritten sign which read 'CASH ONLY'. He rarely carried cash, but just happened to have a ten-dollar bill in his pocket so he passed it through the hole in the glass.

"Here you go," the woman said, sliding a ticket and his change through the hole.

After walking through the second set of doors, Alec looked over to his left to the concession stand. The dimly lit sign above the counter listed a scant list of items. Apparently, the Russell Movie Theatre had not jumped on board with the other ridiculous rates offered by city movie theatres. A large popcorn was listed for only $1.50 and a large pop was a mere $1.00.

"What would you like," barked the same woman who had just taken his admission money. Alec looked at yet another 'CASH ONLY' sign, then dug for the change in his pocket.

"Are these the actual prices?"

"Yes ... why?" asked the confused woman.

"Just checking," he replied, before ordering a popcorn.

Pushing his way through a third set of old swinging doors, he observed that, like most of the other buildings in town, the theatre had not done any renovations since the last time he had been there. The old theatre was narrow with only one small screen. The eighty stained and torn seats desperately needed new upholstery. Alec scattered a few programs on a seat in the back row, where he had always sat in his youth. He sat alone, patiently eating his popcorn while waiting for the lights to dim. Fifteen minutes later, the cashier appeared a third time, and proceeded with some effort, up the incline and out through the doorway at the back of the theatre. Moments later, as he mused that the hunchback was likely also the projectionist, the lights dimmed, and the opening previews began.

The first preview was for a romantic movie and his mind automatically went to Sarah. He thought the next time he spoke with her he would ask her if she would want to go see it. He smiled while imagining the two of them together in that theatre again. He could not recall the last time he had wanted to spend so much time with a woman. He wondered if he was falling for her too quickly and if maybe he should try to take it slower, but before the end of the previews, he'd decided he wouldn't be able to keep his cool. He would be giving her a call to get together again as soon as he returned to the hotel. But for now, and for the next four plus hours, he would sit in the back of that theatre and thoroughly enjoy his time alone with Denzel.

CHAPTER 10

Spending four days in Russell, during his forced vacation, Alec realized he had not put much thought and effort into his work and his life back in San Francisco. This was extremely uncharacteristic of the man, who normally thrived on an eighty-hour work week. With his emails being forwarded to his secretary and his cell phone out of commission, he had been almost completely out of touch and for the first time in as long as he could remember, his career had taken a backseat. He had thought of grabbing another cell phone but was pleasantly enjoying being off the grid, at least for the time being.

When he had returned to the hotel after the movies the previous evening, Edgar had handed him two messages. The first one was from Richard Goldman, which he chose not to bother fully reading, and the second was from Tanya asking him to call her back immediately. It was strange for the condo's receptionist to call him on vacation, but she was a strange girl, and strange happenings were becoming the norm, and now he was curious. Because it had been late, he had decided to return her call first thing the following Friday morning.

"Good morning, this is Bellstar Condominiums. How may I help you?" The unfamiliar, jolly voice took Alec by surprise. He had lived in the condo for several years and did not recognize the voice.

"Hello, may I speak with Tanya please?"

"May I ask what Tanya's last name is so I can look up the resident's number?"

"Who is this? I'm Alec Jenkins. I own one of the condos in the building and I'm assuming you must be new."

"Hello Mr. Jenkins. Yes, you are correct, I am new here. My name is Carlos and I just started this week. I don't know all of the residents yet, but if you can tell me what Tanya's last name is, I can certainly put you through."

"Tanya isn't one of the residents, she actually works at the front desk. She normally works the morning shift on weekdays."

"I'm sorry Mr. Jenkins, but I haven't met anyone by the name of Tanya. Perhaps she is off on vacation."

"Well I received a message from her yesterday asking me to call her, and it sounded important. Do you know if something is wrong with my apartment?" Alec asked, growing impatient.

"Please give me a minute Mr. Jenkins, and I will ask around to see if anyone knows why she was trying to get a hold of you." While waiting, Alec thought it was odd that Tanya would have gone on holidays without mentioning it to him before he had left. He had been avoiding her, but she surely would have mentioned it at some point.

"Hello Mr. Jenkins?"

"Yes Carlos?"

"The caretaker just checked on your condo and there appears to be nothing wrong."

"Ok, well that's a relief," Alec replied.

"I also checked with the other staff and nobody here has heard of anyone named Tanya."

"Nobody has heard of Tanya?" he barked angrily.

"That is correct sir. I've asked everyone here and they all said they've never heard of her."

"Just ask Arnold or Bob for Christ's sake! They'll know who she is, or just ask any of the other residents!"

Arnold and Bob had worked security for the building since long before he had moved in. He often wondered what either of the men would do if their services were ever needed, considering they were both well into their seventies and neither of them looked like they could handle any physical threat. However, they were always very pleasant and attentive so everyone in the building liked having them around.

"I'm sorry sir, but I don't know of a Bob or Arnold either. Is there someone else you'd like to speak with?"

"No, just forget it!" he shouted, before slamming down the phone.

He slumped on the edge of his bed trying to digest the conversation. He had known Tanya for several years. She rarely missed a day of her regular schedule and he could not recall one vacation she had ever gone on since being there. How could Carlos not have known who she or the two security guys were? He stared blankly at the phone when suddenly its ringer screeched, causing him to jump.

"Hello?"

"Hello, Mr. Jenkins. There is a Sarah here to see you."

"Thanks Edgar, I'll be right down," Alec replied eagerly.

After he had returned from the movie theatre, the two had made plans to get together for a coffee. Alec wanted to find out more about Grayson's death but was most excited to see her again. She brought him a coffee and they sat on the courtyard garden around the back of the hotel.

Although the front of the hotel was in much need of a facelift, the back of the hotel looked like something you would find on the cover of a garden design magazine. The owners of the Marby Hotel did not seem to mind that the hotel was falling apart, but apparently had a passion for gardening, as the courtyard garden was magnificent. A row of perfectly sculpted bright green shrubs outlined the large patio. Several potted bamboo and fern plants provided a verdant backdrop to a myriad of gorgeous flowers which concealed most of the uneven flagstone beneath. They sat

129

on a small vintage rickety bench that was surrounded by a bed of orange lilies.

"I've never seen so many beautiful flowers," Sarah said before drinking her coffee. "I wonder what all these beautiful orange flowers are called."

"They're tiger lilies," Alec replied.

"Look at you! Do much gardening back in San Francisco?"

"No, not all. Edgar actually mentioned the name the other day," he replied with a chuckle.

"Who is Edgar?"

"He works here at the hotel. He was at the front desk when you got here."

"I see. Well, they really are gorgeous, and they smell amazing!" She sipped her takeout coffee, while her eyes roamed the garden. "Hey, how were the movies last night?"

"You can never go wrong with Denzel," he replied, smiling.

"No, you really can't. I can't believe you watched two of them."

"I know. I haven't done that since ... actually, probably with you." They smiled at one another as they took in the beauty of the garden around them. "So, tell me what happened to Grayson?"

"He killed himself," she replied.

"Really? Wow ... any idea why?"

"I'm not sure, but I'm guessing it was due to depression. It was well after we had broken up. When we were together, he was pretty messed up, so I can't say it came as a surprise. Poor guy," she murmured as her eyes began to glaze.

"Messed up how?"

"He was really depressed and had started drinking a lot. I thought I could help him, because I mean, that's what I do, but he just kept getting worse each time I tried. Towards the end of our relationship he had stopped confiding in me about any of his issues and I just could not separate the partner from the patient and had to end it. We never spoke after the breakup and a couple years later I read in the paper that he had killed himself. His mom was inconsolable at the funeral."

Alec wondered why his sister had never mentioned anything about his suicide. "Did my sister…" he stopped himself. He wanted to ask if Chelsea brought her kids to the funeral, but still was not sure he wanted to bring up his sister and her mental health problems just yet. Sarah had to deal with mental health issues daily with her job, and Alec did not want to be a burden, at least for now.

"Did your sister what?"

"Oh nothing. So, Grayson never moved out of Russell either?" He asked, changing the subject.

"No, unfortunately he became a true Russelltin, just like me," she sighed.

After finishing their coffees, they continued to sit for a while. Although their talk of death had started on such a dark note, they were uplifted by the surrounding bright thriving environment. The yellow begonias and bright blue lobelias were in full bloom. They sat in silence for a while as they enjoyed the hummingbirds whirring and darting around the nannyberry. The courtyard's ambience was mesmerizing.

"Which ones are you favorite?" Sarah asked, looking around.

"Which flowers?"

"Yeah."

"I think I've got to go with the tiger lilies," he replied.

"You're just saying that because they're the only ones you can name," she laughed.

"Maybe," he chuckled. The two sat quietly for a moment before Alec continued, "Hey, when I die, and I'll certainly die before you, be sure I'm buried here ok?"

"That's morbid," she replied.

"It might be, but just promise me." She looked at him and realized he was being sincere.

"Ok, I promise, but you know there's two problems with that, right?"

"Oh yeah, what's that?"

"Well I might die before you. I mean that's highly doubtful because I'm so much healthier than you, but it's possible," she said, laughing and pushing at him playfully.

132

"Yeah, yeah, doubtful," he chuckled. "And what is the second problem?"

"Do you think the owner of this hotel would actually let me bury you here?"

They laughed and continued to gaze out into the garden. "Maybe I didn't think this out long enough. Well Sarah, where do you want to be buried?"

"Oh god. I don't know. I actually don't want to think about it. It's too depressing!"

Over the next hour, they sat in awe of the garden's beauty, while continuing to discuss everything from flowers to politics. Conversation had always been easy between the two, and it never ran dry. It was not until Sarah's phone buzzed that their discussion would, once again, be put on hold.

"Let me guess, you need to go?"

"Yes, I'm sorry Alec. We're not all on vacation you know," she said, before playfully elbowing him in his side. "Next time we meet for coffee, let's come here."

"I like that idea," Alec replied as they hugged. He could not stop smiling as he watched her silhouette disappear off around the hedges.

After Sarah's untimely departure, he had the urge to try again to reach Chelsea, and decided to take a walk over to his sister's place, this time with backup plans of going by the Spencer home afterwards, hoping that Mrs. Spencer still lived there. He was not sure if his old neighbor would remember him or if even talk with him about it, but he hoped she would be able to shed some light on her son's suicide.

Upon arriving at his sister's front door, he heard some shouting coming from the backyard of the house next door. After knocking loudly on Chelsea's front door and not getting a response, Alec figured he would check around back as it was very odd that she was not home yet again. Entering through the side gate, he could see, while glancing over the fence, that Chelsea's next-door neighbor was arguing with his neighbor on the other side.

After waiting for a few moments at the backdoor, he heard a commotion. Looking over the top of the fence a second time he saw the two men rolling around on the ground. The much smaller man was taking a beating, but just as Alec was about to yell over, they stopped. The fight had only lasted a mere thirty seconds, but the smaller guy had a bloodied nose and his shirt had been torn off completely. As Alec retreated towards the front of Chelsea's home, he saw the shirtless man hop in his truck and peel out of the driveway. Two other neighbors were chatting nearby, but neither seemed to have been bothered by the commotion, and he wondered if this type of thing was a regular occurrence in what had become the "hood".

After yet another disappointment at Chelsea's place, Alec made his way down the street towards the cul-de-sac where the Spencers' and his childhood home still stood. Walking past the homes at the top of his old block, he felt the eyes of the neighborhood upon him. Arriving at the end of the street, he set his eyes on his childhood home.

Memories flooded in as he looked over to the front steps. One of his favorite things to do as a child was to sit on those steps with his family and watch lightning dance across the night sky. His mother insisted with every summer storm that the family gather over a cup of hot chocolate and watch from those very steps. Even now, at the age of fifty, he still enjoyed watching a good storm. Unfortunately, he had not seen many lately as San Francisco rarely had thunderstorms because of the regulating ocean temperatures.

At the curb on the driveway was where he first began developing his skills in sales with the Kool-Aid stands. There were not many hot days where you would not find Grayson and him wheeling and dealing just to make a few bucks. The vacant driveway now showed no signs of life, the steps and foundation crumbling, as it had succumbed to the weather extremes of the Canadian prairies.

He glanced across the street at Grayson's childhood home and wondered if Mrs. Spencer still lived there. Stepping over the curb onto their driveway, he recollected the day that it was finally paved. The boys were beyond excited as the smell of hot tar filled the air. They gazed in awe upon the new black sheet being poured over the lumpy old surface of packed gravel and sand. It was as though their ice rink had just received a fresh flooding from the Zamboni, and now they'd have a brand-new smooth playing surface. He felt the 40 years that had passed, staring down at the contrast of his shiny leather loafers on the tired grey, crumbling pavement. The swaying curtain in the front window of the Spencer home caught his eye, and this time he knew for certain he was being watched.

His knock on the front door was greeted immediately by a woman with an unfriendly glare. As she hovered in the door frame her magnified yellow tinged eyeballs peered through her thick vintage lenses. A waft of both chicken noodle soup and cat pee hit him, as Elvis Presley's *'Are you Lonesome Tonight'* blared from behind the small frail woman.

"Oh, hello. I'm sorry, I was looking for Mrs. Spencer."

"It's Ms. Spencer. What do you want?" she growled angrily.

"Mrs. Spencer, is that you?"

"Yes, but I told you its Ms. Spencer!"

"Oh gosh, I'm sorry Ms. Spencer," Alec replied flustered. He could not believe the haggard stranger in front of him was the same lady he once considered to be a second mother. "I was just in the neighborhood and thought …" but before he could finish, the creature responsible for the urine odor appeared between the woman's feet.

She immediately booted the feline with the back of her heel while shouting, "Get back in there you little shit!" The thin strands of grey hair bobbled in a few rollers atop her head, while she adjusted the thick-rimmed glasses back onto her nose. Her facial lines outlined the current scowl around her mouth perfectly. Her ashen skin and hunched posture were nothing like the warm, motherly, lively figure in his fading memory.

"I'm not sure if you remember me, but my name is Alec."

"Alec?"

"Yeah, I used to live across the street many years ago."

"Alec Jenkins? Is that really you?" she asked, squinting through her thick glasses.

"Yes, it is me!"

"Well I'll be damned" she shrieked. Then, while taking a step back to look up at his face, she shrieked again, "Well I'll be damned! Oh my goodness, it's been a long time." The hardened elderly lady who had answered the door seemed to soften quickly in front of his very eyes, as the warm and loving woman he once knew was now revealed. Mrs. Spencer tried to fight back the tears but failed as one trailed down her cheek. She wiped it with a tissue which she had tucked away up in her sleeve, then placed her hand on his arm and said, "Please come on in. Are you hungry? Let me make you a bite to eat."

Taking a seat at the kitchen table, he replied, "No food for me, thanks. I actually just ate." Although he had not been in that kitchen since elementary school, he felt very much at home, as though he had never left. He peered at the door to the basement, almost expecting to see Grayson appear from the other side.

"Alec, it's so nice to see you," she said, placing a cup of hot coffee in front of him. He smiled, then took a sip while studying the room. From what he could recall, the kitchen looked nearly identical to when he would last have been there. A piece of warm rhubarb pie and blob of vanilla ice cream appeared in front of him as he checked out the clock on the wall. Unlike most of the other items in the kitchen, he was pretty sure the clock was not there when he'd last visited. "When did you get into town?" she asked while taking a seat at the table across from him.

"I've been here for a few days," he replied while watching her take a sip from her mug. Just taking some time off work and figured a trip home was well overdue. It's nice to see you too, Mrs. Spencer. I'm sorry, I mean Ms. Spencer."

"Oh, please Alec, just call me Bev. Geez, I just cannot believe this. I mean, I haven't seen you since … well since your parents' funeral, I guess. I still miss your mother you know?"

"Me too, Mrs. Spencer." She tilted her head down in disapproval. "I'm sorry, I mean Bev." He sat back in his chair while Bev smiled at him from across the table. The room became awkwardly quiet for a few moments before Alec thought of what to say next. "You know I …"

"What?" she asked, staring him down.

"Oh nothing, never mind."

"Come on Alec. I know it's been a long time, but you know you can still talk to me."

"It's just that after all these years I still feel guilty. They were coming out to visit me when it happened, and my mom hated to travel."

"Well that's just silly Alec. Accidents happen and you shouldn't feel responsible for something that's completely out of your hands." She reached across the table and rubbed the top of his hands making him feel like he was a child again. "I just wish your mother hadn't been so scared of planes. If they had flown, they'd probably still be with us today." He thought of the conversation with his sister about their parents' headstone. "Hey how's your sister doing? Does she still live up the street? I haven't seen her around lately."

"Chelsea's doing well. She's been busy lately, that's probably why you haven't seen her." Alec assumed his sister's mental issues had kept her occupied and he did not want rumors to spread throughout the neighborhood.

139

Looking around the room, he noticed the several trinkets spread throughout the kitchen and wondered if they were the same ones, he had seen all those years earlier. Out in the hallway hung the old treehouse clock he remembered seeing so many times as a child. It was a project the boys had worked on in the third grade and Grayson had presented it to his mother one Mother's Day. Alec's own mother cried when she got hers, but it did not stay up on the wall for even one full year. Looking at the one Mrs. Spencer had hanging on her wall; he did not blame his own mother one bit for taking it down.

"And how about those kids of hers?" Bev asked. But before he could answer she continued, "She must have her hands full with Kendra, being a teenager now."

Bev's confirmation of his niece and nephew came with some relief as he had started to question his own sanity with everything that had been happening. His relief quickly turned to concern and sadness for his sister. Ron must have taken off and taken Kendra with him and now she was having a mental breakdown. He also felt bad for his niece as she was only about fifteen, from what he could recall, a tough age to be having your parents splitting up. At least Jason was old enough to already be out of the house. Sitting in that kitchen, he thought that maybe it was time to ask Sarah for her help.

"Yes, I'm sure she does," he replied, trying to think of something else to talk about.

140

They continued to talk of old times and Bev updated him on some of the neighborhood gossip, reassuring his decision to not delve any further into Chelsea's situation. His sister's divorce and mental instability might be a hot topic if the neighborhood found out, but then again Sarah had told him that people kept to themselves. Nobody seemed to bat an eye as Chelsea's neighbors fought outside.

The conversation had yet to include anything about her son, nor his suicide as Alec was hesitant to bring it up. He had planned on waiting for Bev to mention Grayson's name before delving into his suicide. However, as the conversation began to stale, he realized she was not going to bring up her son.

Alec thought about leaving it alone, worrying it was too difficult for her to speak of, but figured it was important he got some answers. He worried he may be heading down the same road so the more he knew about Grayson's suicide the better. While Bev went on a tangent speaking about her large collection of birdhouses, Alec strategized how he would bring Grayson's name into the conversation. He glanced over at the treehouse clock which showed it was twenty past six.

"Hey, I remember making those clocks," he blurted out cutting her off mid-sentence. Bev stared at him blankly as he continued pointing at the clock. "We made those in Mr. Jones' class. Grayson's turned out much better than mine," he said, chuckling nervously. He studied her face for a reaction, but she remained stoic. Her lack of expression had him wondering if she would even discuss Grayson at all. The room had grown quiet and uncomfortable while she continued to stare at him as he babbled on. "We were such good friends."

She leaned forward in her chair and whispered, "Who were such good friends?"

Now uncomfortable and nervous, he wondered if he should change the topic, but figured it was now or never. They had been gabbing about nothing for over half an hour and he had nothing left to discuss. "Grayson and I," he blurted.

She forcefully grabbed his hand with her left and with her right held her index finger to her lips. "Shh … be quiet now Alec. We wouldn't want to wake him".

"Wake who?"

She looked at him, appearing confused, then whispered, "Well Eddy, of course."

"Eddy?"

"Yes, Eddy," she retorted, before peering over his shoulder. "If he finds out that you're here, we'll both be in big trouble."

"Eddy?" Alec inquired again.

"He's sleeping, so we'd better not wake him." She leaned over and whispered into Alec's ear, "He's not very nice when he's awake."

"Bev, who is Eddy?"

"Come on now Alec, you know exactly who Eddy is," she replied with a coy grin, sitting back in her chair. "Actually, maybe you can help me out. I have some things to do later so if he could tag along with you for a bit after he wakes up, that'd be great. I know you're not fond of him, but it would help me out a lot if you could."

"Are you talking about your nephew Eddy?" he asked, sitting back in his chair. "Are you ok, Mrs. Spencer?"

She took a sip of her cup of coffee and grinned, "Yes I'm fine, why do you ask?" He thought of explaining that the boy had died forty years earlier but thought he had better not. He watched in disbelief, as she seemingly transformed back to the elderly, grey-skinned, woman right before his very eyes. He gawked at her as she snickered at him while holding up the coffee pot. "You ok boy? Would you like some more coffee?"

"Oh no, thank you, Mrs. Spencer."

"I told you boy, it's Ms. Spencer!"

Nodding toward the clock on the kitchen, he said, "Sorry Ms. Spencer. I actually should get going."

Her saddened eyes peered over her thick lensed glasses, as he rose from his chair. "So soon?"

"Yes sorry, Ms. Spencer, but I've got a lot of catching up to do while I'm in town. Perhaps I could come visit you again while I'm in town?"

"Yes, that would be lovely," she replied smiling.

143

The incorrigible cat darted for the door as Alec's hand touched the knob, only this time his transgression was met more tenderly by his owner. Ms. Spencer scooped him up and petted the top of his head.

"Who's taking care of you these days Ms. Spencer?"

"Taking care of me?" She asked with a furrowed brow. "Why would I need to be taken care of? Grayson and I are just fine here on our own."

"Grayson?"

"Yes, my son."

"Grayson lives here?"

"Well of course he does silly. He should be home from school any minute now. If you can just wait a little, I'm sure he'd be very excited to see you."

A sense of sadness came over him as he watched her continue to pet the purring cat in her arms. "I actually really need to get going, but please tell Grayson I said hello."

"Sure, I can do that. What did you say your name was again?"

"My name? It's Alec," he replied while bolting backward onto the front lawn.

"Well that'll be easy to remember, his best friend's name is Alec!" she shouted, before closing the door.

Alec stood, head spinning, on the lawn for a moment while recalling seeing a small pair of runners in the entranceway of the home. He wondered how long the small, vintage children's

144

running shoes had been there. The last time he had seen a pair of those were when he had owned a pair in his childhood. Grayson would have worn shoes like that too, but it would have been nearly forty years ago.

Before heading across the street, he glanced back at the Spencer home to see the woman's scowl disappear behind the curtains. Both sadness and eeriness came over him as the once intelligent and loving lady, whom he once considered a second mother, had transformed, and become this bitter angry lunatic. Time and tragedy had clearly destroyed her sweet, lovely appearance and diminished her mental capacity.

Knocking hesitantly on the front door of his childhood home, Alec wondered what the hell would appear on the other side. He had prepared himself for anything outside of normal, after the mind-altering twilight zone he had just witnessed across the street. He knocked louder on the familiar, sun faded solid ash door again, but after no response, he ventured back onto the front lawn to assess the rest of his old family home. The second story soffits and fascia and window trims were neglected and in desperate need of scraping and new paint, while its sun-bleached mangled awnings hung on for dear life. The eaves troughs sagged and were battered down the sides of the home, while the fallen downspouts lay useless on the ground.

The young elm trees which outlined the perimeter of the property were now massive and overtook the front yard. His father had planted those trees the same weekend the Spencers' driveway was being refinished. Alec's parents took great pride in their home and it showed as it was one of the nicest on the street. Its sizeable yard demanded much upkeep, but his parents were able to divide and conquer. His mother took care of the massive garden and several flower beds while his father took care of the trees and maintained its perfectly manicured lawn.

What was once the nicest yard on the street hid neglected, covered by overgrown branches and a decrepit, rusted, old Corvette. The carpet of lawn had conceded to a healthy crop of dandelions and it appeared that the ankle-deep crop had not yet been weeded or mowed that entire summer. The previous horticultural envy had become lost with the others on the now derelict row of neglected yards and gardens.

Alec made his way towards the side of the house where a large wooden privacy fence protected the back yard. It appeared to be the same fence that his dad had built and was now on life support as the harsh Manitoba weather had taken its toll over the years. It now brandished a large safety lock, and without hesitation, overcome with curiosity, Alec hurled himself over, nearly snapping the wood slats in half upon doing so. He smirked with pride as he was reminded of the countless successful covert fence-hopping capers of his childhood. After examining his manicured executive hands for splinters, he began perusing the cherished old backyard.

The fire pit located in the back corner of the yard, where he and Chelsea would often pitch a tent and camp, was still there. His older sister's stories of monsters and boogeymen would deny him of any sleep many nights when they camped. Each time he would promise himself that he'd never stay in that tent again. Chelsea was grounded for one week after their parents found out about the scary stories, but that did not stop her from telling them as it continued for several more summers.

The only thing noticeably missing was the large kidney-shaped swimming pool that once occupied the space adjacent to the fire pit. When the heat of the summer was too much for street hockey out front of the house, Alec and his friends would take refuge in the backyard in the swimming pool. The Jenkins family made good use of their pool as the kids were in it often. Gerald and Susan hosted several pool parties with friends and neighbors. Now the vacant hole in the ground had been filled and replaced with long grass and dandelions.

As he worked his way back through the weeds along the fence, keeping a keen eye on the house for sudden signs of life, it appeared everything else in the backyard was as he had remembered. Approaching the end of the rickety fence, he found the words *'Sarah and Alec forever'* carved into the side of its end post. It was barely legible, but he remembered the two of them etching it there back in high school, not long before he had left. He recalled a promise they made to each other that day to stay together no matter how difficult the distance would put strain on their relationship.

As Alec hopped back over the fence and made his way back down the street, he continued thinking of Sarah and wondered what she was doing at that moment. She was most likely still working, he thought, as she had mentioned that she worked into the evening most days, to allow some of her working patients to set their appointments after hours. Sarah enjoyed being a psychiatrist but mentioned feeling overwhelmed lately, as her patient base had more than tripled within just the last year. Although she did not share the specifics, he got the impression Russell was having some sort of mental health epidemic.

He made his way back to the hotel to have some dinner and hoped Sarah had left him a message. It was just past nine o'clock when he walked through the hotel lobby doors and found two messages awaiting his arrival at the front desk, but to his dismay, neither were from Sarah. The first note was a message the clerk had written down from Richard Goldman which he slid into his pant pocket, thinking he would read it later. The second message was to call Chelsea. After calling her back from the front desk and getting no answer, he decided to grab a bite in the hotel's lounge.

To wash down his pasty chicken alfredo, he polished off a bottle of merlot, promising himself he would have just a couple more drinks at the bar before calling it a night. Three hours later and nine double whiskeys, defeated once more, Alec was feeling no pain. When he had first arrived, every table had been in use, but now as he sat at the bar drinking alone, there were only two occupied. After one of the tables cleared their tab, Alec fixed his stare on the one remaining, which was occupied by what appeared to be a loving married couple. He wished that could be him and Sarah but was saddened at the more realistic conclusion that she'd never settle down with a drunk loser like him. He turned his glare over to his own pathetic reflection in the mirror behind the bar.

"Fuck you, Iron Mike," he slurred, shoving his empty glass aside.

"Would you like another one?" asked the rugged bartender with the thick handlebar mustache.

"Sure, why not," he sighed. Yet another night had developed where he would be dominated by the heavyweight champ. "I'll get you another night, Mikey," Alec muttered.

"What was that?" Asked the bartender, sliding a glass of whiskey in front of him.

"Never mind."

While downing the last mouthful of the whiskey, he noticed, in the mirror, a couple sitting in a booth behind him who had a striking resemblance to the couple he had seen at his parents' gravesite earlier. They seemed to have appeared out of nowhere, as he had just seen the one couple left in the whole place, seconds prior. He gawked at them through the reflection for a moment before realizing they were motioning for him to come over.

He slid off his chair and stumbled off in their direction. He tried to focus on the woman, who was now eyeing him, while whispering into her male companion's ear. Impaired by his blurred vision and sluggish legs, he struggled to make his way across the empty lounge. The man looked very much like some of the photos he had seen of his own father, at a younger age. As he arrived within a few feet of the booth, the family resemblance became uncanny. The man smiled and was about to speak when suddenly a waitress collided with Alec, dumping her full tray of dirty glasses on him and onto the floor.

"Oh my god," the waitress gasped, before squatting down to pick up the glasses and tray from their feet. "I'm so sorry sir," she sighed, looking up at him.

"It's ok, it's not your fault. I wasn't watching where I was going," Alec replied, bending down to one knee to help.

"Oh no, I got your shirt," she gasped.

She quickly took the cloth from over her shoulder and dabbed it over his shirt. Her strong perfume caught his nostrils, while her bright blue eyes met his. She was stunning, and although much too young for him, he was instantly intrigued by her overwhelming sex appeal. He was quickly embarrassed, as his mind immediately had gone to where it should not, as he realized she was probably barely the legal age to be serving alcohol. While picking up the last few shards of broken glass, he caught sight of her name tag, which was half hidden behind her long luscious straight blonde hair.

"It's ok Jenny, don't worry about it," Alec said slowly, trying not to slur. "It looks like you got a lot more on yourself," he chuckled awkwardly, while glancing over her shoulder to look for his intended target, the oddly familiar young couple. To his disbelief, they were gone, leaving only a pair of empty wine glasses behind.

"Can I at least buy you a drink?" Alec stood silent, gawking at the empty booth, still baffled at the couple's disappearance. "Sir?"

His eyes shifted back to the waitress. He knew it would be too difficult for him to resist her request, as it was not too often the fifty-year-old would have such a young attractive female offering to buy him a drink, but he would try.

"Oh no, it's quite alright," he replied, trying not to slur.

"Oh boy, now you're bleeding," she said while looking down at his hand. "Shit, let me grab you something to clean that up at least." The glass was so sharp, it had cut through his thumb like soft butter and he had not noticed.

"Oh, shit! It's bleeding quite badly, isn't it?" he said, staggering, becoming light-headed and weak in the knees.

"Here, hold your hand up above your head," Jenny said, grabbing hold of his wrist. "With a deep cut like that, you've got to keep the bleeding above your heart, or you could pass out. You're actually looking a little pale. Please take a seat and I'll get you a bandage and another cocktail."

"Seriously Jenny, you don't need to buy me a drink, but I will take the bandage." He dropped into the booth, where the young couple once were waiting to speak to him.

"I'm afraid I must insist!" Jenny shouted, making her way over to the bar. He sat in the booth awaiting the waitress' return and realized he was now literally, the only person in the lounge.

"Here you go," said the young waitress who had returned with a first aid kit. Alec reached for the kit as she slid onto the booth beside him. "Here, let me help you with that."

"I can do it. Seriously, you really don't need to fuss."

"It's no fuss, really. Boy, you really did a number on this thing," she said, examining his thumb. She poured some table salt into a glass of water she had brought along with her and then dabbed a cloth from the first aid kit into the glass. "This is going to sting a little," she said before dabbing the cut with the gauze. It stung like hell, but he was not going to let her know. After squeezing some antibiotic cream onto the cut, she wrapped his thumb with the gauze, before placing the bandage over top.

"Wow, you really know what you're doing there," Alec said.

"I've had my fair share of cuts doing this job. Hang tight, I'll be right back," she said before sliding out of the booth. He sat for a few minutes wondering where she had gone and why she'd asked him to stay put.

"Seriously?" Alec exclaimed, seeing the waitress returning with a drink in hand.

"It's the least I can do," she replied while sliding the very large glass of whiskey and coke in front of him.

"Well thank you, but completely unnecessary." He took a big sip from the straw, then asked, "Where did everyone go?"

"We close at midnight."

"What time is it now?" Alec asked, looking at his wrist which a watch did not occupy.

"It's a quarter past midnight."

"Oh well, don't let me ..."

"No, it's ok. I told the others I would close up shop, so there's no rush. Actually, mind if I join you for one?"

"Not at all," he sputtered.

"I'm just going to change out of these clothes and into something more comfortable," she said before leaving.

While waiting at the booth, he pulled out the piece of paper containing the message he had received earlier at the lobby desk from Richard. The message said for Alec to call him as soon as possible. He wondered what could possibly be so urgent but figured it could wait. It was too late now to call, and he was too drunk for a conversation with Richard. However, he would be sure to call him back in the morning.

"Alec, do you want another?" Jenny shouted as she reappeared from behind the bar. "They're free at this time of night!"

He looked down at his large glass which was already nearly empty and replied, "Oh hell, why not."

Her more comfortable clothing consisted of a very short black leather skirt, like one you would see at a strip club. The tiny piece of clothing, which sort of resembled a shirt, barely covered her very large breasts and only a part of one shoulder. As she strolled across the bar, with her arms in the air holding a drink in each hand, he could not help but notice the flatness of her stomach. Her large firm breasts bounced up and down, having him wondering whether they were real. He reminded himself of her age and gave himself a quick talking to, but as she slid into the booth across from him, he caught a whiff of her newly applied perfume and could not help himself.

"I like your perfume," Alec said, realizing the alcohol was taking over control of his actions. *She's just a kid for Christ's sake. Smarten up you old fuck!* He again tried to remind himself of the very large age gap, but the look she was giving him was saying she wanted more than just a drinking partner.

"Oh thanks, it's Santal 33!" Alec nodded like he was familiar with it. "Hey, I'm sorry again for spilling on you. Not a good thing to do on your first day."

"Seriously Jenny, don't worry about it," he replied, trying not to stare at her chest. "Today is your first day working here?"

"Yes, probably my last too," she said sheepishly. "I don't think they like me much here."

"Why is that?" Alec asked, while also wondering why they would allow someone to close the place on her own on her first day.

"I don't think the locals like foreigners here."

"Yes, I can attest to that. So, you're not from around here?"

"God no, I'm from Chicago."

"Chicago? That is a long way away from here. What brought you to Russell?"

"It's a long story," she replied, before taking a long sip of her drink. "Let's just say an opportunity presented itself and I took it."

"An opportunity in the restaurant business?"

"Oh god no," she laughed. "This is just a short-term gig. I'll be out of here soon, even if they don't fire me." She took another sip of her drink, then leaned in towards Alec. "So where is Alec from?"

"San Francisco. Well, I was actually born here, but I left right after high school." She smiled, then lit a cigarette and took a drag leaving her bright red lipstick on its filter. "Are you allowed to smoke in here?"

"Oh, I don't know," she giggled taking another drag. "What are they going to do, fire me?"

"Well maybe," Alec chuckled. "Hey, how did you know my name?"

She stared at him briefly, then replied, "I don't know, I guess the bartender must've told me." She took a sip of her drink, then continued, "I can't say I blame you for leaving here. This place is such a shit-hole," she said while her tongue played around with the straw in her glass. She pulled it in and out of her mouth while playfully stroking its shaft with her fingers. The flirting was blatant, and he wondered if she had meant it to be. "I don't think I'll be staying too long. How long are you going to be here?"

He could not recall mentioning his name to the bartender, but the allure from the waitress had distracted him. He felt the erection of his penis jamming against the crotch of his pants and he envisioned her handling it like she did the straw. He briefly fantasized her lips around his penis, then to having sex with her, before again reminding himself that she was way too young for him. He started to feel a bit off. He was definitely drunk, but his lips had suddenly become numb and his nose tingled. His eyelids felt heavy. He was quickly losing control of his body.

"I think I need to get going. Can you grab my bill from …" he muttered slowly, trailing off.

"What was that Alec?"

"I need to …"

"I'm sorry. I can't understand you," Jenny replied. He tried to speak again but could not. "Alec, are you ok?" The room began spinning and he could tell he was seconds from passing out. "Do you have your room key with you?" He nodded and reached for his pocket, but his hands were not capable of assisting. She reached into his pocket and pulled out his room key, before his head hit the table.

CHAPTER 11

Upon first entering 620, one would assume it was a crime scene. An armchair was tipped over, a lamp hung from a nightstand by its chord, and heaps of discarded clothing lay strewn across the floor. An empty bottle of whiskey and shattered glass spattered the soaked carpet. The red wine-soaked bed sheets that clung to the foot of the bed frame exposed a sagging stained mattress, and across the room the mini bar door hung wide open, displaying only a few sodas on its nearly empty shelves. The room wreaked of stale booze, mixed with strange perfume and old cigarette smoke.

Alec squinted, gradually opening his eyes, gaining focus on the ceiling stain, while trying to assemble any memory of events from the previous night. The last thing he remembered was having drinks at the hotel bar. Up to his left, dangling from the bedside lampshade beside him, was a lace bra. A familiar sick feeling of disgust and regret came over him. Unable to move his head because of the pounding headache, his eyes moved to the foot of the bed, where he discovered the black polished, dainty, female toenails next to his. He slowly rolled to his right and to find a young lady's eyes, inches away, staring back at him.

"Good morning, sleepyhead!" the stranger said giggling, reaching for his midsection.

"Jesus Christ, who the hell are you?" Alec blurted, abruptly sitting straight up. He rubbed his temples trying to numb the throbbing pain.

"Sorry, I didn't mean to startle you," she confessed, laughing, swinging her hand back, and tucking it playfully behind her blonde curls. "After you passed out, I did a few more bumps and couldn't sleep. I tried to wake you for one more round, but you weren't having any of it."

"One more round? Seriously, who are you?"

"Come on Alec, you weren't that drunk," she pouted, propping herself on one elbow. He shook his head, frowning back at her. "Are you serious?"

"Yes, I'm serious," he challenged, frantically turning to confront her directly.

"I'm Jenny. We met in the lounge downstairs." He suddenly had a flashback of the pretty young blonde dabbing his shirt.

"Oh shit, you're the waitress from downstairs!"

"Yes. Wow, were you really that fucked up?"

He looked around the room, trying to gather his surroundings. "Did we ..." he fumbled, reaching for the sheets, as he realized he was completely naked.

"Have sex? Jesus you don't even remember that?" Jenny giggled.

"I don't remember anything," he muttered, half apologizing, while reaching down to retrieve his jeans from the heap of clothes beside the bed.

"Well, you were so hammered I had to help you back to your room. Then one thing led to another. Hey, mind if I have a shower?"

"No, knock yourself out," he replied over his shoulder, preoccupied with a sudden need for a cigarette. Tiptoeing around the broken shards, he found a pack sticking out of a leather purse, so he slipped one out and lit it using the lighter from inside the pack. He pulled back on the nicotine stick hard, with some relief, trying to sort out exactly what the hell had happened. He vaguely remembered stumbling over to the couple in the booth, and then slamming into the waitress. He looked down at his thumb wrapped in bloody gauze, and then recalled this young lady, Jenny, helping him out with the cut.

Flipping the armchair back into position, he sat, scrambling to try to piece it all together, discovering that he had a perfect view of Jenny's body through the steamy glass shower doors. He followed the foamy trail of shampoo from her soapy, long blonde hair down the dimpled small of her back. He wondered how they had ended up in bed together. The last thing he could recall was feeling dizzy while they flirted in the booth. Suddenly, the loud shriek of the vintage desk phone beside him startled Alec, as he jumped to hastily picked up its heavy receiver.

"Hello," he barked, taking another drag from the cigarette, while keeping a voyeuristic eye on the shower scene.

"I've been watching you," hissed a creepy muffled voice. Jumping up, Alec tried to decipher whether the menacing voice was that of a man or a woman.

"Who is this?" he demanded, listening for more of the voice, searching the mouthpiece of the receiver, as though to find some clue to the source.

"You never should have come back here."

A deafening dial tone blared through the receiver, denying Alec a chance to respond. He darted over to the window, peering through the streaked glass, confused, half expecting to find the culprit standing on the ledge just outside. Seeing nothing unusual below the 6th floor window, he continued searching the room. As he hung up the phone, his mind was still focused on the voice, which seemed eerily familiar, but he could not place it. Turning back to resume the tantalizing shower view, he suddenly jumped, once again startled, but this time it would be to find Jenny, a few feet in front of him, posing naked in the doorway, staring directly into his eyes.

"Busted!" she smirked.

"Jesus Christ, you really need to stop doing that!" Alec clutched at his chest defensively, taking another pull from the cigarette. Jenny, while keeping her eyes fixed on him, slid her lace thong up and playfully snapped it in place.

161

"Wow you're jumpy this morning. I also get a little jumpy sometimes, after a night of blow."

"We did cocaine last night?"

She laughed, then replied, "Wow, you must have been really fucked up." Jenny retrieved her lace bra from the lamp, finished getting dressed and headed towards the door while slicking her damp blonde hair up into a tight ponytail. He watched as it playfully bounced from side to side with each step she took. Flashing a tiny bag of white powder, she spun past, with a coy smile, "See you later."

Before he could respond, the door slammed closed behind her. He stared at the minibar as flashbacks from last night began play, interrupted by the telephone ringing again. Agitated in frustration, he picked up the receiver.

"What do you want?"

"Well I was going to ask you how your vacation was going, but apparently there's no need!" Goldman chuckled on the other end of the line.

"Oh, sorry Richard. I just got a prank call and thought it was another. I was just about to call you back. What's up?"

"We've got a problem. The Thompsons are looking to pull out. Apparently, they're not happy with our services lately." Both men knew that "our services" meant Alec Jenkins' services, as Alec solely managed the family's account. He was not sure if Goldman was overreacting or if it was just another one of his

162

ploys to discredit Alec's work, but the Thompson account was one of the company's largest, so it was important not to take any chances.

The Thompson family had been Alec's first big signing and the one that solidified his future with Woodward Financial. When he had secured the contract with the Thompsons, Mr. Rhodes congratulated him for attaining the biggest client that the company had ever acquired over its eighty years in business. He presented Alec with a gold Rolex, with AJ engraved initials and company's logo on its back. He was relieved to see his same valuable possession was still laying safely on the nightstand. Sliding the classic treasure onto his wrist, he cleared his throat, thinking of what to do next.

"Ok, what do we know?"

Goldman continued, "We know that they've had several meetings with the Midula Group and that they're very close to moving everything over to them."

"And how do you know this ... Tom?" Alec surmised.

Tom Neale, a seasoned private investigator the firm had hired back when Rhodes was still President of the company, was often used in these types of situations to gather information. At first, Alec thought his old boss was ridiculous for hiring a private investigator, but Tom had proven to be very valuable over the years. The man was now well into his seventies, but still had a knack of finding out information whenever called upon. Over the years, he had become quite a legend at Woodward Financial.

Over the past fifteen years, several stories had circulated around the office as to what Tom had done before working for Woodward Financial. One of those stories was that he had been working for the CIA and had actually killed several people. Another was that he was a member of the FBI and was a part of the apprehension of several members of the Cosa Nostra gang. But the story Alec enjoyed most was that the television series The Blacklist was based upon Tom's life.

Like everyone else at Woodward Financial, Alec was not privy to much about Tom and his past. However, he did come to find out that Tom had indeed committed at least one murder in his lifetime. One night after several scotches, Rhodes shared a story that he himself had helped get rid of the body of Tom's wife. At first Alec thought Rhodes was pulling his leg, but after divulging such specific detail of what the incident, Alec realized the shocking story must have been true. It also explained why Tom was so loyal and devoted to Mr. Rhodes. After Alec's predecessor's death, Alec assumed the detective was aware of Alec's knowledge of the duo's crime and was confident that Tom's loyalty, partly by default, would be passed on to him.

"Yes, I had him run some surveillance on Jason Thompson," Goldman replied.

164

"I'll deal with it. They must have fed Jason some bullshit information about us. I'll set up a meet with him to set him straight. Have Tom do some digging on the Midula Group. I'm sure they've got some dirt we can bring forth to the Thompsons," Alec ordered.

"Will do boss!"

Although Goldman had shown he was looking to take over Alec's position, he always respected the decisions of his boss. They rarely saw eye to eye on things. However there had been a few occasions where the President and Vice President worked together to close some of the larger deals.

He could hear housekeeping out in the hallway tapping on doors and he did not want them coming into his room. Some breakage had occurred during last night's apparent wild sex party and he did not want staff seeing it before he could tidy up and do damage control. A picture had fallen off the wall and its broken frame and cracked glass leaned against the baseboard. While tucking the telephone receiver between his shoulder and chin, he quickly opened the door a crack and hung out the DO NOT DISTURB sign. Picking up bottles, broken glass, and piling up the stained sheets, he gathered his clothes. While still on the phone, in a flurry of both disbelief and disgust, he could not wait to get off the phone and out of this hell.

"I'll catch a flight tomorrow. Please ask Ellen to book me an early one and have Clive pick me up at the airport."

"I'm on it! See you soon."

Hanging up the receiver he realized that his long time secretary, Ellen, wouldn't be able to send him his confirmation via text as he didn't have a cellular, so he again picked up the desk phone to inform Goldman. With the receiver to his ear, he didn't hear a dial tone.

"Hello?" He said, while examining and confirming the phone wasn't unplugged.

"Go back and don't ever return, otherwise I'll slit your throat ear to ear!" Growled the voice through the receiver.

Before he could reply, a sudden click was followed by a loud dial tone. Alec's trembling hand dropped the receiver as he realized it was the same voice from the previous call. Only this time, the voice was even more familiar, and he tried to recall where he had heard it before.

After running the shower for ten minutes, still unable to get any hot water, and finding an empty shampoo bottle, he gave up, and splashed his face in the tiny, birdbath sink. He threw on jeans and a clean shirt before heading out the door. The phone call had him rattled, and the last place he wanted to be was where that creepy caller could find him.

As the elevator complained its way down to the lobby, Alec hoped its other passenger could not smell his boozy stench. He suspected the slow, hot elevator ride had provided the perfect incubation period to intensify the remaining body odor of residual sweat, booze, and dried seminal fluid.

He was hoping to sneak by the front desk, but the attentive Edgar did not miss a thing. The smile and knowing nod from Edgar confirmed that he was aware of Alec and the waitress's little escapade.

"Mr. Jenkins, how was your night?"

"Just fine thank you," he lied, trying to keep his distance from the man. "Actually, I couldn't get any hot water this morning".

"Oh no, my apologies. This place is falling apart. Between you and I, the owner does not want to spend a dime on anything unless it's on his garden, of course," he whispered out of the side of his mouth, while rolling his eyes. Alec wondered if Edgar might be upset with him for hooking up with the waitress, as Edgar was much closer to her age and likely had a thing for the beautiful young lady. "We had some issues with the hot water on your floor a couple weeks ago and I thought we'd had that solved. I would offer you another room, but we're actually booked solid. You know my room is just over there," he said, pointing at the door off to the side of lobby. "If you'd like to use my shower, go ahead."

"Oh no, that's quite alright, Edgar," Alec leaned back, as Edgar advanced.

"Really, I don't mind." Edgar leaned in further. "No offence meant here, but I think your other lady friend might get wise, if you know what I mean. Just clean yourself up a little." Alec was both impressed and embarrassed as the clever desk clerk patted him on his back.

"Ok thanks, Edgar. I appreciate it."

Although he was slightly uncomfortable using someone's hotel room to wash up, he now winced at the thought of showing up in this more uncomfortable, unimpressive condition, to his upcoming lunch date with Sarah. Edgar tossed him the key, and Alec made his way over to the room.

Edgar was not much for cleanliness. In fact, his room looked like it had not had a visit from one of the housekeepers in months. His room was much smaller than Alec's but had a small kitchenette. It resembled his kitchen back in San Francisco with the dirty dishes piled to the top of the sink and covering the countertop. Edgar appeared to be a big fan of porn, as several videos featuring naked women were stacked on display next to the television. This did not surprise Alec as the young man running the dingy hotel appeared to have no girlfriend, and few prospects, as from what Alec had seen so far, the small town didn't have Jenny caliber candidates to offer. He wrapped his bandaged hand in a sandwich bag, and after a hot, soapy, refreshing shower, he found Edgar's phone and called his secretary.

"Woodward Financial, this is Ellen speaking."

"Hi Ellen, its Alec."

"Hello darlin'! Well for feck's sake, I've missed you. How's your wee vacation so far?" Alec had not realized, until now, how much he had missed the lass, and her thick Scottish accent, which she often used to get away with swear words in an oddly acceptable way. Although Ellen had lived in the United States for more than half her life, she still managed to maintain her lyrical Scottish tongue. Her endearing voice and motherly persona brought him much comfort.

"So far pretty interesting. Did Richard get a hold of you regarding my flight tomorrow morning?"

"Yes, he did, darlin'. I've got you on the seven am flight. I reserved your regular window seat in first class and Clive will be there waitin' when you land."

"Can you also set up a meeting with Jason Thompson for tomorrow evening? I know its short notice, but he can never say no to a Giants game. Oh, and I'll need two tickets for the Giants game."

169

"Yes, brilliant, consider it done. The Yankees are in town so there's no chance of him missing that game. I will get some tickets by their dugout and let Clive know as well. Take care dearie, and we'll see you soon."

"You're the best, Ellen."

"Oh, I know I am, darlin'."

Alec really did think she was an excellent secretary and felt lucky to have her. She seemed to have the answers for everything, and he could not recall one time when she had let him down. Ellen had also taken over the vacant mother position in his life. She had been with him through thick and thin, but he was pretty sure she agreed with the others regarding his need for the vacation. However, in her case, he was not offended as he knew she was only looking after his best interests. Since the start of his downward spiral it upset him most letting her down. He could see the concern and disappointment in her eyes every time he came into the office with a massive hangover and Jack Daniels cologne. She often had to make excuses for his tardiness and forgotten meetings. Her most recent excuse was needed for his last missed scheduled meeting with Jason Thompson.

Hanging up the phone, he noticed a Marby Hotel notepad beside it, with the words *'ALEC JENKINS #620'* handwritten in large print. He sat for a moment, pondering its significance, before picking up the phone again and dialing Sarah's number. They spoke briefly and discussed going for a walk in the park.

Still curious about the notepad, he hung up and left Edgar's hotel room, passing the desk on his way out of the hotel. He would have thanked Edgar again, but the lobby was empty.

It was a beautiful day and Alec sat nervously on the park bench awaiting Sarah's arrival. He was not sure if he had the butterflies in his stomach from excitement, like he'd had previously, or if he was nervous about her catching a hint of last night's activities. Although he had cleaned himself up, he worried that she would somehow still know, as she seemed to have that womanly radar. As she approached, he took a quick sniff of his shirt, confirming once again, he was clear of any external residue.

"Well hello," she said smiling, as she neared. He instantly realized that the anxiousness he felt was guilt. How had he let some harmless flirting end up so beyond control last night?

"Well hello." The words rolled off his tongue tenderly, but his stomach struggled with the telltale lack of authenticity. They smiled at each other, as he tried to hide the developing nausea in his gut.

"What's wrong?" she asked, searching his face, after they hugged.

"Wrong? Nothing … why?" She could read him like a book.

"You just look upset," she said, handing him a coffee before taking a seat beside him on the bench. "Oh no, what happened to your thumb?"

"It's nothing. I just cut it doing something stupid last night. Shall we walk?" he blurted dismissively, before standing.

"Oh, ok sure," she said, springing to her feet.

Last night's festivities were set aside for the moment, as they strolled through the park chatting and drinking the steaming brew. The park was nearly empty, with only a few children playing off in the distance. It was another warm sunny day with just a slight breeze, which made for perfect walking conditions.

Alec was relieved that he'd had that shower, as the new sweat beads began to trickle down his hairline and small of his back. His sense of relief was soon overcome with more feelings of guilt. With every word she spoke, Alec promised himself he would get a hold of his drinking problem because a huge mistake like last night could not ever happen again. He enjoyed every moment they spent together and had no desire to see any other women, especially a random stranger like Jenny. He was soon able to put last night out of his conscious mind as visions of his and Sarah's future together became front and center. A vignette played in his head, of them together, strolling and laughing into their eighties.

After the park, they followed an early dinner with a late movie. Throughout the evening the conversation rarely stalled. Nothing stopped the flow, as they whispered, giggling, repeatedly hushed by the people sitting behind them in the theatre.

"That's so cheesy," Sarah laughed.

"What is?" Alec asked, keeping his eyes on the screen.

"That only happens in movies," she groaned, flicking her wrist in protest, as the main character carried his bride through the doorway.

"You think that's cheesy?"

"Well not really, but that never happens in real life, but they write it into so many love stories."

"Yeah, I guess you're right."

"You mean to tell me you've never carried a woman in your arms like that?" she asked quietly, dodging another shush from behind.

At that moment, Alec wanted desperately to kiss her or at least hold her hand but could not pull the trigger. He normally was not very shy around woman. However, with Sarah, he felt like a kid again. It was not until the last few minutes of the movie, and after their hands accidentally touched, that he finally took charge and pulled her hand over and their fingers interlocked. Her hand squeezed his in return, and she leaned and kissed him fully on the lips. After her brave move, the awkward nerves disappeared, as did the plot twist in the movie, to which they were oblivious. They were completely enthralled in their own movie-worthy make-out session, much to the disdain of the other attendees.

It was not until the movie ended and the lights brightened that they finally released one another's lips. Ignoring the disapproving glares, they pranced, arm in arm, smiling ear to ear, passing the noise police as they left the theatre.

The night air was chilly, as they briskly walked back to Alec's hotel. As they entered through the front doors laughing, Sarah darted towards the elevator pulling him by the arm. He pulled back, suddenly remembering the horrific current condition of his hotel room.

"What's wrong?" Sarah asked.

"Nothing, I just …" Alec sputtered, trying to think of an excuse as to why they could not go upstairs. He glanced over to the front desk until his eyes met Edgar's.

"Mr. Jenkins, welcome back!" shouted Edgar from across the hotel lobby, suddenly galloping over towards them. "I just wanted to let you know that we fixed the hot water issue so there shouldn't be any more problems with your shower going forward," he said with a wink.

"Thanks Edgar, that's much appreciated." Alec nodded, followed by an awkward pause, as Edgar waited for an introduction. "Sorry Edgar, this is Sarah."

Edgar broke into song, while extending his hand out to Sarah. "Sarah, Sarah, storms are brewing in your eyes. Sarah, Sarah, no time is good time."

"Starship?" Sarah offered, as they shook hands.

"You know your music," Edgar smiled, giving a second wink.

"Not one of my favorite songs as I'm sure you can imagine, but I must say you sang it beautifully."

"Well thank you, Sarah. You're very kind."

Alec's mind frantically scrambled for solutions to avoid taking her up to his room and realized the plumbing staff may have already reported him, and no possible explanation came to mind.

"Oh, and by the way Mr. Jenkins, you left the DO NOT DISTURB sign on your door again, so I figured, after seeing you leave earlier, you'd want your room cleaned. I hope you don't mind, but I took the liberty of sending in housekeeping." After Edgar's third wink, Alec was assured he knew exactly 'what time it was'.

"Thanks Edgar, that's great. You're a real life-saver!"

Relieved, he turned and pressed the elevator button, before pulling Sarah close to him. The elevator ride seemed short, but in that time, they had managed to lock lips while she jammed her hand down the front of his pants and massaged his penis. After the doors opened, he picked her up and carried her down the hallway, then through the doorway into his room.

"See it doesn't only happen in the movies," Alec said while placing her down on the bed.

"I didn't know you were such a romantic," Sarah said, removing her blouse.

"I'm not, but that movie inspired me," he said laughing, as he dove onto the fresh clean bed.

The touching was soft and exciting. He kissed her all over her body, then pulled her pants off. As their eyes locked, he slowly rubbed his fingers up her inner thigh until they were inside her. She moaned while kissing him, then tugged at his belt buckle. He frantically undid his belt before sliding his pants and underwear off. Sarah licked her hand, before stroking his erect penis. He moved his fingers to enter her again, but she pushed his hand away, then grabbed his buttocks, pulling him in closer. She guided his erect penis into her. He entered her slowly, until he was fully buried deep within. As he pulled out, her nails dug into his back and he thrusted back in hard this time, causing her to shriek.

"Sorry, too hard?" he asked softly, pulling out.

"No, give it to me harder!" She moaned as his shaft slid all the way back into her.

Each time he plunged into her; she dug her nails into his backside, pulling him deeper inside. His smooth belly slid up against hers with each thrust. His tongue ran along her moist neck. Then she kissed his salty neck, suddenly digging her teeth into his shoulder. As the intensity maximized, he exploded inside her.

They lay quietly for a moment with their bodies loosely intertwined as Sarah continued to kiss his neck. She lovingly ran her nails through his hair as they giggled before picking up the conversation that they had earlier at the park that day. At that moment, Alec knew he still loved her and wanted to let her know, but it was too early.

"That was amazing," she said, examining his shoulder for marks, as she tossed her sweaty, fiery red hair off her face.

"You're amazing," he replied.

As they continued caressing one another, he could not recall a happier moment in his life. For the moment, all his worries were behind him and all he could think about was their future together. After Sarah had fallen asleep in his arms, he continued to think of the possibilities of their future, while stroking the back of her thick, silky hair. His arm was numb from being pinned beneath her head, but he would not dare wake her. He watched her as she slept, thinking he would never leave her behind again, as he drifted off to sleep.

Alec was abruptly woken by a loud thump coming from out in the hotel hallway. After another thump and laughter followed, Alec, still half asleep, glanced at the clock reading 3 a.m. He dismissed it as just some lost partying hotel guests, until there was a third much louder, deliberate thump on his own door. He quickly slid his arm out from under Sarah's head and slipped silently out of bed. Without touching the door, he peered through the peephole.

"Oh fuck," he gasped, seeing Jenny's face gawking back. He stared at her through the peep hole then back at the bed, pondering what to do. "Fuck, fuck, fuck," he gasped again, before pacing silently back and forth. He remembered her words as she had left earlier about seeing him later, but he did not think for a second that she was speaking literally. As he peered again, he prayed that she had left, and could just see her wrist cocked and ready for another wrap on the door. In sheer panic, to prevent her knocking, he quickly opened the door a few inches, as he braced his body against the door with his foot firmly blocking potential entry. "Hey Jenny," he whispered. "Sorry, but I'm not feeling well."

"You've got to be kidding!" the waitress bellowed. She appeared to be high, which was quickly confirmed when she held up a small bag of the white powder. "You know what I had to do to get this shit?" After Alec did not respond, she retorted with intense awkward laughter. He glanced back over his shoulder to

178

see if the noise had woken up Sarah, and to his relief it had not. As he watched, she was starting to toss and turn. He needed Jenny to leave immediately.

"Sorry Jenny, but I really need to go back to sleep."

"Is there someone in there with you?" The look on his face provided confirmation. "Hey, I'd be down for a threesome if you guys are." The strong odor of cheap tequila wafted through the narrow opening, as Alec attempted to quietly close the door. "Oh, come on Alec," she whined.

"Listen Jenny, I still don't remember what all happened last night, but can we just talk about it later? Now is definitely not a good time." This time Alec's tone was much more hard-nosed.

Jenny laughed again, this time even louder in an obvious attempt to wake Alec's guest. She had now pushed his buttons, and he wanted to tell her to fuck off but didn't want an even louder confrontation.

"Fine, it's your loss," she snarled.

As he checked back over his shoulder again to see if Sarah was still asleep, Jenny grabbed his hand off the door and forced his fingers into her mouth. She sucked on his fingers as a mock blow job. Repulsed, he wrenched his hand back, scowling his disapproval. Finally conceding, she hobbled away on one broken heel, while flipping a middle finger, and fumbled, with the other hand, pulling down one side of her pants, exposing her right ass cheek.

"Who was that?" Sarah asked, half-awake, as he climbed back into bed.

"Oh, just some drunk girls."

"What did they want?"

"Nothing, they just went to the wrong room." He was fairly confident that his lie would hold up as Sarah was still half asleep, but he was ashamed that he'd even been involved, and so recently, with someone like that. Suddenly there was another loud thud at the door.

"What the hell was that?" Sarah called out, now wide awake and sitting up in the bed.

"For fuck sakes! The drunk chicks are probably back," he grumbled, darting toward the door.

He assumed it was Jenny, but prayed it was not. As Alec tried to open the door just slightly, it burst open forcefully, smacking against his forehead. In the door frame, now stood the young waitress. Unlike earlier, she was not displaying her usual fun, playful demeanor.

"Did he tell you that he likes it rough?" she shouted at Sarah. "I could barely walk this morning because he fucked me so hard last night." As Alec bent forward, holding his forehead in pain, she reached out and jammed her fingers, now covered in white powder, under Alec's nose. She then turned, still unsteady on her broken heel, and stormed out of the room, licking her powdered fingers while shouting down the hallway, "Thanks for nothing asshole!"

Alec could not bear to look back at the bed. Wiping the cocaine from his face he tried to find words, but there was nothing he could say to refute Jenny's accusation. Sarah, stunned and fully alert, stood up from the bed and methodically dressed.

"Sarah let me explain."

"Last night Alec? Seriously … last night?" she interjected, pulling her blouse on over her head.

"I know this really looks bad, but I …"

"Alec, there's nothing to say here. I don't know what I was thinking," Sarah motioned a stop signal with her hand, as the tears streamed down her reddened face. "I thought, ugh, I mean I thought … never mind."

Alec reached for her as she pushed past but she swatted away his arm before fleeing toward the elevator. He hesitated in the doorway for a while, listening for the ding as the elevator closed, and as he caught his own reflection, he caught sight of the ridiculous white cocaine moustache smeared under his nose. He hated himself for what he had done and understood how Sarah must have felt. He tried to admonish himself for making poor decisions while in the wrong frame of mind the previous night, but then denied himself any possible justification. Although he still had a complete blank spot between flirting and waking up in bed with Jenny, it was crystal clear that he had lost another bout and had screwed things up royally. Things between Sarah and him had been moving forward so well, he should have put on the brakes with the waitress right away.

The defensive self-talk continued. If he had only known that drink she'd brought over would have put him over the edge, of course he would have said no. Brushing off his upper lip, Alec turned back into the room and as the door closed behind him, he continued trying to fill in the lost time of the previous night. He recalled being pretty hammered at the bar, surely drunk enough to knock over Jenny's full tray of drinks, but could he have been so out of it that he needed help back to his room? In all the years he had been drinking, he could not recall one time he had lost total control of his body's physical function. And how the hell would he and Jenny have had sex if he was such a mess. He started to wonder if maybe she had made it all up because he did not remember one second of it. He then thought back to when he had started to lose control and the first thing that happened was his lips became numb.

"Did that crazy little bitch roofie me?" he said aloud, flopping down onto the edge of the bed.

He made a conscious effort to return his thoughts back to Sarah. He wished Jenny had not shown up. Sarah would still be in his arms, unaware of his regrettable mistake. Now he was going to be single and lonely again, and in just a few hours he would be on yet another depressing flight back to San Francisco.

Another lonely trip, and there would now be no loved one who would miss him or excited, awaiting his return.

There was not anything he could do now, so he figured he would at least try to get some sleep before his early morning flight. An important day with Jason Thompson was on the horizon and he needed to be mentally prepared. He would have to try and patch things up with Sarah when he returned. With the scent of Sarah's perfume still looming, he lay his head on the pillow and sniffed the sheets, staring blankly at the water mark on the ceiling. He tried to strategize a plan to successfully recover the Thompson account, but was too upset to focus on business. He resolved to fall asleep with images of Sarah. The morning would arrive very shortly. It was going to be a long and challenging day.

CHAPTER 12

It seemed like mere seconds after closing his eyes that Alec was jolted upright by the Captain's loud voice, announcing their final descent. Alec had slept the entire three-and-a-half hour flight but felt as though he had momentarily blinked. Glancing at his well-earned Rolex, he realized that the whole morning had been a complete blur. He barely recalled the lengthy drive to the airport that morning and the debacle at the airport, where he narrowly missed his flight.

He had been away on vacation only one week, but it had felt like months since he had been in San Francisco. He had flown thousands of times; however, this return flight home came with a new sense of nostalgia. As they flew over the Golden Gate Bridge, he recalled seeing the iconic landmark for the first time. He had been on his initial trip to San Francisco from Vancouver soon after he had graduated university. Uncle Perry had set up an interview for him in one of the top investment firms in the United States. Through Uncle Perry's business travels, he had become good friends with Harold Rhodes. Woodward Financial was not looking to hire anyone at the time, but as Harold was the President of the company, he offered to at least meet with the nephew of his friend in case a position opened in the future. That was the only break Alec Jenkins needed to start his long and prosperous career.

Two days after his interview with Harold, Alec received a call from Woodward Financial saying they would like to bring him in for a one-year apprenticeship. Before reaching the end of that apprenticeship, he was hired on with the company as a full-time employee and it was not long before his relationship with Harold grew stronger. Harold had a knack for spotting potential and a good business fit in young starters, and Alec Jenkins was certainly no exception.

Upon first moving to San Francisco, Alec lived in the basement of a fellow employee's home, but soon after becoming his landlord's supervisor at work, Alec decided it would be best to find a new place to live. By that point, he had saved enough money for a down payment on his own home, where he currently still lived, at the Bellstar Condominiums.

He was quite a loner in his early years as a new resident of San Francisco. This suited him fine as it was what he had grown accustomed to since moving away from home. The lack of friends had not bothered him much, but holidays were always a little rough on the young professional. In his university days, he at least had his uncle to spend Christmas. His coworkers had friends and family close by; he only had his sister back in Russell to speak with over the telephone. He was single, his parents were deceased, and besides his sister the only other family was his

Uncle Perry, who was not much for conversation. While his coworkers were with their families celebrating the holidays, Alec would try to keep busy to avoid the loneliness. The bottle helped with some of that loneliness at first, but eventually the holidays and his life in San Francisco became desolate. His desire to succeed made him rich financially, but poor in his personal life.

He could have purchased a large house with his extravagant income, but his condo at Bellstar had its sentimental value with its lasting reminder of his early beginnings in the business world. He eventually purchased the condos on each side of his, then proceeded to knock out the walls between, updated the floorplan, thereby tripling the living place to 3,600 square ft. The building contained only four units per floor and he desperately wanted the fourth unit, so as to occupy the entire floor. He was denied by the other unit's owner, even after offering her more than double its value. He never would understand why the stubborn old bat refused to sell it to him. The haggling between them damaged the once neighborly relationship beyond repair.

The harmony between Alec and the other condo owners had also deteriorated over construction noise and other disrespectful behavior, reaching its boiling point the evening he drove his Porsche through the front door of the building. He had lost another title fight with Iron Mike and passed out behind the wheel after several glasses of Jack Daniels. Luckily for Alec, nobody had seen the act and the cameras that surveilled the area had coincidentally been vandalized that very same evening. The other owners had attempted to have him evicted, but there was nothing they could do without evidence. The nods and smiles he had once received in the hallways had recently turned into scowls, averted eyes and whispers.

As he exited the turnstile of the San Francisco airport, he dreaded having to see those scowls again. His thoughts turned to the new staff who now apparently worked in his building. Who was this Carlos guy and why did he not know Tanya? And what was Tanya's urgent message regarding? Although he was anxious to get answers to these questions, he currently had more urgent work issues to deal with. He was tired and still was not fully prepared for his meeting with Jason Thompson.

"Good morning Mr. Jenkins. How was the flight?" Clive asked, as Alec approached the car.

"Just fine Clive, thanks for asking."

Clive closed the door behind his passenger as Alec sat in the back of his limousine. Pulling away from the airport, Clive asked, "Are we heading to your place, sir?"

"No time, just take me to the office please."

After all these years, Alec still enjoyed the fact that he had a chauffeur, mostly because it further solidified his success. The luxury of having a driver also allowed him to get some work done while in transit, which he often took full advantage with his busy schedule. On this occasion however, he took full advantage of having a driver by getting caught up on some well-needed sleep.

As they pulled up to the entrance of Woodward Financial, he was awoken by Clive.

"Here you are, sir."

"Thank you, Clive," he mumbled, wiping the drool from the side of his mouth. Stepping out of the car, he was greeted by one of the company's young attendants.

"Good morning, Mr. Jenkins! Let me take your luggage. Have you had breakfast yet, or would you like to have someone bring some to your office?"

"I actually haven't eaten, so that'd be wonderful. Coffee with a couple of espresso shots please."

"Right away, sir."

One of the many perks of carrying the title of President of the multi-million-dollar company, was having people taking care of the little things. Woodward Financial occupied the top four floors of a twenty-two-story building, while the other floors were occupied by several smaller businesses. Some luxury items on the top floor included a massive marble washroom, steam room, sauna, a sprawling patio that overlooked the San Francisco Bay, an indoor golf simulator equipped with the layout of every PGA golf course, a fitness room, and a miniature basketball court which included a game-used Chicago Bulls backboard that Michael Jordan had signed for his friend Harold Rhodes. This was usually the first thing Alec would show to impress his new clients on their first tour of the establishment. Like his former boss, he too was a huge fan of the five-time MVP. Michael Jordan was also the biggest professional athlete name that Alec Jenkins could refer to as a client. He was able to get tickets to almost any big sporting event which included all San Francisco Giants baseball games.

He exited the elevator onto the twenty second floor. As the attendant rolled Alec's suitcase outside the elevator doors, he said, "I'll have your breakfast sent up right away sir." As the doors closed behind him, he turned to see his long-time secretary standing to greet him.

"Hello dearie, how was the flight?" Ellen was the only one in the building who did not refer to him as Mr. Jenkins. It was either Alec or dearie, or darlin' in a strong Scottish accent and that was just fine by him.

"Flight was good. I just need some coffee to wake up. Did you get a chance to ..." but before he could finish, she handed him a pair of tickets. He chuckled, "On top of things as always."

She nodded heading back towards her desk. "I need to rinse off, can you get a hold of Tom?"

"I spoke with him this morning. Your meeting is scheduled for noon, so he'll be here shortly."

"Of course. What would I do without you Ellen?"

"You'd bloody starve to death or half drown in that there bottle o' whiskey," she raised an eyebrow and set down a tray before turning and marching away.

"Nice to be back, Ellen," he chuckled sarcastically.

Alec kept several suits and other clothing in his office as working through the night was not out of the ordinary. After using the shower and then the spa, he sat at his desk and ate the breakfast that was waiting for him. While sipping on his coffee he began reviewing his messages. There was one message from Goldman that mentioned he would be handling everything working abroad and that if needed, could be reached on his cell. He wondered where he meant by abroad and why he was being so vague. Goldman was up to something, but he would have to investigate that later.

"Hello Mr. Jenkins," came a loud deep voice, startling Alec, as he had not seen the large man enter the room.

"Jesus Tom, I didn't hear you come in," he gasped, before motioning to a seat across the desk from him. "Alright, so tell me what you've got."

Tom could be an intimidating figure, as his deep loud voice came out of his six foot five, two-hundred-and-forty-pound stature. But for those who knew Tom, as much as anyone really knew the private man, they would describe him as a kind and gentle person. He was soft spoken and did not say much, but when he did speak, people listened.

"Well, the Midula Group is surprisingly clean. I couldn't find anything substantial on them but did manage to get you some interesting photos of Jason that you could use." He slid a large envelope across Alec's desk, then continued, "They should do the trick."

"Who's the woman?" Alec asked, holding up one of the photos from the pile.

"Amanda Perrins. She works at Midula." Tom watched Alec as he smiled, while continuing to scroll through the photos.

"Oh boy," Alec posed, with one hand on his chin and the other holding up another photo.

"Find any women like that in Russell?"

Continuing to scroll through the photos, Alec kept his focus downward and replied, "I wish." After finishing he continued, "Most of the Russell women are either missing teeth or married to their first cousin."

Tom nodded, then chuckled. For some reason, he did not want Tom knowing of his relationship with Sarah. They smiled again at each other before Tom rose to his feet and began to walk away.

"Oh, by the way Mr. Jenkins, Amanda Perrins carries Valtrex tablets in her purse."

"Valtrex?"

"It appears the lady may have genital herpes."

"You've outdone yourself this time Tom, nice work!" Alec shouted at the large stocky man as he stood waiting for the elevator to arrive.

Over the next few hours, Alec sat as his desk, reviewing the Thompson files in preparation for their meeting. Jason's father was a smart man who started the family business with a brilliant invention and then went on to buy several other various patents. Many were for products that had been struggling, that he went on to turn into big sellers at top retail outlets across the US. He seemed to have a sixth sense for knowing how to make undesirable products desirable. When Alec had acquired Jason's father as a client, their company had the rights to fourteen patented products, three of which were among the top ten selling items of the Target Corporation. At the climax of their success, the Thompson family had the rights to over fifty patented products. However, as Alec reviewed their current list of products, the count was down to just sixteen, none of which were amongst the top ten of any mass chains.

Since Jason had taken over his father's company it had taken a nosedive, and most of the blame fell on Jason's lap, as most thought it was due to his lack of business knowledge, combined with his irresponsible party boy behavior. The family business was handed down to him when he was only twenty-five, which was around the same age that Alec had been when he first started working for Woodward Financial. As Jason was fed with the silver spoon, and had no drive, Alec had little respect for him.

It was not until Jason married years after taking over, that he began to mature, slow down on the partying and take his business more seriously. He met his wife Ana on one of his many trips overseas at a yacht party off the coast of Peru. It was love at first sight when being introduced to the former Miss Venezuela. Jason being a relatively good-looking man, with oodles of money, still did not impress the sophisticated lady, as she was still way out of his league. He pursued Ana for over three years until she finally gave in and married him. Then children soon followed. The incriminating photos would, without question, crush their marriage, especially the one that showed Miss Perrins giving him oral sex in the car on the family's own driveway.

"Alec, darlin', I have Jason Thompson on line two for you."

"Thanks Ellen."

Picking up the receiver, he hoped Jason was not calling to cancel, as he wanted to get this meeting over, as he suddenly felt an urgent desire to return to Russell to try to make things right with Sarah.

"Mr. Thompson, how are you sir?"

"I'm doing well Alec, thanks for asking! Looking forward to the game tonight. I heard the Yankees pulled Sabathia off the disabled list to pitch tonight. Not sure if it's a good thing or not because that fat bastard is so unpredictable."

Alec was a fan of the San Francisco Giants and considered himself quite knowledgeable of the game of baseball, but not to the extent of Jason. Mr. Thompson took Jason to hundreds of games and molded him into the informed loyal fan he'd become. Jason was not only a big fan of baseball; he was also once an elite player. Several major league scouts had him projected to be drafted in the first round before he blew out one of his knees in a skiing accident. No team in the majors was willing to take a chance on a nineteen-year-old catcher with bad knees, so that was the end of his dream of becoming a major league baseball player.

"I hope so, Posey is hitting over five hundred on Sabathia this year," replied Alec showing off his knowledge of the game.

Anyone who knew Jason knew of his dislike for Buster Posey, the starting catcher for the Giants. Alec wanted it to be known that their evening together would not be one with him groveling to keep the Thompson family business, so just his mentioning of Posey would help deliver that message. Alec believed that Jason

194

was lucky to have him looking after his family's investments and he would be damned if he would have to suck up to the man who was destroying his father's legacy, just to keep his business. If Jason did not see Alec's value and wanted to move his business elsewhere, Alec would have no other option but to use the photos. He tried to convince himself that part of the reason he would use the photos was for his empathy for Ana, but deep down he knew that was not the case.

"Don't even get me started on Posey blowsy," Jason snarled. "That loser couldn't hit a beach ball. The guy is only batting two hundred this year. Why they haven't released him yet is mind-boggling."

"Yes, he's really struggling this year. Hey, listen, I'm just finishing up some work then I'll be ready to go." Alec interjected to avoid a rant that would have gone on for hours. "Pick you up at your office around six?"

"Yeah, that's actually what I was calling about. I was hoping we could go a little earlier to talk and maybe even see some batting practice, so six would be perfect. See you then!"

Alec was looking forward to seeing some baseball and although he did not have much respect for Jason and his business dealings, he did enjoy his company. The thought of blackmailing him was not appealing in the slightest, but if it had to be done to save his business and potentially his own job, he intended on doing it. The photos would only be used as a worst-case scenario.

He had only been at the office for a few hours and had smoked more cigarettes than the entire previous week in Russell. He glared at the overflowing ashtray on his desk, then finished off responding to the last of the emails sitting in his inbox. After peeling back the bandage on his thumb to find the cut had fairly healed, he tossed the blood-stained bandage into the garbage. He thought back to Jenny and that crazy wild night. The more he thought about it the more he believed the waitress had put something in his drink. His thoughts then turned back to his disastrous treatment of Sarah and how he was possibly ever going to make things right. In dialing her number, he realized he had not prepared what he was going to say. Her voicemail came on and Alec froze in silence for moments before any words finally came.

"Sarah, it's me ... Alec. I um ... just wanted to let you know that I'm really so sorry ... and I miss you. I will try to explain ..." Staring at the bloodied bandage in the trash, he continued, "And I uh ... love you."

He hung up, instantly regretting allowing those last three words to blurt out of his mouth. He knew he had a lot more investigating and explaining to do, before bringing any confessions of love to the table. Flustered, he shot back a half glass of whiskey before heading down to his ride.

Traffic was worse than usual and although Clive did some fancy driving to get them to the game quickly, they arrived with only a few minutes left of batting practice. The over 41,000 in attendance were loud and the atmosphere was electric. After grabbing two beers and some popcorn, Alec and Jason Thompson took their seats along the first base line. For the first few innings they only spoke of baseball. The home team was dominating, and the mood was upbeat. In the top of the fifth, the mood began to sour as the Yankees began to take over, going through their whole batting order.

With the game tied, Alec contemplated how to bring up his knowledge of the meetings between Jason and the Midula Group, but as he eyed Jason nervously chewing his nails, he decided to wait. In the bottom of the seventh, Buster Posey stepped into the batter's box and proceeded to absolutely destroy a pitch from the tiring Sabathia, sending the ball into the upper deck for a monster three-run homerun. The crowd went crazy as they watched the catcher jaunt around the bases. The mood became upbeat once again and after the crowd quieted, Alec figured the timing was right.

"Jason, are you happy with the work we've done for you since you've taken the helm?" Alec shouted loud enough so Jason could hear him over the rambunctious crowd.

"Yes of course, why?" he shouted back, keeping his eyes on the game.

"Well, I know about your meetings with Midula."

"What the hell are you talking about?" he replied, turning his attention to Alec. "I mean …" he paused, studying Alec's face, realizing there was no point in trying to lie. "Ok yeah, I met with them, and to be brutally honest, have been considering moving my investments over to them. Listen man, my father loves you and you've always been good to him and my family, but lately we've been hearing things."

"What things?"

"Listen Alec, can we be straight here?"

"Of course, please."

"Midula came to us a couple months ago, saying Woodward was going to be folding soon."

Alec rolled his eyes, "Come on man, tell me you didn't fall for that bullshit!"

"I didn't! We didn't," Jason replied, before taking a sip of his beer. "At least we didn't at first, but then they came to us again with some pretty concerning information."

"What information?"

Jason reached into his pocket and pulled out an envelope, then handed it to him. Alec pulled out three photos showing himself standing beside his smashed Porsche, with one hand wrapped

198

around the neck of a whiskey bottle, while relieving himself with the other.

"Dude, I didn't know you had it in you. I mean I've been there, and I totally understand, but I'm not sure we can have someone like this looking after our investments."

Alec sat in silence, baffled as to how the Midula Group could have obtained the photos. He dug into his pocket to retrieve the photos of Jason, but then refrained. He was so disgusted with himself. Perhaps it would just be best if Jason did move their investments over to another firm whose leader was more capable. The two sat quietly while the Giants fans continued to celebrate as another three runs came across the plate.

"Listen Jason, I'm not going to lie to you. I've been going through some shit in my private life and I'd be lying to you if I said I wasn't absolutely shit faced that night. I've actually been a disaster for the past few months. I was just lost. I know that is no excuse, but if it means anything, I have cleaned up my act or at least I've been trying to. I have made a mess of things in my private life and I assure you it hasn't affected your investments. If you were to go to Midula, I would completely understand." Jason appeared shocked to hear his confession. Alec continued, "I'm serious. If they've done that kind of due diligence, to get your business, I'm sure they'd also put that kind of effort in managing your family's interests. Your family's account has always been my main priority. Did you know your dad was my first big client?"

"Yeah, I did."

"I was just a kid and I was so nervous meeting him," Alec said smiling. "Your dad can be intimidating when he wants to be, you know?"

"Oh, I know," Jason laughed.

"He was always tough, but fair. He gave me, a young impressionable guy, a chance and I've never forgotten. That's why your family has always been my top priority. I remember thinking my father would have been proud of me that day. You're so lucky that you have such a good relationship with your father. I think I was always a bit jealous of that relationship if I'm being honest."

"Jealous of me, really?"

"Oh yes. I was close with my dad once, but things changed. Then he died, and I lost that chance and I think I kind of resented you because of that. I think the relationship you have with your dad has made you an excellent father yourself. I've seen you with your kids and they absolutely adore you. The people that work for you also love you. I don't know how you manage to balance your friendships with the people that work for you because I've never been able to do that. I know you and I haven't always seen eye to eye, but I just wanted you to know that."

"Thanks Alec, that's nice of you to say and I really appreciate those words." He sat back in his chair and let out a sigh. "You know I've been jealous of you as well?"

"Of me?"

"Yup. Well, I've always thought you were an uptight prick, but my dad ranted and raved about you all the time. I think he hoped I was more focused like you and if I'm being honest, I've always resented you for it. I've made lots of mistakes in my life and it's actually nice to see you're human and make mistakes as well," he said before swigging the last of his beer. "Listen, I've been there dude; feeling like your life is spinning out of control, drinking every night, drugs, hookers …"

"Hookers?" Alec blurted.

"Oh yeah, when I was at rock bottom, there was nothing I wouldn't do."

"From hookers to Ana. That is quite the turnaround. Maybe there is hope for me yet," Alec chuckled.

"Ugh, man I really fucked things up with Ana."

"What do you mean?"

Jason took a moment before replying. "I've been cheating on her." Alec did his best to appear surprised as Jason continued, "I don't even know why I did it. I don't even like this other broad and I have the most amazing wife. The worst part is what this will do to my kids."

Another roar from the crowd while Jason sat slumped in his seat with his fingers intertwined on top of his head. Alec felt badly for him.

"Didn't you say earlier that we all make mistakes? Maybe this was just your one mistake. I mean an idiot mistake at that but ..."

"Yeah, I know, so stupid. I've made lots of mistakes with drugs and broads over the years, but not with Ana. At least not until now. She made me a better man. I finally got my shit together and things were going so great. Then I went and do this and fuck it all up. She's going to leave me when she finds out, and she'll take the kids and move back with her family. Ana and the kids have been there for the past two weeks visiting and it's given me some time to reflect on how empty my life would be without them."

"Maybe she doesn't have to know," Alec said, sitting up in his seat. "If you know it was a horrible mistake and it's something you would absolutely never do again, maybe it's best she just doesn't know about it. Jason, you're a great guy and you made a mistake, so why let that ruin all your lives?"

"I see what you're saying, but I just don't think I can live with that lie. I just ended the affair this morning and it's killing me not to tell Ana, but it would crush her if she found out."

"Well, if you were trying to make me feel better you succeeded," Alec said with a smirk. They looked at each other and let out a deep simultaneous exhale, which was immediately followed with laughter.

"Fuck, what a mess we are, hey?" Jason said, patting Alec on the shoulder. "Maybe this is rock bottom for both of us and we can turn it around."

"Yeah, I can't see it getting much worse than this."

Alec went on to explain some of what had occurred during his stay in Russell, including things with Sarah and Jenny. Jason seemed impressed that the fifty-year-old could still land a twenty-year-old. He thought Sarah would come around after she had some time to cool off. After all, they were not exactly in a committed relationship at the time. For the first time since he could remember, Alec felt as though he had made a new friend in Jason and the thought of losing him as a client had taken a backseat.

"We'll take two," Jason shouted to the young girl carrying a tray of beers. "Cheers," he said, after passing one to Alec. They bumped their cans into one another.

"Cheers," Alec said, before taking a seat.

"I figured you probably weren't vacationing in Greece like your office had said, so I appreciate your honesty," Jason said, sitting back in his seat. "You know, even though we haven't always seen eye to eye, I don't think we're all that different. He took a sip and appeared to be in deep thought before continuing, "You know my dad has always trusted you, and I think it's time that I do the same." He took another sip then continued, "Yeah, fuck it, and fuck Midula. We're going to stay with you guys."

"Are you serious?" Alec gasped.

"Yes I am. You may have been a disaster lately, but you've always done an excellent job for us. And hey, we all make mistakes. Just do me a favor and get your shit together so I don't regret this decision."

"I don't know what to say except, I promise you won't regret it. You can trust me, and you can trust the people that work for me. Thank you for giving me another chance," he said while reaching out and shaking Jason's hand.

"Ok, now enough of this sappy shit," Jason said, laughing and looking out onto the field.

"What's the score anyway?"

"Jesus we're up by eleven runs. How did that happen?" Jason said, laughing while checking the scoreboard.

"Time flies while you're having fun!"

"Who would've thought that you and I would ever be friends?" Jason asked, putting his arm around him. "We are friends now, aren't we?"

"Yes, of course," Alec replied with a big smile, before they bumped beers a second time.

Alec tossed the envelope Jason had given him into a garbage can while walking out of the game. Getting into the back of the limo, Alec passed Clive the other envelope containing the photos of Jason and the estranged woman. After pulling up the driveway to the Thompson home, Clive opened the car door and Jason got out.

"Hey Alec, thanks again for taking me to the game and thanks for being so candid tonight. You don't see that kind of thing these days, so it was nice to see."

"Thanks Jason, and same to you." As the car began to roll away Alec watched him turn and walk up his driveway. Alec stuck his head out the window and shouted, "Hey Jason just a word of advice, get a STD test." After getting a strange look he continued, "You just never know."

Jason smiled, then nodded, before the car pulled away. Not only had he gained a friend, but he had managed to save a big client for Woodward Financial. For the first time in a long time, Alec felt like his old self. The feeling was reminiscent of the time Jason's father had first signed the contract with Woodward Financial.

"Where to now, sir?"

"To my place please. Thanks Clive."

"And what do you want me to do with this?" the driver asked, holding up the envelope.

"Burn it."

As the limo rolled through the streets of downtown San Francisco, Alec took in the breeze as the wind from his window blew through his hair. Mr. Rhodes would have been proud and the two of them would have stayed up late, sipping on some single malt scotch.

"Have a good evening sir," Clive said as he held open the car door.

"You too, Clive," he replied, stepping out.

As the limousine pulled away Alec noticed the entranceway to the Bellstar Condominiums was much darker than normal and unusually quiet. Upon reaching the front door, he found it increasingly odd that nobody, including the concierge, were around to greet him. In the over twenty years he had lived there, he had never recalled having to use his key. After his key would not fit into the lock, he peered through the front window to see that the lobby was completely empty. No person or furniture were on the other side of the glass and the place looked as though it had been sitting empty for quite some time. Laying on the dusty floors were a couple of paint cans, brushes and several empty energy drink cans.

He went across the street where he noticed a payphone and frantically dialed the number of his condo building.

"Frank's Pizza, how can I help you?"

"Sorry, I must have dialed the wrong number," Alec replied before hanging up. After dumping in more coins, he dialed the number again, only this time paying extra attention to each number he hit. This time it was answered after the first ring.

"Hello Frank's Pizza, how can I help you?"

"Frank's Pizza?"

"Yes, this is Frank's Pizza and we're very busy. What can I get for you?"

"Sorry, but I'm actually trying to call someone else and for some reason it keeps dialing your number."

"Well, we've had this phone number for over ten years so not sure what to tell you bud," snarled the voice from the other end. Before Alec could reply, a dial tone blared through the receiver. Although he did not know most of the numbers in his cell phone, he was certain of Bellstar's as he realized it so happened to be 415-alc-ohol, an irony Tanya had introduced to him.

His next call went to one of the only other local numbers he knew, to the home of his secretary, Ellen. She answered after the first ring and as usual was very accommodating. It would not be the first time he would be sleeping on her couch as he had each time his place was going through renovations. Staying at his Scottish secretary's home had always included a hearty breakfast from a warm motherly host. Memories of his early childhood arose each time he stayed at Ellen's home.

He could not recall what Clive's number was, so he flagged down a taxi. As the cab pulled away, he glanced back and observed the large '*Lundar Meats*' sign atop the building. Only a week earlier, that same very sign had the words, '*Bellstar Condominiums*'.

As the taxi made its way past the industrial zone of run-down storefronts and onto the low-income houses, and Ellen's modest little house, Alec told himself it was time to give his secretary a well-deserved raise. Until now, he had not paid much attention to the neighborhood in the past. It was too rough and unsafe of an area for a vulnerable sweet old lady like Ellen to live. Walking up the pathway through the old rickety gate, Alec was greeted at the front door.

"More renovations to that massive condo?" Ellen raised a brow, smiling, while re-tying the belt on her tartan robe.

"Something like that," he replied, before giving her a hug that lifted her wee body off the floor.

"Come on in dearie. I'll make us a cup o' tea."

He could tell she wanted to talk about his evening, but exhaustion had set in and he did not want to get into a discussion about his history, sorting out the strange occurrences and missing time gaps. He really hadn't a clue where to start, as he couldn't make sense of any of it. After several yawns and refusal of a second cup of tea, Ellen directed him to the pullout sofa, which had been set up for his arrival. He was happy to be in a familiar cozy place, and although the old sofa was not very comfortable, he felt a sense of calm. The Seinfeld rerun on the television kept his attention for a few minutes, but it was not long before he was fast asleep.

CHAPTER 13

The Paw Patrol theme song blaring from the tiny television woke him abruptly. Although he had tried his best to fall back asleep, the loud shouting and sound effects at Adventure Bay were too intense for any sleeping couch surfer to ignore. Ryder and his team of pups were on a very important mission to save the Polar Bears, while Alec was on a mission to find the remote.

After lowering the volume, he glanced at the clock on the wall to see it was just after ten a.m. San Francisco time. Perched on the edge of the sofa, he stuffed his legs one by one into the two pools of pant leg piles that lay ready on the floor beside him. Pulling out a cigarette, he was about to light it, when he remembered the stern brogue lecture from Ellen about smoking in her house, so he quickly slipped it back into the pack.

"Ellen?" he shouted, then listened intently. "Ellen ... are you home?" he shouted again, before realizing she must have left.

In the dining room draped over the back of a rocking chair, lay a knitted afghan, the true trademark of a loving grandmother. On the wall was a clock which was identical to the one in his sister's home back in Russell. He had not spoken with Chelsea in a few days, so he picked up the phone sitting beside the sofa and dialed her number. After three rings, a man's familiar voice came through on the other end.

"Hello?"

"Hello, is this Ron?" Alec asked, expecting his sister's voice on the other end.

"Yes, who's this?"

"You're back?"

"Back? From where?"

"I was there the other day and you weren't home."

"The other day?" Ron asked, sounding skeptical.

"Never mind. Is Chelsea home?"

"No, she isn't."

"Well can you tell her to call me when she comes home?"

"Sure, if I remember."

"Thanks man, I really appreciate it," Alec replied in a thick sarcastic tone.

He wanted to tell him to go fuck himself, but out of respect for his sister, restrained. Having hung up the phone, he wondered how his sister was going to explain the reappearance of her husband the next time he visited. He was not positive but thought he could hear his niece in the background as well. Alec figured Ron and Chelsea must have reconciled because he and Kendra had returned home. Alec could not stand the man, but thought his sane sister having a shitty husband was a better alternative than what he had witnessed.

The next phone call went to Sarah, but again there was no answer. He waited for her voicemail just so he could hear her sweet voice. He then left her another voicemail, letting her know he would be back in town soon and said he hoped to meet up with her at the hotel's gardens to talk.

Ellen had not booked him a return flight to Russell, as he was not sure how long he would need to be in town. Now that the fire had been put out, and everything was ironed out with Jason, he was anxious to get back to see Sarah. Also, after his surprising conversation with Ron, he was also anxious to get to the bottom of the confusing conversations with Chelsea. He called United Airlines and booked the last flight out that same evening.

Wanting to tie up some loose ends at the office before he left again, he found Clive's number in Ellen's old rolodex, and dialed it on her phone.

"Industrial Light and Magic, this is Tina speaking. How may I help you?"

"You've got to be fucking kidding me," Alec barked.

"Pardon me," replied the woman.

"I'm sorry. Who did you say this was?"

"Tina from Industrial Light and Magic. Did you dial the wrong number?"

"No, I'm pretty sure I dialed my driver's number. Sorry for the inconvenience."

Slamming down the receiver he noticed a set of keys laying on the coffee table. Out the window, he could see what he imagined was the vehicle associated with those keys. After doing a quick search of the house and not finding Ellen, he left a note informing her that he had borrowed her old rusted Ford Taurus.

As the rust bucket made its way up Bay Street, Alcatraz loomed outside its driver's side window. Alec glanced at the island and recalled his first trip to the prison with one of his coworkers. She had told him everyone should see Alcatraz at least once and after Alec had, he thought of how much his father would have loved touring it, as he was a huge history buff. While waiting at a red light he watched as a young family posed for a photo, with the prison in the background. Even though he and his sister were not very close anymore, she was the only family he had left. As the light turned green, he told himself he needed to be a better brother and would spend some time with the niece and nephew upon his return to Russell.

On Howard Street, he could now see the large twenty-two story building towering over the other nearby buildings where his office resided. He was very proud when he first started, to be working in one of the most prestigious buildings in all of San Francisco. As he plowed up to its front doors, in Ellen's deteriorating Taurus, he still felt just as proud. He was quickly greeted by the parking attendant.

"Hello sir. How can I help you?"

"I'm with Woodward Financial," Alec replied.

"I'm sorry sir, but I meant which company are you here to visit?"

"Woodward Financial. I work here," he snarled. "I'm the President."

"Woodward Financial?"

"Yes, it's on the top floor. Are you new here?" His waning patience was not missed by the young man.

"No, I've been here for three years and I've never heard of a Woodward Financial. Swinerton Builders owns this building and occupies the top floor."

"Swinerton Builders?"

"Yes, that's right. Sir … is everything ok?" he asked, leaning closer, before two other parking attendants quickly appeared at his side.

"Yes, I'm fine!" Enraged, Alec piled out the car and slammed its door, before jamming his finger into the man's face. "Listen pal, I don't know who you are, but I'm Alec Jenkins and I'm the President of Woodward Financial and it's located on the top four floors of this fucking building!"

"Take it easy sir," warned one of the other parking attendants.

"What the fuck is going on here?" Alec demanded.

"I think it's time for you to leave sir," said one of the other parking attendants. Alec looked over to see some onlookers had begun to gather.

"I'm not going anywhere. This is my fucking building, buddy," he replied, poking the other attendant's chest. "Don't you know who the fuck I am?" Security quickly surrounded him and after you a short struggle, he was thrown forcefully to the ground. Alec's suit jacket ripped in the armholes, and was covered in mud, while he twisted an ankle in the exchange. As the three attendants lined up blocking his entry, he angrily picked himself up off the sidewalk and hobbled away.

"Sir, what about your car!" shouted one of the security guards, pointing at the Taurus.

For the next few hours Alec roamed the downtown streets of San Francisco, wondering if he had completely lost his mind. He thought about going back to Ellen's home, but was worried what he would find, or not find, there. Now that his condo and office had vanished, he wondered if Ellen's place would have as well. Walking around a corner, he was knocked to the ground by a large man walking past with a group of friends.

"Watch where you're going, asshole," Alec barked, struggling to get to his feet.

"Fuck off," replied someone from the group, before another pushed him back down to the ground.

"Fucking bum!" shouted someone else from the group.

215

"Get a job!" shouted another, as they walked away.

After dusting himself off, he caught sight of his sad reflection in a store window. He needed to get back to Ellen's so he could shower and possibly wash his clothes, so he headed back towards the building where he had left the Taurus. He could not help but look at his pathetic appearance each time he passed a store window along the way. He suddenly noticed he was being followed by a man wearing a cowboy hat and a tan overcoat with blue pockets.

Alec made several quick turns to confirm he was indeed being followed. He tried to catch a glimpse of the man's face several times but failed as his admirer kept his distance. He was convinced he had seen the man earlier that morning as he had been leaving Ellen's home.

Upon approaching the building, he was relieved to see Ellen's car had not been towed and was still parked where he had left it. When the parking attendants were busy, Alec hopped into the Taurus and sped off.

He lit a cigarette on the way to Ellen's place, holding it outside the car window, but another lecture was the least of his worries. After Ellen did not answer her front door, he used the house key from the Taurus keychain to enter her home.

He wondered where his secretary had gone, before thinking Ellen may have also vanished. Beginning to unravel, he resorted to his usual composure mechanism, and searched the home for alcohol. Knowing the granny did not drink anymore, he finally dug deep to find an aged bottle of brandy back in a kitchen cupboard. Rubbing off a layer of dust; he poured the last few ounces into a coffee mug with the words *'what happens at grandma's stays at grandma's'* written on one side along with a cartoon picture of an elderly woman smoking a cigar on the other. He belted back the contents in two swigs, and then realizing it was a few hours before he would need to be at the airport, he watched another rerun of Seinfeld. He laughed and related to one of his favorite episodes as Kramer slammed his money on Jerry's kitchen counter divulging that he was no longer the master of his own domain. As he watched Elaine shell out some cash for also losing the same bet, his mind shifted to Sarah and his desire to return home heightened.

There was not much left for him in San Francisco now, as the city literally seemed to be disappearing around him. Putting his feet up on Ellen's antique coffee table, he lit another cigarette, then rested his head on the back of the sofa, while playing out all that had transpired since his return to San Francisco. He tried to make some sense of it all but was not able.

Perhaps once he returned to Russell, and spoke with Sarah, she would help him make sense of things. He had resigned to the fact that his sister was not the only one having a mental breakdown of sorts, and that Sarah may be his only hope. Even if she angry with him, after he told her what was going on, there was no way, at least from a professional level, she would turn him away. He threw his clothes in the washer, then headed into the bathroom.

During a long hot shower, he told himself that all the chaos must have some reasonable explanation, and it would get better. All the crazy events must be somehow linked, and if he did not start to get answers soon, his head would explode. He was desperate to sort out the apparent blackout night with Jenny and hopefully, it would repair some damage done between him and Sarah, and everything would be better.

After towel drying his hair, he used a corner to wipe the mirror above the bathroom sink. As the fog cleared away, he was suddenly startled by a familiar face staring straight back at him. Jolting backward, he slipped on the wet tile, whacking his head on the toilet as he fell to the floor. He sat on the floor, dazed for a minute before picking himself up. Leaning into the sink, feeling his scalp for blood, he gathered his courage to look back at the person again, but was frozen with fear. After what seemed like several minutes, he finally was able to look up into the mirror, only to see his own reflection. What had he seen exactly? It was a child's face; it was Eddy's face.

"Jesus fucking Christ! I need some drugs, strong drugs," he said aloud. Before leaving the bathroom, he looked back at the mirror once again, then over to the bathtub, but saw nothing out of the ordinary.

He needed to get back to Russell as soon as possible. After tossing his clothes in the dryer, he made toast with some of Ellen's homemade jam, then sat back on the couch, wearing a towel wrapped around his waist. As he searched the channels, he thought back to the flashes of white light. He thought of Grayson and Eddy and wondered if they were somehow connected to what was happening with him now. After pulling his clothes out of the dryer, he got dressed and called a cab. While waiting, he decided to try his sister again.

"Hello?"

"Hey Chelsea, its Alec."

"Hi Alec. How's San Francisco?"

"Fine. I'm on my way back to Russell tonight. I tried calling you earlier, but Ron said you weren't home." He paused waiting for a response but received nothing. "Anyway, I have something to ask you."

"Yeah, what is it?"

"Do you remember Eddy Sutton?"

"Yes, Grayson's younger cousin? He was the little one with the creepy eyes, wasn't he?"

"Yeah, and the chalk-white skin. I've been having some dreams lately about him, and I um …" Alec paused, debating whether he should inform her about what had just happened and decided he'd better not.

"Yes Alec? And what?"

"Well some weird stuff has been happening lately and I don't know how to explain it, but something isn't right."

"You haven't seen him, have you?"

"Seen who?" Alec asked.

"Eddy."

"Have I seen Eddy? How could …" but before he could finish, he heard a click followed by a loud dial tone coming through the other end of the phone. He frantically tried calling her back several times, but each time received only a busy signal. A car horn blasted from outside letting him know his cab had arrived.

CHAPTER 14

Air Canada flight number 8336 touched down in Winnipeg just before six in the evening. The airport was oddly quiet, as Alec waited by the baggage carousel number four for his luggage to arrive. Looking around, he did not see one person from his flight but after double-checking the screen above, it was confirmed that his luggage was to arrive at carousel number four.

"Alec Jenkins?"

"Yes?" Alec said, turning around.

"Remember me?" asked the tall skinny man.

"Yes of course. Tim Boyd isn't it?

"Yes, well it's Byrd, but close enough. What's it been like thirty years?" It was either the strongest case of déjà vu or Alec had just had this conversation with this same man just one week earlier. The baggage carousel kicked into gear behind Alec making him jump. "Geez, are you ok," Tim asked.

"Yeah, just a little jumpy. I think I had too much coffee on the flight."

"Oh yeah, I've been there. My wife tells me I should really start drinking more decaf. Wow, it's been a long time! It's so great to see you," Tim said with a large smile.

"Ha, funny," Alec replied sneeringly.

"What do you mean," asked Tim perplexed.

"Well, we just ran into each other here last week."

"Huh?"

"You don't remember?"

"Must've been someone else," Tim replied.

"No, I'm sure it was you. You mentioned your youngest was just about to graduate from high school. Come on, you seriously don't remember?"

"Well now I know you're speaking of someone else. I don't even have any kids!" He thought of the scene in Groundhog Day where Bill Murray punched his old classmate in the face and contemplated doing the same to Tim. As that scene played out in his head, Tim continued, "Listen Alec, great seeing you, but I actually need to run. Maybe we'll grab a coffee while you're in town."

"Sure Tim, sounds good," Alec replied, seeing his suitcase approaching. "Oh, there's my luggage. Sorry, just one second Tim." After pulling it off the carousel he turned and said, "Hey Tim, if you …" but stopped mid-sentence as he saw the man was gone, appearing to seemingly vanish.

Alec glanced up at the clock above the carousel to see it was 6:20 p.m., then rushed over to the large desk beneath the ground transportation sign and was immediately greeted by a smiling, much shorter, heavyset woman.

"Good evening sir. How can I help you?"

"I'm looking for a ride to Russell."

"Do you have a reservation?"

"No sorry, did I need one?"

"Usually, but we may have something. Let me just take a look," she said before casually navigated the mouse. She stopped to take a sip of her coffee, then slowly went back to navigating the mouse. She stopped for a second time to take a bite of her donut and another sip of the coffee.

"Is there a ride available? Sorry, but I'm in a bit of a rush here," Alec urged.

She moved her hand away from the mouse slowly, while rolling her eyes. "Listen sir, without a reservation I'm not sure we'll even have a driver for you. Now, give me a minute and I'll see what I can do here," she replied bitterly.

"I'm sorry. I didn't mean to be a dick. Do you have a phone I can use?"

Without moving her eyes away from the screen, she passed Alec the cordless phone she had tucked behind the desk. He quickly dialed his sister's number only to receive a busy signal. Upon trying her number, a second time, he recognized the man coming out from the door behind the desk.

"Denzel!" Alec shouted.

"Excuse me?" replied the man, before taking a sip out of the mug in his hand.

"It's me, Alec. You gave me ride a few days ago."

"Sorry bud, wasn't me."

"Yes, it was definitely you!"

"Dude, you've got the wrong guy. My name is David."

"Come on Denzel, you drove me ..." Alec started, but before he could finish the man was gone back behind the doors.

"Ok it's your lucky day sir," said the woman from behind the counter. "I've got a driver for you, but you're going to need to wait for about an hour as he's just on his way back."

"An hour? What about Denzel, can't he take me?"

"If you're referring to David, he's not one of our drivers."

"But he was my driver on Monday," Alec pleaded.

"I can assure you sir, that David was not your driver."

"Listen lady, his name is Denzel and I'm telling you he drove me last week."

"Listen sir, that man's name is David, and he doesn't even work here. I should know, he's my boyfriend," she snarled back. "He's just waiting for me to get off work, so he can give me a ride home. Now take this pager and I'll buzz you when your driver is ready." After handing Alec the buzzer the woman also vanished through doors behind the desk.

Alec took a seat on the bench across from the desk, while thinking of the previous times he had seen Tim and Denzel. Panic began to set in as he began to wonder how things with Chelsea and Sarah would be once he returned to Russell. Wild thoughts raced through his head, as he rested it on the back of the bench. Fifteen minutes later, after he had nearly fallen asleep, the

224

buzzer in his pocket went off, letting him know his driver was ready.

CHAPTER 15

The headlights of the sedan lit up the vehicle parked in Chelsea's driveway. Alec knew the car was Ron's as he had seen it in a few of the photos his sister had sent him. Although he was not interested in seeing or talking to Ron, just knowing he was home brought on a sense of normalcy and relief.

"Thank you," Alec said to the attractive blonde driver, as he exited the vehicle.

"You're welcome. I hope everything works out with the girl," she replied before backing out of the driveway.

After a few heavy knocks, Ron finally appeared at the door looking angry and more ragged than he had seen him in the photos, but Alec was just relieved that the man actually existed.

"Hello Ron, nice to finally meet you," Alec said, as the door swung open.

"Do I know you?"

"It's me, Alec. We have spoken on the phone a few times. I'm Chelsea's brother. Is she home?"

"I think you've got the wrong house, bud," he snarled, before attempting to shut the door.

"Wait," Alec said, holding his arm out, stopping the door from closing. "You are Ron, aren't you?"

"Do I know you?" he asked.

"Well we've never met, but we've spoken on the phone several times."

"Dude I don't know who you are, but you're starting to weird me out."

"Ron, I told you, I'm Chelsea's brother. Can you just get her for me?"

"Listen man, I don't know who you are, and I don't know any broad named Chelsea. Did the boys at the Legion put you up to this? Those fuckers are always pulling shit like this on me," he said, looking over Alec's shoulder as if to see if the Legion boys were watching.

Looking past Ron and into the home, he realized that it looked nothing like what he had seen just days earlier. From what he could see, the layout appeared to be the same, but the paint on the walls was completely different and none of the furniture matched. The home was quite bare, with not a trinket in sight. Alec backed away from the house and his body began to tremble. Tears began to stream down his face.

"Oh shit, dude, are you ok?"

"No, I'm far from ok. Nothing makes sense anymore and I don't know what to do." Ron stared at him blankly as Alec turned and walked away.

With no moon in the night sky, the streets were dark as were most of the homes he walked past, while making his way over to Sarah's place. It was not quite ten o'clock, but it appeared everyone on the street had already gone to bed. Besides the humming of the streetlights, the only other noise he heard came from a barking dog in the distance. With each step the barking grew louder.

Walking up the path to Sarah's front door, the barking abruptly stopped, following a loud yelp that echoed throughout the street. With no answer at her door, he wondered if she had fallen asleep but then panic set in as he thought there was a good chance there may not even be a Sarah Edwards at this point. He sat on the front step and lit a cigarette while thinking of the time they had spent together. It had to have happened, but he was starting to doubt everything. If Sarah vanished, he worried he would not be able to cope. Maybe he'd end up doing what Grayson had done.

Before long, a small pile of cigarette butts rested at his feet. With his face in his hands, he watched a colony of ants maneuver their way through the pile.

"Alec?"

"Oh, thank god," he sighed upon hearing Sarah's voice.

"What are you doing here?" Sarah scowled.

"I just needed to see you," he replied, still with his head in his hands.

"Well, I don't really want to see you. Not after ..." she began as Alec raised his head. "Jesus Alec, you look like shit. What's wrong?"

"I think it's time I let you in on some things Sarah."

As Alec began to go through the list of odd things that had happened, the psychiatrist patiently sat back and listened without interrupting. The pile of cigarette butts continued to grow, while he explained that places he'd been had changed and people he knew had started disappearing. He anticipated her stopping him at several points throughout his story, however she did not say a word. It was not until the mentioning of his most recent run-in with Ron, that she interrupted.

"Did you say you saw Chelsea a few days ago?"

"Yes, why?" he asked, wiping the tears from his eyes.

"I think you need to see something." Rising to her feet, she held out her hand to help him up. "Come with me."

Sarah drove down the main street in town until they reached the town's perimeter. No other cars were in sight as they hit the highway. Their car rolled through the darkness of the night. Upon hearing the Tragically Hip song, Sarah turned up the radio.

"Yeah that's awful close but that's not why, I'm so hard done by," she quietly sang along.

229

"Where are we going?" Alec asked before watching her glance over and completely ignore the question.

"In an epic too small to be tragic, you'll have to wait a minute cause it's an instamatic," she continued. Her expressionless demeanor was eerie and concerning.

A few minutes later they arrive at the gates to the cemetery and Sarah stared straight ahead as Alec watched her intently.

"What are we doing here, Sarah?"

Still, she did not answer. After placing the car in park, she opened her door and stepped out. After noticing he didn't follow, Sarah leaned her head through the window.

"Coming?" she asked, before turning and walking away.

"Fine," Alec said, climbing out of his seat. "Why aren't you telling me …" he said, before realizing Sarah was too far ahead to hear. He picked up the pace to a jog, trying to narrow the gap, but had difficulty maneuvering through the gravestones in the dark. After stumbling over a headstone, he shouted, "Sarah, slow down!" Making his way past a row of shrubs, he saw her sitting just a few feet away, staring back at him.

"Over here, Alec."

"Why did you bring me here?" Alec whined. She remained stoic and did not respond, while she continued to sit on the bench in front of him. He watched her as she kept focused on one of the gravestones. "Seriously I already came to visit them," he muttered while looking over to see what she was eying. "What the hell ... No, that just can't be ... But Sarah, I just saw her!" Sarah watched him as he continued to gawk at the headstone which read:

CHELSEA JENKINS
BELOVED DAUGHTER OF SUSAN & GERALD
AND SISTER TO ALEC
THERE ARE NO BUSSES IN HEAVEN

After moving to sit beside him on the ground, Sarah began to stroke his back as he sobbed. His body shook, while the snot and tears streamed down his face.

"It's ok Alec," she said softly.

"Sarah, I don't understand what's happening. None of this makes any sense."

"I think all the trauma you've experienced in your life has caused a great deal of stress and anxiety," she said, continuing to comfort him. "Stress can do crazy things to people, and I think in your case, it's led to a chain reaction of delusional episodes."

"So, you think I'm delusional?" he asked, wiping the tears and snot away with his forearm.

"Well, it's a little early for me to give you an actual diagnosis, but I'm thinking you never truly dealt with the loss of your family. You probably threw yourself into your work and did not allow yourself to mourn. I have seen this kind of thing before. Taking ten, twenty or even thirty years, to truly mourn the loss of loved ones is not as uncommon as you would think. Perhaps this is the reason for your lack of memory and your black outs. Maybe since you came back to town, you're finally allowing yourself to mourn the loss of your family and all these memories are too much to handle."

Although the panic inside felt insurmountable, her diagnosis was oddly somewhat comforting to him, even though he was not sure he believed it completely. His recent memories of Chelsea just seemed much too real to not have happened.

"Is that possible? I mean, it was so traumatic that I've made up all these other memories in my head?" he asked, continuing to stare at Chelsea's headstone in disbelief.

"The mind is a very powerful thing Alec. You've heard of people having multiple personalities, right? Well many of them have created those alternate personalities internally to deal with things that were too traumatic for them to handle." After moving onto the bench across from his parents' gravestone, they sat in silence for a few moments while Alec contemplated what she had said.

"There is something else that has been bothering me though, which I can't figure out."

"What's that?"

"I used to be really close with my parents when I was a kid, but then for some reason, we drifted apart when I was a teenager, and I don't understand why."

"That's not uncommon with teenagers, Alec."

"Yes, I know, but we were really close and then it felt like overnight we weren't. By the time I had moved away, we barely spoke. I think they were actually relieved when I left."

"I seriously doubt that Alec. Your parents loved you very much. I could see that when we were together."

"You could?"

"Yes, of course, but I really only saw things from the outside. If you're saying things changed that quickly, there must have been something that happened. Was there a specific event, that you can think of, that possibly changed your relationship with your parents?"

"No, not really."

"Nothing at all?" she asked, sounding skeptical.

After taking a moment he replied, "Well I do remember them always making such a big deal about my birthday every year, but then one birthday it all changed. They actually did nothing, which I remember thinking was odd. Then going forward, they didn't do much of anything for any other birthdays."

233

"Well that is strange. Do you remember what birthday it was when it all started?" Although his life was in shambles, he could not help but be impressed with Sarah's professionalism.

"I don't know for sure, but I think I was fourteen or maybe fifteen when that happened."

"Hmm."

"I argued with her about their gravestones," Alec blurted, motioning to Chelsea's gravestone.

"What do you mean?"

"When I saw Chelsea a few days ago, we spoke about their gravestones."

"Well Alec, I think we both know that isn't possible," she said softly, while rubbing his back. Her warmth was comforting and her perfume, intoxicating. Her allure was certainly helping take his mind off his troubles. Their eyes grew intense upon one other and he was certain she desired him. Feeling the moment, he leaned in for a kiss, but she quickly pulled back. "I'm sorry Alec, I just can't."

"It was just a stupid mistake Sarah. That girl meant nothing to me. I was drunk, and I know that's no excuse, but I actually think she may have slipped something in my drink."

"It's ok, Alec, you don't have to make excuses. You didn't actually do anything wrong," she interjected. "It's not like we're a committed couple or anything. It threw me off because I just didn't think you were that type of guy."

"I'm not. I just …" he began to say, putting his hand into hers.

"Listen Alec, let's just get you better," she interjected smiling. He smiled back, realizing it sounded like she had not completely given up on them.

Suddenly, a twig snapped behind them. Although Sarah had not seemed to notice, Alec had, and quickly turned to see who was there. It was the same man who had been following him back in San Francisco and it appeared he had been creeping up on them.

"Hey, come back here!" Alec shouted, hopping to his feet.

"Where are you going Alec?" Sarah shouted. "Alec, wait!"

The cowboy hat bobbed and weaved through the trees and trail of gravestones, as the overcoat flapped wildly in the wind. Although he had told Sarah about most of the strange events that had transpired, he had not mentioned he was being followed.

As Alec navigated his way through the headstones after the stranger, he heard Sarah calling out to him. Her voice quickly quieted, eventually disappearing, as he maintained his pursuit of the cowboy hat. The mysterious man was clearly running away from him and he was having difficulty keeping up. Each time he thought he had lost him; the cowboy hat would reappear, seemingly floating through the graveyard. After nearly running the length of the graveyard, Alec stopped to catch his breath. He had nearly given up the chase before seeing the man again, standing off in the distance, looking back at him. He appeared to be taunting him.

Suddenly, a bright white light came over him. It was so excruciating blinding that it brought Alec to his knees. His head throbbed and he was not able to open his eyes even though he tried several times. A high-pitched ringing screamed between his ears. He felt lightheaded and knew he was seconds away from fainting. Before losing consciousness, he heard people talking in the distance, then suddenly directly above him.

"Come on Eddy, you can do it," begged a woman.

"Nice and easy. Come on son," said a man's soothing voice before everything went dark.

CHAPTER 16

Grayson and Alec arrived at the tracks to see the back of the caboose heading in the other direction, towards the mill. They followed along the set of tracks, slowly catching up to the caboose while continuing to call out for Eddy. The train slowly made its way past the thick trees that lined one side of the track, while a second set of tracks and gravel road lined the other. As they approached the back of the caboose, they neared a second parked train sitting on a parallel set of tracks. Dust from a passing vehicle blew over them while they investigated each railroad car of the stationary train as they walked past.

"I bet the little fucker went back to the house to tell on us," Grayson growled.

"I don't know man. Would he even know how to get there? We are kind of far from our place." Alec wanted to believe his friend was right but was very concerned for Eddy's wellbeing.

"I'm sure the little shit is just fine. Oh wow, check it out," Grayson said, pointing at the engine to the motionless train up ahead.

"Jackpot! It still has all its windows too!" he shouted, before proceeding to throw rocks until smashing one of its windows.

"Boom! Did you see that?"

"Nice one," Alec replied, unenthusiastically.

Walking past the engine, they neared the back of the moving train and its caboose which continued to slowly crawl along the tracks. After making their way past the caboose, they started checking into each of the railroad cars of the active train. It began picking up speed, so they started jogging alongside to keep the pace.

"Check this out!" shouted Grayson, holding up some old rusted tools he had pulled out of one of the cars.

"Sweet," Alec replied, now faking his enthusiasm.

The boys would hide their collection of treasures from the trains behind a shed in Grayson's back yard. They would often get together just to look at them while making up wild stories of the people who had left them behind. Pirates were often involved in their stories, even though they had never seen one and Russell was nowhere near any ocean. Their imaginations ran wild and sometimes Grayson's vivid stories would keep Alec from sleeping at night.

The boys used their walkie-talkies to communicate after their parents had gone to sleep, often talking of their treasures. They would sometimes sneak out at night and head to the train tracks just to hang out inside the trains. Their parents were unaware until the evening Alec's father barged into his room after overhearing their plans to meet at the tracks. That was the first time, but certainly not the last, his father would lecture him of the dangers of playing on the trains. The walkie-talkies were confiscated that evening, but later returned, as their parents figured the boys had learned their lesson. They were wrong, as the boys would use them several more times when planning their late-night adventures.

What their parents did not know was their kids played on the trains regularly, and often in the middle of the night. They would play a game that involved hopping on and off the moving trains to see who would stay on the longest. Alec had once stayed on too long and ended up breaking his ankle while jumping off the train as it sped along. They lied to their parents, telling them that he had fallen off his bike while doing tricks at the park, to avoid getting in trouble.

The marsh between their homes and the railroad tracks was where they would tell their parents they would be playing anytime they would go to the railroad tracks. As their homes were close to the lumber mill, there would often be trains stationed there overnight, waiting to be loaded the next day. The boys would take full advantage of the stationary trains by playing on them at all hours of the night. Four sets of parallel tracks lead to the entrance of the mill, where the workers would load and unload materials. Two hundred yards out from the mill, the four sets of tracks would consolidate into two sets of tracks.

On one occasion, a fleet of engines was stationed overnight, and the boys threw rocks at them smashing over forty windows. The next morning the town was a buzz as several Royal

Canadian Mounted Police surrounded the engines, conducting a thorough investigation. Although they were never caught, Mr. Jenkins was quite certain his son had a hand in the destruction and for the following month, Alec's chores around the house increased substantially. The boys steered clear of the trains and marsh for the rest of that summer. By the next summer, they were back there playing, but never again did they do any insurmountable damage to the trains.

Grayson's parents were not as strict and allowed him to come and go as he desired. He would regularly talk back to his mother; however, he would not dare talk back to his father. To Alec's knowledge, the only thing Grayson feared in life was his father. Mr. Spencer was a large burly man who rarely spoke around the boys. Alec had seen him angry on several occasions and feared the man. Mr. Spencer was not around much, as he worked shift work at the mill and often worked overtime. When he was home, he was usually seen sleeping on the sofa chair in front of the television, always with a beer nearby.

Grayson's mother was a lovely lady and was no match for a bratty kid like Grayson. She was timid and soft spoken, something Grayson took advantage of while his father was not around. For as long as Alec could remember, his friend had a very dark evil side. He would disobey his mother constantly and almost without fail each time she would threaten punishment, once his father got home. Alec wondered why Mrs. Spencer

240

would never follow through with her threat, always keeping her husband out of the loop. She, too, was probably scared of the man.

Grayson's parents started dating in high school and when she was only a sophomore, Mrs. Spencer got pregnant. By the time grade twelve had rolled around, she had dropped out of school and Mr. Spencer's father had insisted he marry her. Alec got the feeling that Mr. Spencer never wanted kids, as the boys were together nearly every day and he had never once, seen the man speak to his son, unless it was to discipline him.

Alec had a great appreciation for his own father, as he always made time for him and Chelsea, even though he also worked long hours with all the extracurricular activities that came with being a schoolteacher. Mr. Jenkins was an affectionate man, which was not as common in those days. He insisted on a hug from his children nearly every morning and night until Alec had gotten to the age where he would shrug off his father, telling him it was not cool anymore. Thoughts of his crumbling relationship with his mother and father saddened him throughout his adulthood, but nothing bothered him more than the memory of the disappointment his father showed after he told him he was done with his affection.

Each time he disobeyed his father, he felt guilty. He knew, even at a young age, that he had a good father who was only looking out for his children's best interests. The problem was his best friend liked to get into mischief, so Alec would often have to disobey his father's rules in fear of losing the respect of his best friend. Even though he was an active participant in Grayson's mischief, he was almost always reluctant.

After passing several empty cars, they heard something scurrying around in the second-to-last car connected to the engine. Grayson put his finger to his lips signaling to Alec to be quiet. As they approached the car, Eddy's head popped out from the side. Even with the wind blowing, his thick black hair remained glued to his head, while his ghoulish eyes searched for a place to land.

"There he is!" Grayson shouted, before proceeding to pick up a handful of stones.

Eddy ducked back into the car after Grayson began throwing rocks. Alec reluctantly joined in the rock tossing but purposely threw them nowhere near where Eddy had appeared. They continued running alongside the moving train while throwing rocks. Eddy popped his head out a few times while attempting to jump off, each time drawing more rocks from Grayson's hand. As the boys began having trouble keeping up to the train, Alec stopped.

"Hey man, maybe we should stop. He really needs to get off the train, it's starting to go pretty fast."

"Yeah, ok," reluctantly, Grayson agreed.

"Eddy jump off! We're not going to throw anymore rocks!" Grayson shouted.

When Eddy did not appear, Alec pressed on, "Come on Eddy, jump off! It's picking up speed and you won't be able to jump off soon!"

They continued running alongside the train while pleading for the young boy to listen, but to no avail. Alec briefly worried that Grayson might have hit him with another rock, knocking him unconscious. However, as he caught up with the train, he could see that Eddy was no longer inside.

CHAPTER 17

The wonderful aroma of sizzling bacon and freshly brewed coffee filled his nostrils. The bed squeaked as he rose to a sitting position. He listened to Sarah speak on the telephone in the other room while stretching his arms. After putting on his boxers, he made his way into the kitchen.

Taking a seat at the kitchen table, he was met with a hot cup of coffee. While she continued with her conversation, it became apparent to Alec that she was speaking with one of her patients whose panic attacks were affecting his or her job.

"If they think they need help, tell them to get in line," Alec muttered.

She giggled, then put a finger to her lips, motioning for him to be quiet. He smiled, thinking their relationship may still have a chance, as it appeared as though all may be forgiven. After apologizing to her patient for giggling, she examined the bandage on Alec's head, a bandage that he was unaware of having until that moment. She squeezed the receiver between her chin and shoulder, while giving advice to her patient and removing the bandage on his head, before replacing it with a new one.

Alec tried to remember what had transpired at the graveyard, but the last thing he could recall was chasing after the man that had been following him. Before hanging up, she informed her patient she would prescribe Alprazolam to help with the panic attacks so he could return to work.

"Good morning Eddy," she said, before placing a kiss on the back of his head.

"Eddy?"

"Huh?" she replied.

"You just called me Eddy."

"No, I didn't," she said, pouring herself a cup of coffee. "I think you're still half asleep," she said with a chuckle, before taking a sip.

"I'm pretty sure you called me Eddy. Anyway, what day is it today?" Alec asked, feeling the bandage.

"Tuesday and don't touch that," she said, swatting his hand away. "So, are you going to tell me what happened?"

"I was hoping you would tell me. The last thing I remember was sitting with you at the cemetery."

"You don't remember running off like a lunatic?"

"No, why would I do that?" Alec asked, knowing well why he had run off. For some reason, he did not want to explain to the psychiatrist that he thought he was being followed.

"I don't know, but it sure was strange. You took off running and I could not keep up. By the time I found you, you were on the ground unconscious."

"Really? I don't remember any of that."

"Well you've got to stop doing stuff like that, at least until we figure out what's going on in that noggin of yours. It's a good thing that man was there to help with getting you into the car. How's your head? Looks like you cracked it pretty good on that headstone."

"Headstone?"

"Wow, this is still bleeding," she said, examining Alec's head wound. "I'm going to find another bandage." She made her way across the kitchen as Alec tried to piece together what had happened.

"So, someone helped you get me into the car?"

"Yes, that's right," she replied, digging through the drawer.

"And you don't know who he was? I thought you knew everyone in this town?"

As she stood over him, replacing his bandage, she replied, "I guess he wasn't from around here. He did look kind of familiar though. I was so concerned with you that I didn't pay much attention to him. He seemed nice, but a little creepy though."

"Creepy?"

"Yeah, it wasn't anything he did, it was just the way he looked at me, I guess. Also, when I got there, he was just standing there looking down at you but not really doing anything. Then he just stared at me for a bit before helping me get you to the car."

"What was he wearing?"

246

"Well that was also weird. He was wearing an overcoat. Who wears an overcoat when it's warm out?"

"Was he wearing a cowboy hat?"

"A cowboy hat?" she laughed. "No cowboy hat. Why?" Alec sat back, looking confused and said nothing. "What's going on Alec? What is it?"

"Nothing …"

"Why do I get the feeling you're not telling me something?"

"There is something, but I just didn't want to tell you." He let out a big sigh and continued, "Now you're for sure going to think I'm completely insane and at this point, I think I just might be."

"What is it?"

"That man, I've seen him before, back in San Francisco. He's been following me."

"The guy from the cemetery?"

"Yes," he replied reluctantly. "At first I thought I was just being paranoid, but then I kept seeing him and now I'm sure he was following me."

"Was he wearing an overcoat when you noticed him in San Francisco?"

"Yes."

"Did you notice anything different about his overcoat?"

"Listen I know this all sounds crazy and you probably don't believe," Alec began to say before she interrupted.

"Alec, was there anything different about his overcoat?"

"No, not really. It was just a tan overcoat."

She gave him a skeptical look and replied, "Well, the guy I saw was wearing a tanned one too."

"Oh wait, did it have blue pockets?" Alec asked. He could tell immediately that it had by the look on her face.

"Yes! Why, is this guy following you? Who is he?"

"So, you saw him too? Maybe I'm not so crazy after all! I don't know who he is or why he's following me, but after I saw him at the cemetery, I ran after him to find out what he wanted."

"Can you think of a reason why someone would be following you?"

He thought for a moment, then said, "Well there is a competitor of mine that could have possibly hired someone to follow me, but I doubt it."

"I have to finish up with a couple work calls, then let's go see if we can find this mystery man. Sound good?"

"Sounds great! So, we're going on a stakeout, hey?" Alec replied, still riding on the excitement that he may not be insane.

"Yes, I guess you could say that," she chuckled.

"Just like a couple of detectives from 21 Jump Street!"

"And what, you think you're like Johnny Depp? You wish … actually, I should say I wish. I would love to be partners with Johnny. Those detectives were both men, so I'd say it's more of a 'Murder She Wrote' kind of thing."

248

"Oh, ok so you're Angela Lansbury?"

"Yeah sure, why not?"

"Because she was a hundred years old," Alec chuckled.

"So what? She was brilliant and always solved the crimes."

"Listen Sarah, if we're going to do this, we've got to do it right. Usually on these stakeouts there's some sexual tension, and I don't want to be visualizing a blow job from Angela Lansbury. Let's go with T.J. Hooker."

"Blow job? I don't think so. And you think Lansbury is too old, but the old and fat Shatner is ok? You've got the same double standards as Hollywood," she scoffed.

"Hey, Shatner might be old and fat now, but he was a total stud back when he was Sargent Hooker."

"That's true, ok you make a good point. T.J. Hooker it is," she snickered, then left the room.

He hopped into the shower while Sarah made her phone calls. After getting dressed, he heard her still on the phone, so he sat on the bed and turned on the television at the foot of her bed. Flicking through the channels, he passed over the Oprah show and was reminded of his mother's and Mrs. Spencer's love for the show. The next channel he stopped on was CNN, where they were yet again referencing idiotic tweets from President Trump.

"Find something else to talk about," he muttered, before changing the channel. The next channel was playing the movie

Groundhog Day and he thought of the two run-ins he'd had with Tim Byrd.

"Alec," Sarah said, as she appeared in the doorway, startling him. "Geez you're jumpy. Are you ready to go?"

"Yeah, let's get out of here," he replied, looking back at the television to see Bill Murray punch his old classmate.

Driving through the streets of Russell, Alec did not think they would find the mystery man but enjoyed spending time with Sarah, so he obliged. She seemed to be genuinely enjoying their stakeout as they searched. Her enthusiasm and excitement had become contagious. The television show references continued between the two as they portrayed their detective roles. Again, there was no lull in the conversation as Sarah rambled on for hours, during their surveillance.

Sarah had several false alarms as she so desperately wanted to catch their perpetrator. Yet most of her suspects were not close to matching the description of the actual man they were hunting. At one point, Alec asked if she should be wearing glasses.

With Sarah still defending her capable vision, they pulled up to the end of the driveway of Alec's childhood home. He thought about his relationship with his sister and how close they were when they were kids and wished things could have been the same in their adult years. While staring out the window, he came to the realization that he was completely to blame for their lack of closeness. Even though she could be annoying at times, Chelsea was the one that made all the effort in keeping in touch. She was his sister, his own flesh and blood, and he should have made more of an effort.

He remembered walking home from elementary school while the whole school followed behind as Jerry Pinks, a much larger and older classmate, pushed and shoved him along the way. His parents taught him not to fight back, and that's what he did, but as the other children encircled the two boys, he had been cornered with no other choice but to fight back. Jerry Pinks landed the first punch knocking Alec, the much smaller of the two, to the ground. Alec tried to fight back but couldn't see because his eyes were full of tears. After taking a few more punches to the back of his head, he turtled until he was rescued by his older sister.

She pulled the kid off her brother's back before proceeding to lay a beating on the bully. After only a few seconds, Jerry Pinks lay whimpering on the ground as the other kids watched and laughed. Jerry Pinks was no longer the school bully after that, and his sister became her little brother's hero along with several of the other kids around Alec's age. Chelsea made Alec promise never to tell their parents what had happened, and he never did.

A tear rolled down the side of his cheek as he sat there looking out the window, wishing he could see his sister again.

"What are you thinking about?"

"Nothing," he replied, subtly wiping the tear from the other side of his face.

"You've been awfully quiet looking out that window. I can tell you're thinking about something."

"Did they ever have sex while out on a stakeout?"

"Who?"

"T.J. Hooker and Locklear's character," he said with a smirk.

"You're such a pig! Of course, that's what you're thinking about. My mom was right, you men are all the same."

They sat there in silence for a few moments before Alec asked, "Do you miss her?"

"My mom? Yes, every day. Do you miss yours?"

"Yes," he replied, looking at the house. "Did you know I didn't even cry at their funeral? What kind of son doesn't cry at his own parents' funeral?" The car remained silent for a few moments then he continued, "You know I've been thinking a lot about my sister and all the conversations we've had since my parents' death. If Chelsea did in fact die along with my parents, then all those conversations were just made up in my head?"

"I'm afraid so, Alec," she replied, reaching over and rubbing him on the leg. "I know it seems impossible, but the mind is very fragile, and those things can and do happen, especially when

252

someone goes through a traumatic experience. It must've been really hard on you losing all of your family at once."

"I don't remember it happening that way and I just can't see how all those conversations I've had with her on the phone over the years weren't real. And having coffee with her a few days ago wasn't real?"

"All in your imagination. Apparently, your brain has created altered memories for your well-being, Alec. Like those people with split personalities, but instead of your brain creating an alternate personality, it created an alternate life."

"It just seems impossible. How do I know that you're not a part of this alternate reality?"

She looked at him and smiled, before planting a big kiss on his lips. Groping his groin until he became hard, she continued, "You tell me, is this an alternate reality?"

As they continued to make out, he understood what she was saying, but was not completely convinced of her diagnosis. He did trust her and had just seen Ron, who had no idea who he was, so he was resigned to the fact that it was a good possibility.

"What about schizophrenia?" Alec asked.

"What about it?"

"Maybe I'm schizophrenic? That would make the most sense wouldn't it?" She became quiet, staring out the windshield and he continued with a sense of panic in his voice, "Sarah, do you think I'm schizophrenic?"

"It's too early to tell, but I won't lie to you, the thought had crossed my mind." They sat in silence, while looking out the windshield, before Sarah suddenly hissed, "Oh my god!"

"What?"

"Don't look now, but I think I see our guy!"

"Where?" Alec whispered, trying to follow her eyes.

"He's standing behind the big oak tree. The second last one on the right."

"Holy shit, that is him!" Alec confirmed.

"What should we do?"

"Ok, no sudden movements because I don't want to scare him off. Slowly grab your door handle, and on the count of three, we'll go after him." They casually reached for their door handles and on three, they simultaneously opened their doors and jumped out. The man, still wearing the tan coat with blue pockets, immediately bolted in the other direction.

"Hey stop!" Sarah shouted as they chased after. Only a few feet out of the car, Sarah quickly fell behind as Alec raced ahead. Although Alec was a fast runner, he was not able to catch up to the man. Seconds later, the man disappeared through the trees at the back of the yard.

A feeling of nostalgia came over him as he stood there looking out at the marsh now in front of him. It seemed identical to when he had last been there as a child. The combination of the rotten-egg smell and sounds of the chirping crickets and frogs, brought back old memories of all the time he had spent back there in his youth. Sarah finally caught up to him a few seconds later.

"Where did he go?"

"He's gone," Alec replied. "No telling which direction he could've taken beyond those trees." With their hands on their hips, they remained standing there while trying to catch their breath.

"Look!" Sarah shouted, pointing at a tree where the man's overcoat dangled from one of its branches. After carefully lifting it off the branch she held it out for him to see the blue pockets. "Well we may not have caught the guy, but at least we've got his jacket!"

"Well, at least we have that," Alec replied, taking hold of the coat and throwing it over his arm. "But that's all we had on him, so now how are we going to recognize him?" Together they laughed at the ridiculousness of the situation. Still gazing out at the marsh he continued, "You know it is amazing, besides the trees being much bigger now, this marsh hasn't changed at all since I was a kid. I mean it really looks exactly how I remembered."

They stood in silence for a few more moments as she watched Alec while he continued to look out at the marsh. Finally, after Sarah had turned and started walking back to the car, he followed.

"Did you check the pockets? Maybe his wallet is in there or something," Sarah said, forging ahead.

As he rifled through the pockets, he found a used tissue, a gum wrapper, and a folded piece of paper. After putting the other stuff back in the pocket, he opened the folded piece of paper.

"What the hell?" he gasped.

"What's on it?"

"My name and room number at the hotel."

"That's strange."

"I saw this note in Edgar's room at the hotel."

"So, Edgar must know this guy. Did he mention anything about this?"

"No, he didn't," Alec replied intrigued. "Let's go talk to him."

By the time he reached the car, Sarah was behind the wheel, staring at him impatiently.

"Let's go slow poke!" she barked. As the car pulled away, a loud rumbling came from behind the marsh. "What the hell was that?"

"The train. They bang around when they start to move," Alec replied.

"Wow, that's loud. How did you ever sleep as a child with all that noise?"

"I actually find it soothing in weird way. Actually, a lot of the time, we were playing on them in the middle of the night," he replied, thinking of his and Grayson's escapades.

On the drive over to the hotel, he thought of what he was going to say to Edgar once they arrived. Edgar must have been working with the mystery man. and if he was, Alec wondered if interrogating him was a good idea, but he needed to find out exactly how much Edgar knew.

As they pulled up in front of the hotel, Alec quickly jumped out before the car had come to a complete stop and rushing through the front doors, he motioned to Sarah to wait in the car. Moments later he returned to the driver's side window and she rolled it down.

"What did he say?"

"He's not here. They said it's his day off, but he'll be back in the morning. I knocked on the door to his room, but he didn't answer. I'm going to stay here tonight so I can catch him in the morning."

"Ok just be careful." He leaned in through the window and they exchanged a kiss before he turned to walk away. "Oh, and T.J ..." she said out the window.

"Yes?"

"I love you too." She winked at him, then drove away.

He had forgotten about the voice message he had left her while in San Francisco. He smiled as he entered the hotel, wondering if there was any sincerity to what she had said or if she was just teasing.

He checked back into the Marby Hotel. They put him up in the same room. Apparently, Edgar had saved the room in case he returned. As Alec opened the door of room 620, he was baffled that the only perfume that still lingered was not Sarah's, but the strong scent of the waitress from the previous night. "Jesus Jenny, you might want to take it easy on the perfume," he muttered to himself aloud, while closing the door behind him.

"Sorry, is it too strong?" The voice darted from the bathroom doorway, startling Alec. He looked up to see Jenny, now standing in the middle of the room, wearing only a towel. With her wet, slicked back hair, she fixated on him.

"Jenny, what are you doing here?"

"Surprise! I saw you in the lobby, so I thought I'd surprise you."

"How did you get in here?"

"I still had the key from the other night. Guess your lady friend isn't joining us. What a shame, I'm totally into redheads."

"That lady friend is actually my girlfriend. A girlfriend I nearly lost because of you the other night. You should go."

She stood up and untied the towel, allowing it to drop to the floor. Standing naked in front of him she replied, "Should go, or should stay and have some fun? I haven't been able to get you out of my mind since the other night."

"Listen Jenny, you're a great girl …" he paused, watching as she continued trying to seduce him by squeezing her breasts together. Although he was trying not to get drawn in by her seduction, it was difficult to resist. Rubbing up against him, she began kissing his neck and caressing his groin before he leaned away and interjected. "Jenny, seriously, I'm twice your age. Surely there's some twenty-year-old that's more suitable." He placed both his hands on her arms and steered her away. "I really think you need to go," he continued, but even he was not convinced of the sincerity of the words coming out of his mouth.

"I don't think he wants me to go," she replied, looking down at what was protruding from his pants. "Tell me one more time to leave and I will," she said, before putting his fingers in her mouth while attempting to unzip his fly and shove her hand down the front of his pants.

She fixed a wide-eyed stare at him, dropping to her knees, and Alec stood momentarily transfixed, watching. As his pants hit the floor, he finally snapped. "Seriously Jenny, please leave," he said, with a much sterner tone, while pulling up his pants.

"You're such a tease," she whined, rising to her feet. She stepped back and reached for her sundress off the bed. After slipping it over her head, she playfully pranced, attempting a runway model walk towards the door. "You know where to find me when you change your mind later," she sighed, as he ushered her out the door.

After his erection softened, he felt a little better about himself for being able to resist the sexy twenty-year-old. He turned on the television to try to take his mind off Jenny, and what might have transpired. The Giants game was showing on one of the channels. It was just past 9 p.m., and they were on the road in Seattle, so the game had just begun. He hoped the game between the Giants and Mariners would help to take his mind off the game he had turned down.

The Giants were on a bit of a tear lately, and by the fifth inning they found themselves with a large lead. He thought of his conversation with Jason during the baseball game back in San Francisco, and grinned thinking of how they had missed the Giants scoring a slew of runs because of their intense conversation. He then started to wonder if the game had happened, or if maybe he had just imagined it had. Was there actually a Jason Thompson? Was there a Woodward Financial? If there was no Woodward Financial, then there was certainly no Mr Rhodes. What things and people of his memories were real, and which had he just imagined? As he sat back, searching through his memories for answers before the phone on the nightstand rang vociferously.

"Hello?"

"I thought I told you never to come back here, yet here you are." He recognized the voice as it was the same one from the previous prank calls.

260

"I've got your jacket asshole. Why don't you come get ..." but before Alec could finish, the person hung up. Suddenly, there was a loud knock at the door. "That was quick," he muttered before hanging up the phone. As he approached the door, his hand trembled as he wondered if he was finally going to meet the mysterious man who had been following him. His heart raced as his sweaty palm reached for the doorknob. He turned the knob then pulled it back towards him quickly, only to find three drunk young women on the other side.

"Oh, sorry sir, wrong room," shouted one of the girls as the others giggled. Alec stared at them, wondering how old they were, as they looked to be around the same age as Jenny. After turning away, they continued to laugh, entering the room across the hall. One of them shouted to another inside the room, "Who's the old creep across the hall?"

After the door slammed closed behind them, Alec was abruptly reminded what it usually felt like to be a fifty-year-old man socializing around such young ladies, which made him suspicious as to why Jenny seemed to find him attractive. He then wondered if he actually had hooked up with Jenny, or if he had just imagined the whole thing.

Sprawled out on the bed, he returned his attention back to the baseball game. The Mariners had scored a few runs, narrowing the gap, and were now making a game of it. After almost dozing off, he looked up to see the game was heading into the bottom of the ninth and the Giants had their ace on the mound. He propped up a couple of pillows, then placed his head on them and was now ready to catch the unfolding drama.

A blast of white light suddenly filled the room and a sharp pain drove through his temples. The sounds of the baseball game distorted into shouting voices from afar. The shouting then appeared to be right over him, but Alec was unable to open his eyes as the blinding light made it impossible.

"What's going on?" someone asked to his right.

"Everyone calm down!" shouted another to his left.

"Eddy, can you hear me? Please, baby ... please," whimpered a familiar voice directly over him.

CHAPTER 18

As the train continued to pick up speed, the boys ran as fast as they could but struggled to keep pace. Alec saw the eight-year-old's head pop out the side of one of the cars again and pleaded for him to get off the train.

"Eddy jump now! We have got to get him off that train before it's too late! Did you see where he went?"

"No … oh wait, there he is," Grayson shouted, pointing to the top of the train. They watched in fear as Eddy's legs trembled, struggling to steady himself, while standing atop the train.

"Eddy, get down please!" Alec shouted, nearly out of breath.

"Sit down!" Grayson pleaded.

"Can you get to the caboose?" Alec hollered at Eddy. "It might be easier to jump off back there."

The train began to pull away from the boys, as it continued to pick up speed. Eddy nodded, then went to his knees and began crawling along the top of the train, attempting to get to the back. The older boys cheered Eddy on while he struggled to get to his feet, nearly falling several times. They watched helplessly, until finally the eight-year-old reached the last car before the caboose.

"He's only got one more to go Eddy!" Grayson shouted, as they continued watching as the train began disappearing into the horizon.

"I can barely see him anymore," Alec whimpered.

"I can, he's climbing onto the caboose," Grayson replied. They watched nervously as Eddy struggled to reach the caboose. He stretched his short arms across, reaching for the ladder on the caboose, while his unsteady legs remained on the last car before suddenly, disappearing in between the cars.

"Oh my god, where did he go?"

"Fuck, I think he fell between the cars!" Grayson gasped, almost completely out of breath.

Sharp pains ripped through Alec's stomach, as he worried about Eddy's safety. He continued chasing after the train, now nearly out of site, with Grayson close behind. Finally stopping to catch their breath, Alec noticed something up ahead on the tracks.

"What is that?"

"Oh no," Grayson whimpered.

Alec thought it might have been Eddy sitting to catch his breath. But as they approached, he could see it was Eddy, but he wasn't just trying to catch his breath, the eight-year-old boy was completely mangled.

"Oh god," Alec moaned.

His body ended landing in the sitting position, with his head and shoulders slouched over his torso. His legs appeared to be broken in several places, as they lay in a heap completely drenched in blood. They stood silent over the lifeless body for several minutes, while tears streamed down their faces.

"Fuck," Grayson groaned.

"Is he dead?" Alec whimpered. Grayson placed his fingers on Eddy's neck for a few seconds, then looked back at Alec and nodded.

"Yeah, I think so. I'm not feeling a pulse." They sat down beside Eddy's maimed body. Alec began to cry uncontrollably. Grayson tried to console him but was not able. "Why didn't he just jump," Grayson whined, getting to his feet. They both knew the answer to that, but he was looking for his friend to help lessen the blame.

"We should've stopped," Alec said, dusting off his pants, before turning and walking away.

"Alec, where are you going?"

"I'm going to get some help."

"Some help? He doesn't need help, he's dead."

"Yes, I know Grayson, but we need to tell someone."

"I don't think that's a good idea."

"Why not?" Alec asked, after stopping and turning to face him.

"Because we could go to jail!"

"I'm pretty sure they don't send ten-year-old kids to jail. Now come on, let's go! We need to tell someone."

Alec turned and Grayson pleaded, "What's your dad going to say about you playing on the trains again? You'll be grounded for the rest of your life, and once he finds out what you did with Eddy you'll probably end up in a foster home."

"What I did?" he shouted, turning back. "You're the one that insisted on throwing rocks at him."

"So what? You threw stones too, so don't put all the blame on me. You're just as guilty as I am," Grayson fired back. Alec hated that he was right and began to cry again. Grayson made his way over to him and put his arm around him.

"It's ok Alec. It's not like we meant to hurt him. It was an accident. So why should we have to suffer the rest of our lives because of it."

"What are you saying we should do?"

"I don't know," Grayson replied, surveying the area. "Nobody knows we were here, and nobody has to know. If we stick to the same story, nobody will ever know what happened."

Alec convinced himself that his friend was right, after all they had not meant to harm Eddy. They never could have predicted that this would happen. They sat on the tracks for several minutes, quickly concocting a story that they hoped would keep them from getting into trouble.

They would tell everyone that the three of them had been chased by a wild dog, then got split up, losing Eddy in the melee. Whatever happened to Eddy, happened when they were not around because after splitting up, they were alone in the abandoned shack behind Grayson's house, looking at their treasures. It was a good cover as their parents knew they spent lots of time back there. Mr. Spencer would often tell the boys to go play in the shack when he didn't want them around.

Alec agreed to go along with the story and the boys swore to never tell another soul what really happened. After finalizing their alibis, they decided to move Eddy's body to buy themselves some time. After agreeing that the stationary train was their best option, they lifted the distorted body.

Alec had the morbid task of lifting Eddy from under his armpits. He tried not to look at his bloodied face, but curiosity got the best of him and he immediately regretted looking. Eddy's eyes were shut, but the blood oozing from his ears and nose was gruesome. His broken legs swung from side-to-side as the boys struggled to move his body. After they managed to lift him into the car, Grayson hopped inside to pull him further out of sight.

"Alec, there's a crate in here, come help me put him in it," Grayson ordered. Alec hopped in and the boys quickly lifted the body and placed it into the crate.

"What should we do about all the blood?"

"Let's use those pails we have to catch tadpoles, to wash the tracks."

"This is really bad," Alec said, as tears continued to stream down his face.

"I know, but crying isn't going to help us right now. Come on, let's get this over with."

After twenty minutes, there was little to no evidence of what had just transpired. The boys sat on the tracks with their heads buried into their hands, without saying a word for several minutes, before hearing footsteps coming towards them from the other side of the parked train.

"Fuck, someone's coming," Alec whispered, quickly rising to his feet. Grayson stood, then they waited, before hearing more steps heading towards them.

"Get down," Grayson whispered. The boys retreated down towards the marsh and ducked behind some thick shrubs. They watched on their bellies as the silhouette of a large man closed the doors to a few of the open cars, including the one holding Eddy's dead body. Moments later the man was gone.

"Who was that?" Alec asked.

"Just one of the guys that works on the trains, I guess."

"Do you think he saw us?"

"No, we would've known by now," Grayson replied, rising to his feet. "Let's get out of here."

After the boys started making their way down the tracks, they heard a thunderous boom behind them, startling them both. Looking back, they could see the train carrying Eddy's body had begun moving in the other direction. They stood in silence while watching the train until it completely disappeared. They headed back to the shack and prepared themselves for the chaos that was surely to ensue once they arrived without Eddy.

They went over their story one last time before heading into Grayson's home. As the door slammed behind them, Eddy's mother's eyes darted over to Alec.

"Where's Eddy?" she asked. Alec stood frozen, unable to move or speak, as his preparation completely failed him. His lips quivered uncontrollably.

"He isn't here?" Grayson quickly interjected. Eddy's mother stared at the boys silently as her eyes darted back and forth between the two of them.

"What's going on?" Mrs. Spencer asked after she appeared from the hallway.

"I just asked them where Eddy was and they said they don't know," replied Mrs. Sutton nervously. The desperate look on her face sickened Alec. He wanted to tell her that everything was ok and that her son would return soon, but he knew that would not be true. Her son was in fact dead, and all alone in a box in a train heading to some unknown location.

"Boys, where's Eddy?" demanded Mrs. Spencer. Alec could not bear to look at her, instead he stared out the window hoping all of this would somehow just magically disappear or that he would wake from this nightmare. He wanted desperately to be at home in his bed where he would be safe, where no one would ask him anymore questions. After neither boy replied Mrs.

Spencer continued, this time with sheer panic in her voice, "Grayson, did you hear me? Where is your cousin?"

"I have to go," Alec said, darting out the door, leaving Grayson to fend for himself.

Grayson went on to tell the story they had rehearsed. He mentioned that a wild dog had chased them, and that they had gotten split up. It was not until a while later that Grayson and Alec ran into each other that they realized Eddy was alone, but they had just assumed he had gone back home.

"You ok Alec?" asked Mr. Jenkins, after seeing his distraught son walk through the door. Without saying a word, Alec fell into his father's arms and started bawling. His father continued to ask what was wrong, but Alec was unable to speak as he sobbed uncontrollably. Mrs. Jenkins came barreling into the room upon hearing the commotion and squeezed him tight, helping to console her son.

"It's ok Alec. Everything is going to be ok, my boy," she said softly.

"We're here son. We're here," Mr. Jenkins said, rubbing his son's back.

Alec went on to tell his parents that Eddy was missing before delving into the rehearsed story that he and Grayson had fabricated. They appeared to believe him as Mrs. Jenkins continued to console him while Mr. Jenkins watched out the front door as neighbors began to gather in front the Spencer home.

Alec later found out that upon hearing Grayson's story, Mrs. Spencer frantically called several neighbors asking if any of them had seen Eddy. Soon after, several police cars appeared in the Spencer driveway and the whole town was quickly put on alert of the missing eight-year-old boy.

CHAPTER 19

The knock at the door of room 620 woke the fifty-year-old from his deep sleep. The housekeepers were doing their usual eight am rounds and had reached his door.

"Please come back later," Alec shouted, sitting up on the edge of the bed.

He rubbed his dry eyes, taking in his surroundings, before heading over to the bathroom sink to get some water for his dry mouth. He hopped into the shower for a hot twenty-minute steam. Getting out of the shower he sat on the toilet seat, letting the steam clear his congested lungs. All those years of smoking had taken its toll.

After making his way over to the vanity, he wiped the mirror clear, so he could see his teeth while flossing. The washroom countertop displayed an array of the hotel's soaps and lotion, which he used to moisturize his face and hands. He clumsily knocked the lid of the lotion and watched as it dropped to the floor. After drying his hands, he bent down and picked up the lid and returned to the vanity. He began flossing his teeth before wiping the mirror a second time as it had become steamed up once again. In the reflection the handwritten letters 'E-D-D-Y' suddenly appeared on the wall behind him. He whipped around to look, only to see that the wall was bare, the writing was gone.

Alec dropped onto the toilet seat, and with his head in his hands, he broke down. Tears poured down his cheeks. All the images of that day, and the gruesome reality of Eddy's mangled body came rushing back. It was as though a protective curtain of secrets had been lifted, and a barrage of traumatic childhood memories came flooding back.

He remembered every detail about the day at the train tracks with Grayson and his cousin Eddy. He thought of the panic and chaos that occurred that awful day, and how every person in the town, along with police from surrounding towns, began a massive search for the missing boy. The town filled with reporters from all over the country. Even the FBI was called in to do a thorough investigation of the boy's disappearance as they thought it may be related to a case involving several missing children from the northern United States. Eddy's mother pleaded on television to whomever had taken her son to return him home, unharmed.

He and Grayson were questioned several times by several different officers as well as the FBI, and each time their well-rehearsed story remained unchanged. Finally, the boys' fathers put a stop to the questions, as they felt their children had been through enough. The authorities felt the pressure of having an unsolved crime, while the locals became paranoid that their children might be next. The chaos continued for weeks, until the day an arrest was made.

273

The man accused, was unknown to nearly everyone in the town, as he had recently moved to Russell just days before the boy's disappearance. The man in question, Allen Bishop, had a criminal record and had no alibi for the day of Eddy's disappearance. He had also been seen on the street around the same time the boys had lied and said the wild dog had chased them.

During the trial, the prosecuting attorney showed the jurors a receipt from a hardware store that was found in Bishop's wallet. The receipt contained conspicuous items that would be used for an abduction and it was dated the day just before the boy's disappearance. The final nail in the accused's coffin was a late addition to Grayson's initial sworn testimony. He added that he remembered seeing Eddy walking away with Bishop. Although his testimony was not collaborated by Alec, it was all the prosecution needed.

The case was completely circumstantial, and although no body was found, the prosecutor managed to impose his will on the jury. They convicted Allen Bishop for kidnapping, initially because there was no body, but later added the murder charge after it was deemed Eddy Sutton was dead, after missing for over two years.

At Bishop's sentencing, people from all over showed up outside the courthouse, carrying signs demanding the maximum penalty for Eddy's killer. To the utter shock of the criminal defense team, the people got what they wanted as Bishop was sentenced to twenty-five years in prison without the chance of parole.

Many defense lawyers on CBC and CNN said that Bishop had not received a fair trial because it took place in Winnipeg. The jurors would have been biased, as they would have seen plenty of coverage of Bishop in prison attire and handcuffs in the news before being sequestered. Most of the coverage had portrayed the man as the perpetrator even before the circumstantial evidence was presented.

Although Alec never knew Allen Bishop, he was sickened at the thought of the man going to prison for a crime he did not commit. Because of Alec and Grayson's ages, the court decided they would not be required to testify at the trial. Instead, both were interviewed on video as to their account of what transpired the day of Eddy's disappearance, which was later shown to the jury. The boy's parents protected them from all the reporters and other sensational media coverage that revolved around the trial.

After the conviction, the citizens of Russell went back to their regular lives. However, the town and its people would never be the same after the trial. Grayson and Alec never spoke of that day to each other and quickly grew apart soon after. Nobody ever suspected the two of them for any wrongdoing, especially after Allen Bishop's guilty verdict.

The Jenkins home life drastically changed after Alec came through the front door that dreadful day. Afraid of having to speak of Eddy's disappearance, or of letting something slip, Alec avoided his parents and others. The Jenkins tried to help their troubled son, but it seemed the more they tried, the further he retreated. They tried family counselling on several occasions, but each time found it did not help, as Alec continued to guard his words and keep his emotions to himself.

Now the memories flooding Alec's entire body became unbearable, causing him to vomit in the toilet. He continued sobbing, suddenly realizing his withdrawal was the reason his relationship with his parents had suffered. He had always blamed them, but now realized that his own fear, shame and guilt had consumed him and would be the cause of his unhappiness.

How had he blocked such an event from his mind for all those years? He thought of what Sarah's reaction was going to be, once she found out what he had done. How does someone as intelligent as Sarah react when finding out such an evil dark secret? She was a psychiatrist and had surely heard some terrible things people had done, but he wondered if she had ever heard of something this brutal.

He composed himself, and wiped his face, before stumbling over and slumping down on the bed. After staring at the telephone for a few moments, he straightened up, picked up the receiver and with his trembling hand, dialed her number.

"Hello?"

"Hey Sarah, it's Alec."

"Did you talk to him?"

"Talk to who?"

"Edgar! Jesus Alec, I've been anxiously waiting to hear from you!"

"Oh, no not yet. I just woke up."

"What are you going to say to him?"

"I don't know yet. Edgar and this mystery man are the least of my worries right now." He tried to think of the best way to explain how he had assisted in the murder and cover-up of an eight-year-old child, then let someone else take the fall. He thought of Eddy's mangled body again and was sick to his stomach.

"What are you talking about?" she persisted, but he struggled to find the right words. "Hello, Alec, are you there?"

"Sarah, I don't even know where to begin. Let's just say I woke up from a nightmare that wasn't quite a nightmare. At least, I think it happened, but I don't even know what's real anymore."

"What in god's name are you talking about?"

"I think I've had some sort of awakening, or some sort of memory breakthrough, of something I'd blocked out in my past."

"Oh, I see, tell me about it," Sarah replied.

He continued sitting on the edge of the bed, clutching a hand towel, dabbing his face and neck, while relaying the details of all the initial bullying, and resulting tragic events that had transpired

277

on the day of Eddy's death. Sarah said nothing and only listened, while he told her of his transgressions. At one point he stopped and asked if he should stop before confessing any criminal act, but she reminded him that he was technically her patient, and patient confidentiality would protect him.

Attempting to console Alec, Sarah confirmed that he was only a ten-year-old child at the time, who was scared and impressionable. Alec was relieved by her understanding, professional approach and was comforted that she did not hold him completely accountable for Eddy's death. He continued to tell the story without any interruption from the psychiatrist. It was not until the revelation that an innocent man had been sentenced for the boy's murder that Sarah stopped him.

"Oh my god Alec," she gasped.

"I know it's terrible."

"Yes, it is. But I guess you would not have heard the news about Bishop, while you were away all these years."

"Heard what?"

"Allen Bishop escaped from prison years ago and has never been found. The town was in shambles after he escaped because everyone thought he was going to come back and murder again. I told my patients that no escaped convict would ever come back to the same town they were caught to commit another crime … My god, you mean to tell me he's been innocent all this time?"

"Yes. I should have told the police or my parents, but I guess I was just too scared of the repercussions if I had. I never should have listened to Grayson. I can't believe I let that happen."

"Oh my god!" Sarah shrieked.

"What?"

"Oh my god. I think that was …"

"What Sarah? What is it?"

"I'm not positive, but I think the man at the cemetery may have been Allen Bishop."

"Really?"

"Yes! I mean I can't be certain, as he would be much older now, but now that I think of it, I knew he looked familiar. I just could not put my finger on it at the time. Those eyes were so dark and creepy, exactly like Bishop's."

"How old was the guy from the cemetery?"

"If I had to guess, I'd say around seventy."

"Well Bishop would be around that age. Sarah, how sure are you?"

"I'm pretty sure, but just can't be certain."

"We need to find a picture of Bishop. Maybe we should go to the police?"

"I think that's a good idea Alec, but let's not tell them about your involvement with Eddy's death. At least not yet, we need to think about how we're going to handle that first. By the way, I had a prank call last night after I dropped you off."

"Really?"

"Yeah, and it was very creepy."

"How so?"

"They just sat there, breathing deeply into the phone."

"Maybe it was Bishop. I've been getting prank calls too. If he's the one that's been following me, I bet it's him making those phone calls."

"Oh shit! Alec, he saw me with you yesterday. What do you think he wants?"

"I don't know, but it can't be good. Maybe he found out about my involvement with Eddy. If he did, he'd have known about Grayson's involvement too." He sat back and put his hands on his head, trying to piece things together.

"What are you thinking Alec?"

"I'm thinking Bishop paid Grayson a visit."

"You think he killed him?"

"It's possible. Or maybe Bishop questioned him about Eddy, and he told him what really happened. Maybe Bishop killed him, then staged his suicide. I don't know, but since Grayson's death, I've had this guy following me and been getting prank calls. Seems like a pretty big coincidence, don't you think?"

"Yes, it does." Her voice had become unsteady. "Alec, I'm freaking out."

"You have nothing to fear Sarah. It's me he's after."

Moments passed with complete silence, as they continued to think of the possibilities. Suddenly, a loud thud sounded through the receiver of Alec's phone.

"Sarah?"

"Shit, there's somebody at my door. One sec, I'll be right back," she said, sounding panicked. Another thud was heard before she placed the receiver down. A few moments passed, then suddenly a scream.

"Sarah? Sarah!" Alec pleaded, rising off the bed.

Alec listened intently, trying to hear what was happening on the other end of the telephone but there was only silence, and then seconds later, there was only a dial tone. He frantically dialed her number only to receive a busy signal. After two more attempts he was out the door pounding on the elevator button, anxiously waiting for it to arrive. The seconds felt like hours and he could not wait any longer, so he plummeted down the stairwell until he reached the hotel lobby. Making his way towards the front exit, he glanced over at the front desk and saw no sign of Edgar.

It was about a twenty-minute walk to Sarah's place, but Alec got there in just six. By the time he arrived, she was gone, and her home looked nothing like it had the last time he had been there. The normally meticulously clean home was now looking more like an apparent crime scene. Furniture was tipped, items dumped, with evidence of a struggle. Sarah was missing.

Alec immediately thought of Bishop and assumed his involvement. After flipping the table back over, he flopped into one of its chairs while trying to piece together what may have just happened. He figured Bishop escaped prison, interrogated, and possibly killed Grayson, started following him around the streets of San Francisco and Russell, called and threatened him a few times, and now had kidnapped and potentially killed his girlfriend.

Alec surmised that Bishop had probably figured out the truth about what had happened to Eddy and wanted revenge for all those years he had wrongfully served behind bars. Grayson must have confessed and that was why he was coming after him now. But if that was the case, why hadn't Bishop just killed him when had his chance back at the cemetery? Perhaps he was going to, but then Sarah showed up. Maybe he did not hit his head on a headstone, and Bishop hit him instead.

He decided he had better get the police involved. He continued sitting at the table, and avoided touching anything else, as he noticed Sarah's home phone receiver had been put back in place. While he surveyed the room for other clues, he tried to figure out how he could explain this to the police without incriminating himself in the process. After calling 911, he sat waiting for the police to arrive at Sarah's home, continuing to iron out his story. He would have to find a way to get them to help him focus on Sarah, without revealing his own involvement in Eddy's disappearance, all those years earlier. He was not ready to confess, at least not yet. He needed to find Sarah, and the key was likely Bishop.

A police officer arrived at Sarah's door. Alec informed him that his girlfriend had just been abducted, by who he believed to be Allen Bishop. Although the police officer was aware of the escaped convict, he could not understand why the man would randomly attack Sarah in her home. As Alec became more emphatic that Bishop must have been involved, the officer decided it would be best if they discussed the matter at the police station, so the two men got into the police car and headed there.

Upon arriving at the police station, Alec was led to a back room where the officer informed him that one of the lead detectives, who was working on Allen Bishop's case, was on his way. He was driving in from Winnipeg and would be arriving in a few hours to speak with him.

Waiting in the small room, Alec continued to iron out his story while trying not to panic about Sarah. Looking around the room, he began to get very nervous. The sickening feeling in his stomach was reminiscent of how he felt the first time he was questioned by the police about Eddy's disappearance forty years earlier. The police station had not changed, and he realized the room where he was sitting was the exact same room he had previously been questioned.

Nearly four hours passed while he waited. As the two men entered through the doorway, Alec was startled, jolted upright, then gathered himself and braced himself for the questioning. His palms began sweating instantly, and his chest pounded. Beads of sweat collected and ran down his jaw, as he quickly wiped them subtly with his sleeve, trying to show concern, rather than guilt. The uniformed police officer, who had escorted Alec to the police station, directed the man in plain clothing, who was wearing a detective badge on his hip, towards the table where Alec was sitting. The detective hesitated for a moment while assessing Alec before proceeding to gruffly dump himself into a seat across the table.

"Thanks officer, I can take it from here," said the detective. After waiting for the officer to leave the room he turned back and eyed Alec from across the table. "Alec Jenkins is it?" he queried with his deep loud voice.

"Yes," Alec mumbled, nearly inaudible. "Yes, that's me," he said after clearing his throat.

"I'm Detective Cole. I am the lead detective on the Allen Bishop case. Can I get you anything? A coffee or some water?"

284

The detective was smaller in stature, but his assertiveness made him seem much larger. His long-slicked back hair, dark rimmed thick glasses, and deep voice made him seem much taller than his five foot eightish inches.

Alec tried to steady his voice, before replying. "No thank you."

"So, the officer gave me a rundown of what you had told him. Your girlfriend, Sarah is it?"

"Yes. Sarah Edwards."

"Oh, Sarah Edwards," replied the detective.

"Do you know her?"

"Of course, I do," said the cop, pushing his chair back to put his right foot up across his left knee. "I know everyone involved in this case," he grumbled. "So, you say Sarah is missing and you think she was abducted by Allen Bishop. Is that correct?"

"Yes. Well, I'm not certain it was Allen Bishop, but I'm pretty sure."

"And what makes you think Bishop had anything to do with this?"

"Sarah told me a few days ago that she'd been getting prank calls from someone who sounded like Bishop, but figured it was someone just playing a bad joke. But after someone started following her, she thought it was him after catching a glimpse of man. She said he was wearing a tan overcoat with blue pockets."

"Blue pockets?" the detective asked, taking notes.

"Yeah, weird I know, that's what I said. Anyway, she called me this morning in a panic because she had seen him again yesterday. Then while we were on the phone, she got a knock at the door and when she went to answer it, I heard her scream. Then the phone went dead." Alec paused, eying the detective, hoping to find some indication of the impact of his story, but the detective remained stoic, giving him nothing.

"Go on," said Detective Cole, looking up from his notepad.

"I tried calling her back a couple times and couldn't get through, so I ran over there. Unfortunately, she was already gone by the time I got there."

"She was already gone, eh?" smirked the detective. Alec was starting to get the feeling the detective thought he had been involved in Sarah's disappearance. Another bead of sweat was about to trickle down his fifty-year-old's receding hair line, as he dabbed it quickly, hoping the detective would not notice. "Why are you so nervous?"

"I'm not nervous," Alec replied, only this time he was not successful in hiding his shaky voice.

"You sound and look nervous to me," he replied, with his eyes darting across the table.

"If you're insinuating that I'm acting nervous because I had something to do with Sarah's disappearance, you're wrong," Alec fired back.

"I'm not insinuating anything Mr. Jenkins. I'm just stating the facts."

"As I'm sure the officer already told you, her place was trashed, and you could tell that there was some sort of struggle. I would check her home phone for fingerprints as I'm pretty sure whoever took her was the one who hung it up." The detective sat back in his chair, keeping his eyes focused on Alec.

"Yes, I have all the communication between you and the officer, and I assure you, we'll be acting accordingly. Did Sarah tell you why she thought Bishop would be following her?"

"No, but she inferred Bishop was one of her patients while he was incarcerated. She wouldn't tell me more because of the whole doctor patient confidentiality thing." After receiving a look of confusion from the detective, he continued, "As I'm sure you're aware, Sarah is a psychiatrist."

"Yes," he replied, before slurping loudly from the cup of coffee that had been steaming in front of him. "But I've only been working on the Allen Bishop case since his escape, and this is the first I'm hearing of him seeing a psychiatrist."

"Well I don't know much about it," Alec replied, leaning back in his seat, getting more comfortable. "I assumed from our conversations that he was one of her patients, and that was possibly why he went after her. At least that is the impression I got from Sarah, but when she mentioned the confidentiality, I didn't press her any further for information. She did say, at first she thought she might've been just paranoid, but then she was emphatic that he was coming after her." The detective sipped on his coffee, while readjusting himself in the chair.

"Alec Jenkins. Why does that name sound familiar to me?" he asked, staring at his note pad.

"You would've read it in Bishop's case file. I was questioned by police in the trial when I was a kid."

"Ah yes, that's it! I knew I recognized the name but could not put my finger on it. You were one of the older boys that was with Eddy the day went he went missing."

"Yes, that's correct."

The two spent the next hour going over the Bishop case while discussing Alec's testimony from forty years earlier. Each time the detective pressed him as to his recollection of that day Alec kept his answers vague as he did not want to slip and tell the detective something he had not already told before. The longer the conversation went, the more he felt like the detective was more interested about his involvement in Eddy's disappearance than Sarah's whereabouts. He had held his cool for as long as he could and was starting to feel himself unravel while the detective pressed on for more answers.

"I don't want to scare you Alec, but Bishop was being investigated for the disappearance of someone else before his arrest on the Eddy Sutton case."

"I remember hearing that the man who had abducted Eddy, had a criminal record, but I don't recall hearing anything about another missing person."

"That's because that information was never released to the press. The judge suppressed all information involving the investigation, as it was still an ongoing investigation. I guess she did not want it affecting the jury's decision in Eddy's trial. The detectives working the other missing person investigation didn't have enough to charge him, but they were fairly certain he had also killed his ex-wife."

"You think Bishop killed his ex-wife?"

"Well, the guys working that case did."

"And why are you telling me this, detective?"

"I just want to be straight with you Alec. If Sarah was abducted by Bishop, you need to be prepared for the worst. If he is involved, she may already be gone. And the longer she is missing, the less likely she is alive. So, we'll need to work quickly here. Sarah told you she had seen Bishop, but did you ever see him?"

"I saw a guy wearing the same coat Sarah had described, but I never got close enough to see his face."

"And how tall would you say this guy … in the overcoat was, approximately?"

"He was tall, like around six foot five or six foot six. He was much taller than me and I'm just a little over six feet. How tall is Bishop?"

"He's six foot six," Detective Cole replied with a coy smile. "If you saw Bishop, do you think you would recognize him?"

"No, I doubt it. I haven't seen him since the trial and that was so long ago."

"Didn't you see his face plastered all over the news when he escaped?" Detective Cole asked, somewhat confused.

"No, I've been living down south. I just came back to town a little over a week ago for the first time. I didn't even know the man had escaped until Sarah told me."

"Surely you would've heard about it from someone in Russell though?"

"Listen detective, I haven't kept in touch with people from this town since I moved," he said, thinking of Chelsea. "I don't know why anyone still lives in this shit hole."

The detective pulled out a folder he had tucked away, then slid it across the table. "Take a look at these."

On the outside of the folder it had Allen Bishop's name along with the words 'case number' followed by a combination of letters and numbers. Alec stared at the folder, and while assuming it contained photos of Allen Bishop, did not want to look inside. He had never seen, nor did he want to see, the face of the man he had helped send to prison. However, as he did not want to raise any suspicion, he reluctantly opened the folder and looked inside.

The first few photos were mug shots of a man who appeared to be in his mid-thirties. His dark eyebrows furrowed beneath his buzz cut, while his nostrils flared above his thick black moustache. Alec's stomach turned as he flipped through the old photos while looking into the eyes of the poor man he so cowardly allowed to be sent to jail. He thought he might be sick but managed to keep it together in front of Detective Cole. To Alec, Bishop's eyes screamed of his innocence, but maybe only because he knew the truth. He concentrated on Bishop's eyes until realizing they seemed oddly familiar. He continued to flip through the photos as he felt the detective's eyes upon him. He hid his emotions well, until he flipped to one of the last photos. His mouth dropped and his eyed widened before he let out a gasp.

"What is it Alec?" Detective Cole asked eagerly.

"What is this? What's going on here?" Alec barked, jumping to his feet.

"What do you mean?"

"These all can't be of Allen Bishop. Why is this one in here?" Alec demanded, holding up the last photo he had seen.

"Yes, they are. That one was taken after his last parole hearing which he was denied. He escaped just after that photo was taken and nobody has seen him since. That was taken about fifteen years ago."

"It just can't be him …" Alec sputtered, examining the photo.

"Why? Have you seen him?" The detective eyed Alec as he continued gawking at the photo in complete silence. "Alec, have you seen him?"

"Yes, I have seen him," he replied, still staring at the photo in disbelief. After tossing the photo on the table, he took a seat and continued, "His name is not Allen Bishop though, at least it's not anymore. It's Tom Neale. He's a private detective who works for Woodward Financial. We hired him … about fifteen years ago."

CHAPTER 20

Sitting alone quietly on the bench amid the gorgeous gardens of the Marby Hotel, Alec sipped his coffee in disbelief, as he searched his memory through the numerous interactions he'd had with Tom Neale (AKA Allen Bishop) over the years.

He had first met the man at a rare surprise company meeting conducted by his former boss. Without notice, all upper management were sequestered to the boardroom on an early Monday morning, to find Harold Rhodes sitting at the head of the table along with a large burly man at his side. Harold began the meeting explaining that he had suspected someone had been embezzling from the company and the man sitting to his left was a private investigator, whom he'd hired one month earlier to find out who was responsible. He then handed the meeting over to the detective who he introduced as Tom Neale.

As the six-foot-six man emerged from his chair, his presence was immediately revered by everyone in the room. With his loud domineering voice, Tom showcased damning evidence against their Vice President. He showed the group several images and bank statements displaying how the woman went about embezzling over half a million dollars during her employment. He then went on to discuss the preventive measures that should have occurred to stop someone like her from doing so, before handing the meeting back over to their angry, red-faced boss.

In graphic profanity, the group was informed that not only had the thief been fired, she had also been arrested. Rhodes went on to explain that Tom Neale would be staying on with the company, in a part-time role, to keep any eye on things going forward. Shortly thereafter, the President proudly informed the management group that Alec Jenkins, at the age of thirty-five, would be the new Vice President of Operations.

At first, Alec's interactions with the private investigator were few and far between, as Tom was rarely seen around the office. When he was in the building, he was usually in private meetings with Harold. It was not until years later, after Rhodes had died and Alec had taken over, that Alec's interactions with Tom became more frequent.

As President, Alec confided in Tom for his investigative prowess on several occasions. One of those occasions was a personal matter involving a woman who was trying to extort him, which was quickly extinguished after one visit from Tom. On all occasions, Tom did his job quickly and effectively, often saving the company and Alec from potential disaster. Yet, in all those years working for Woodward Financial, the private investigator somehow managed to keep his personal life to himself.

Thinking back, Alec realized he knew very little about Tom Neale's personal life. Tom seemed to deflect attention when it came to his past, but until now, Alec had always allocated it to the man's aloofness.

Taking in the ambience of the beautiful garden, Alec continued to try to piece together Allen Bishop's transition into Tom Neale. He began to make sense of some of their interactions, which before seemed odd, but now made sense. Tom was well-travelled and extremely knowledgeable of the globe yet seemed to be quite ignorant when it came to the country sitting atop the US. He recalled Tom taking a ribbing when saying he would like to go to the Calgary Stampede if he ever visited British Columbia, even though the least knowledgeable person in their office new Calgary is in Alberta. If Alec would have been suspicious of the man back then, he would have known Tom was overplaying his ignorance of Canada.

Another memory came to mind while he emptied the last mouthful of much needed caffeine into the back of his throat. Alec had just returned from a long trip to Chicago a day earlier than expected and decided to swing by the office on his way home from the airport. Upon his arrival, he ran into Tom in the lobby of the building, which was odd, as they had not scheduled a meeting and it was also middle of the night. He had not thought too much of it, as Tom had been working on something for

Goldman at the time, but later that evening, he noticed someone had been rifling through his desk drawer and had left the key to Alec's top drawer in the lock. The top drawer had confidential client information and Alec would never have been so careless. Looking back now, Tom must have been looking through his drawers that night and perhaps left the key in haste, due to Alec's sudden arrival.

There was no doubt that the photo at the police station of Allen Bishop was also Tom Neale. He wondered why the escaped convict would track him down all those years later, posing as a private investigator. All that time he had been posing as Tom Neale, he had also been on the run from the Canadian authorities.

Before Alec left the police station, Detective Cole mentioned that they had not been able to track Bishop once he had gotten past the US border. He also pointed out that he had been working on Bishop's case for several years with little, to no leads, and had no real hope of catching him. Alec excused himself from the interview by informing the detective he had an appointment he could not miss. The detective obliged before mentioning he would be in touch soon with more questions and to update him on his investigation into Sarah's disappearance.

Alec was still eager to speak with Edgar about the note he had found in the pocket of the overcoat, but the hotel clerk was still not around when he had returned to the hotel earlier. After tossing his empty coffee cup into the garbage, he made his way through the hotel lobby where he saw Edgar assisting a woman checking into the hotel. Alec stood behind the guest, fidgeting anxiously, eying Edgar while he wrapped up his conversation.

"Mr. Jenkins, how are you?"

"I need to talk to you in private, right now," demanded Alec.

Sensing his urgency, Edgar directed him towards the side of the desk. "What's going on?"

"I'm not mad, but I need you to tell me about the guy who came in asking for my room number."

"For your room number?"

"Listen Edgar, this guy has been following me and I know for a fact that you gave him my room number, so stop fucking around! Did he say why he wanted it?"

"Mr. Jenkins, I'm so sorry," Edgar conceded. "I shouldn't have given it to him."

"Why did you then?"

"I got a knock at my door the other night from this guy saying he was an old friend of yours and that he wanted your room number so he could surprise you."

"At the door to your room? How did he even know you worked at the hotel?"

"I have no idea, but I asked the other staff working that night. They said the same guy asked them your information and they wouldn't give it to him. After I told him we are not allowed to

297

give out that information, he insisted. He first offered me a hundred bucks and after I turned that down, he said if I didn't tell him he'd come back with his gun."

"A gun?"

"Yeah man, this guy was fucking crazy!"

"Why did you write it down on that paper instead of just telling him?"

"While he was at the door, my phone rang, and he told me to pick it up. He said if I said anything to whoever was on the other end, I'd regret it. It was my mom on the phone, and she can talk for days, so he passed me the pen and paper and told me to write it down. I wrote down your room number, but when I looked up, he was gone. I think he got scared off by a group of drunk broads coming down the hall because they stumbled into my room right after. I think that asshole took my shades too."

"Your sunglasses?"

"Yes, after I hung up, I noticed he scooped them from me. They were expensive too!"

"That's weird. So, all he wanted was my room number?"

"Yes, I think so. Hey man, I'm really sorry."

"Don't worry Edgar. I think I know who this guy is. I just don't know what he wants," Alec replied, before turning to walk away.

"Well, when you find him, tell him I want my sunglasses back!" Edgar shouted across the lobby, as Alec headed out the door.

Bishop must have been the one following Alec to Russell, probably in hopes of finding evidence that tied him to Eddy's disappearance. The escaped convict appeared to be desperate. So desperate that he had risked returning to the place where he was on the run from. Alec envisioned the burly six-foot-six beast snapping Sarah's neck, and a sharp pain ripped through his stomach. He needed a stiff Jack Daniels badly as the stress was mounting, but it would have to wait.

Using the payphone out front of the hotel he dialed Sarah's phone number, but it again went straight to her voicemail. As he listened to the sweet sound of her voice, his eyes filled with tears. He felt guilty for the possibility that he was responsible for her disappearance. Whatever happened to Sarah was completely his fault because if he had not returned home, none of this would have happened. After reluctantly hanging up the phone, he used his sleeve to wipe the tears from his face before noticing a man and woman arguing across the street.

On further inspection, he realized the woman was Jenny. He could not tell who the large man was that she was arguing with as he was facing the other direction. The two were entrenched in a serious bickering match. He watched intently as Jenny's arms flailed about in the man's face, knocking his hat to the ground. Alec chuckled, figuring it was probably some other guest the waitress had hooked up with before being cast aside. Alec wondered if she drugged that guy too, as he watched the man pick up his hat before placing it back on his head. The two continued to squabble as they climbed into the dark-green Chevrolet Silverado parked out front the liquor store.

After the truck did a U-turn, it neared the front of the hotel. As it approached, he could hear its two passengers shouting at one another. Alec quickly held up the phone to shield his face from Jenny. As the Silverado made its way past, Alec peered in to catch a look inside, seeing Jenny's face clearly. However, the driver's dark glasses and a hat hid his identity. It was not until he heard the driver shouting at Jenny while passing by that he discovered the driver was none other than Tom Neale, or as the locals knew him, Allen Bishop.

Dumbfounded, Alec wondered why they would be together and what connection the two could possibly have. It was possible that they had just gotten together for a night of partying, but it was unlikely as Tom was way too old, even for Jenny. It was more likely that she was helping Bishop in some way. Thinking back to the first time he had met Jenny, he started to believe their bumping into one another was not accidental. Bishop must have wanted her to get closer to Alec to help find some damning evidence that tied him to Eddy's disappearance. Now it made more sense as to why the much more attractive, younger woman would want anything to do with the fifty-year-old man. When Jenny came by, it was not for round two; she was probably snooping around, and he had walked in on her in the process.

After the truck sped off, he hopped into one of the taxis sitting outside the hotel's entrance and pleaded for its driver to follow the truck. He asked him to stay far enough back, so they wouldn't know they were being followed, and the driver obliged. The truck made several turns throughout the town, but the taxi driver was able to stay behind without the two in the Silverado knowing they were being followed.

From two cars back, Alec looked on as the Silverado's passengers continued their heated conversation while it sat stopped at a red light. Jenny's hands flailed all around before Bishop swatted them away. The light turned green, but the truck did not move, irritating the old man driving the rusted-black Volvo behind it. After the old guy leaned on his horn, the Silverado peeled ahead, not before Bishop placed his hand and erect middle finger out its window.

The Silverado turned right on the first street past the set of lights, but the Volvo continued going straight, leaving no obstruction of view in between the taxi and Bishop's vehicle.

"Ok, turn right but just stay back a little more. I don't want them to know they're being followed," Alec instructed.

"You got it," replied the cab driver, who appeared to be enjoying the moment. The taxi followed a few car lengths behind for the next several blocks. A large moving truck pulled out in front of them from a side road, causing the driver to hit the brakes. "Fucking asshole!" shouted the cab driver, before leaning on his horn. After a few more blocks, the moving truck slowed down to 40 kilometers per hour. "What the fuck is this guy doing?"

"I think you pissed him off," Alec replied, looking out his window trying to see past the large truck with the words 'U-Haul Moving & Storage' plastered across its wide behind. "Can you pass him?"

"Sure," replied the cab driver, trying to glance past the truck out his driver's side window. After putting his left signal on to pass, he began making his way into the left lane, but the moving truck quickly followed leaving the cab in its shadow. "This fucking asshole," shouted the cab driver.

"For fuck sakes," Alec growled from the backseat, trying to see past the truck. The cab driver leaned on the horn again. Seconds later the moving truck's left-turning single began to flash, as it slowed down to almost a complete stop, before finally turning off on to a side gravel road. "Shit, where did they go?" Alec asked, staring at the empty road in front.

"I don't know," replied the driver.

"They must've turned off while we were trying to pass that idiot. Quick, turn around and go back," Alec ordered, and the driver obliged. For the next few blocks, they drove back in the opposite direction, and Alec surveyed the left side of the road. "There! Up on the left," he barked. "They must've turned down that road."

"Ok," replied the driver.

After making the turn, they drove down the long narrow gravel road, while Alec watched out the window in hopes of seeing the Silverado. After driving for nearly five minutes, Alec feared they had lost them. About to give up, he noticed a driveway up on the right-hand side of the road where there was dust whirling in the air.

"Slow down," he said to the driver.

"Want me to turn down there?"

"Yes, but slowly though." The taxi turned and made its way slowly down the long gravel driveway, until Alec saw the back of the green Silverado. "Stop, I'll get out here." He looked at the meter, then handed the driver two twenty-dollar bills and said, "Keep the change."

"Want me to wait?"

"No, it's ok, thanks."

"Are you sure?"

"Yeah, thanks. Great job by the way," Alec said quietly while sliding out of the cab. He glanced at the narrow driveway then leaned his head back into the cab. "I don't think you'll have enough room to turn around. Would you mind backing straight out from here?"

The driver looked through his windshield, then at his rearview mirror and replied, "Yeah sure, no problem. Good luck with whatever you got going on here."

"Thanks," Alec replied, slowly closing the door to the cab.

He waited until the front bumper of the taxi disappeared before continuing on foot, down the side of the driveway. As he approached the end of the driveway, it widened making way for three or four parking spots in front of what appeared to be a large abandoned shed. Trying to keep the element of surprise, he moved into the trees for some cover, then continued making his way towards the green truck. He was close and could see the truck was empty as it sat parked outside the dilapidated old building.

He surveilled the area and wondered if Sarah was possibly inside, and if so, after what the detective had said, could she still be alive. He tried to think positively, that Sarah may not be in Bishop's hands, but he could only envision those same massive hands being capable of strangling her to death.

Alec thought back to Harold's story about helping bury the body of Tom's ex-wife, as the knot in his stomach continued to tighten. Harold had not given much geographic detail but did mention they'd buried her where nobody would find her, beneath a shed on the outskirts of a small town. Alec's mind raced, as he realized that Russell would be Bishop's town, and with his vehicle parked outside, this could very well be the actual shed where he had buried his ex-wife. After several single malt scotches, Harold had also confessed to Alec that they had poured a concrete floor over top the body to ensure the woman would never be found.

The shed he described was very much like the one Alec was looking at, except Harold's description involved several skylight windows and this one did not have any, that Alec could see from the bushes. However, Harold had mentioned that the shed was old and dilapidated with a sagging roof and bowed walls, much like this one.

After reaching the back of the Silverado, he noticed its bed contained several construction tools. He carefully picked through the tools, grabbing a hammer and a large wrench, thinking they would make the best weapons if needed, before making his way over towards the shed. He walked gingerly along the front of the shed while trying to look inside but the windows were blacked out from the inside - yet another detail Rhodes had described about the shed.

As he continued over to the corner of the shed, he wondered why Bishop would have a jackhammer in the bed of his truck. Alec decided instinctively, as he thought about the concrete floor, and a way to fuck with Bishop, that he should remove it from the truck. Without hesitation, he laid down his tools and crept back to the truck bed. He quickly and quietly opened the tailgate before slowly pulling out the heavy jackhammer. It made a large thud when hitting the dirt driveway and Alec ducked behind the truck, while keeping an eye on the front door to the shed. After waiting a minute, while anticipating the door bursting open, he then dragged the jackhammer over the grass to the side of shed and laid it on the ground with the other tools. He crept back towards the truck to close the tailgate, but suddenly voices approached so he quickly scurried back to the building.

Bishop's deep voice bellowed out the front door of the shed as it swung open. Alec dove around to the side of the building, laying in the deep grass, unscathed, watching the beastly man place a padlock on the front doors to the shed. Jenny stood at the passenger door to the truck, checking her reflection in the side mirror, while waiting for Bishop. Alec laid still, praying that the tools would not be noticed, until the two got back into the Silverado and peeled away, leaving a huge cloud of dust behind.

After checking the padlock, Alec walked along the side of the building, but was unable to see anything through each blacked-out window. It was not until he came around to the back, that he could see the back side of the roof which housed several large skylight windows. His stomach dropped as this detail became the final confirmation that this was indeed the shed Allen Bishop's ex-wife was buried beneath.

After breaking a small window with his elbow, he managed to crawl through before lowering himself to the cold concrete floor inside. He found piles of old, rusted, metal scrap and other discarded dusty junk which looked like it had been there for years. The scrap metal and wood parts scattered in heaps throughout the shed were reminiscent of his and Grayson's treasure collection, and he was reminded of their wild treasure stories as he stepped over the pile of rusted wrenches.

The skylight brought enough light into the shed for him to see that Sarah was nowhere on the premises. Alec was relieved to find no sign of her nor any evidence she had ever been there. Sarah was also clearly not with Bishop and Jenny in the truck.

The cold concrete floor gave him chills, and he found himself curious about the body that was probably buried beneath.

He thought of running to get Detective Cole to inform him of the body, but thought he'd first better make certain it was still there. He smiled, while using the crowbar to pry open the front door, as his instinct to grab the jackhammer had paid off. After dragging the jackhammer inside, he stared at the concrete floor, trying to guess where they would have buried the body. He decided to try the center of the shed floor first as it would have been the spot he would have chosen. After several attempts of starting the jackhammer, it finally jumped to life.

An hour later, he was knee-deep in crumbled concrete and dust, but still found no sign of a body. Alec remained determined and after two more hours, the hammer suddenly hit something. He used the hammer to scoop away the soil, until he noticed he had dug into a black garbage bag completely wrapped in duct tape. He sat beside the rubble for a few minutes, staring at the garbage bag which was still mostly buried. After taking a moment to collect himself, he dug some more until the bag was nearly fully exposed. After laying the jackhammer aside, he found a retractable knife and used it to tear a small slit through the tape and plastic bag. As he crouched knee deep in the pit, he lifted the end of the bag onto his lap, and saw within the bag, a head of long human hair and skeletal remains.

He retracted in horror at the thought of holding, in his arms, what was once a living, breathing human being. Scrambling up out of the pit, he began to vomit several times, crying uncontrollably, as his mind raced. He tried to imagine what might have been the poor woman's last moments. He was sickened by the anguish of her loved ones when she was never found.

He began to sob, thinking of what he and Grayson had also done by denying Eddy's family the same closure. Eddy was just an innocent eight-year-old boy, who had tragically died, and because they hid his body where it was ultimately never found, he and Grayson had only exacerbated their grief. Overcome with sadness and guilt, combined with difficulty breathing in the dust clouds that clouded his lungs and view, he staggered toward the door to get some air, but before he got there, he was met by the six-foot-six man, who he now knew went by the name Allen Bishop.

"Hello Mr. Jenkins."

CHAPTER 21

Although the man standing in front of him was well into his seventies, Alec knew he was no match for Bishop. He feared for his life, so he briefly thought of lying as to why he was there. He quickly realized there was no point as the skeletal remains of the man's ex-wife were exposed, just a few feet behind him.

"Hello Tom, or should I call you Allen?" Alec smirked, attempting to mask his fear.

"I wondered when you were going to put that together," Bishop replied with a grin, before glancing over Alec's shoulder. "What were you planning on doing with her?" he asked, after his grin disappeared.

"I don't know." He did know, but saying he was going to inform Detective Cole did not seem to be the safe thing to say at the moment.

"I told Harold this would happen," Bishop whined. "He goes all those years without telling a soul. Then you come along, and he blabs. What the fuck was he thinking?"

Although Alec tried to appear calm, his trembling hands and bug-eyes were surely a dead giveaway. Just out of his reach, lay a large rusted hammer. Alec pondered grabbing it momentarily, but then decided he had better not. "I won't tell anyone," he conceded, hoping it sounded believable.

"Don't worry, Alec," he replied, glancing over at the hammer. "I'm not going to hurt you. I just came by to try and talk you out of whatever you came here to do."

"How did you know I was ..."

"You left the tailgate open." Bishop looked over Alec's shoulder again before continuing. "So, what did Harold tell you about my ex-wife?"

With his voice still trembling, he replied, "Not much, just that he helped you hide her body after you had killed her."

"Did he actually say after I killed her?"

Alec thought for a moment before replying, "I guess not, I guess I just assumed ..."

"Assumed what, that I killed the one person I ever loved?" Bishop interrupted. "Jesus," he said, shaking his head. "So, I presume he didn't mention Rosa's health problems?"

"No, he didn't."

"Take a seat and let me explain," he said, gesturing toward a couple of chairs just inside the doorway.

The two men sat for several minutes, while Bishop explained what had happened the night his ex-wife was put to rest. He admitted that he had indeed taken her life, but only because she had begged him to do so.

At the age of only forty-two, Rosa was diagnosed with early-onset Alzheimer's, and after a long battle with the disease, she no longer wanted to live. Although the Bishops had been

311

divorced for several years, she knew Allen was the only one she could count on to follow through on her burdensome request.

Rosa and Allen married young and were well on their way to a long happy marriage, until the sudden loss of their only child. Like many couples who have lost a child, their marriage did not overcome the tragedy. Even after several visits with a grief counsellor, Rosa was barely able to function after their son's death. Rosa shut out everyone in her life, including her husband. Two years after their son's death, the divorce was finalized. Although they were no longer married, he still loved her very much and would have done anything for her. Less than a year after she was diagnosed, Rosa had deteriorated to only a mere glimpse of the woman she had once been. She begged Allen to help her die for months. A request he continued to deny until finally one day, he could not deny her any longer.

In her last few months, Allen visited her home regularly, and watched helplessly as her mind and body deteriorated rapidly. On her final day, he had gone to check on her, but she was not home. He found her a few blocks from home, walking down a back lane in the dead of winter, wearing only a thin bathrobe. She had not been out long, as she surely would have died from hypothermia if she had, but that was when Allen realized it was time to grant her dreary request.

Helping her into the passenger seat of his car, she no longer recognized the man she had once married. Drool dripped from

312

her chin while she rambled on about the evil spirits chasing her from her home. He thought back to an earlier conversation they'd had, not long after she had been diagnosed with the disease, where she made it clear, she did not want live to the point where she'd have to be permanently hospitalized.

Later that evening, while Rosa was asleep, he injected her with a large dose of secobarbital and pentobarbital drugs and seconds later, she was gone. Although there was some suspicion from the police that he was involved, no charges were laid. Allen buried Rosa in her small hometown in Saskatchewan.

Not long after his wife's passing, he moved to Russell for a fresh start, but was soon arrested and convicted for the crime he did not commit. He later escaped and relocated to San Francisco to track down Alec. He knew he and Grayson were more involved in Eddy's disappearance than they had let on because of the lie Grayson had told where he had seen him with Eddy. He had never heard of Eddy Sutton until the day of his arrest.

Allen wanted to get close to either one of the boys to find out what had really happened, but as Grayson was still living in Russell and he could not be seen there, he picked San Francisco to find Alec. He did catch up with Grayson before his death, but assured Alec he never laid a hand on him. He only spoke with Grayson on the phone and he told him the truth about everything. That was when he discovered the boys had stuffed Eddy's body into a crate on the train. Grayson swore to him that he would go to the authorities and confess but said he just needed a couple days to tie up some loose ends. He never thought the loose ends meant his suicide.

After Grayson's death, Alec was Allen's only hope of proving his own innocence, so that's where he focused all his attention. He couldn't afford to have Alec run or push him too hard where he'd end up dead like Grayson, so he decided he would first get close to Alec to find evidence that he could share with the police, that would prove his innocence.

While Allen continued to tell his story, Alec knew he was sincere, believing every word. He felt bad for Allen as he could not imagine how difficult it must have been for him. He felt worse that Allen now had to deal with the remains of his unearthed ex-wife's body yet again.

Allen had gone over the transcripts of the entire court proceedings of his case countless times, and something about the testimonies of the two older boys did not seem right. He also thought it was odd that the parents of the two older boys put a stop to the police questioning, since the whereabouts of the missing boy was still unknown. While still in prison, he kept tabs on the boys and hoped that one day they would come forward with some missing information, but he grew tired waiting.

He managed to escape prison and at first, planned on just approaching Alec and asking him directly about the day he'd spent with Eddy before he'd gone missing, but knew if he had, there was a good chance he would have ended up back behind bars. He figured he would work his way into Woodward Financial to get closer to Alec where he could potentially later find some evidence that would ultimately clear his name.

Allen first met Harold Rhodes at a men's club. Harold believed the meeting was completely random, but he had planned out the whole thing. He knew Harold went to the club every Wednesday to play squash, so he joined and befriended Alec's former boss. He introduced himself as Tom Neale, a semi-retired police officer who had just moved to the area. It was not long after, the two would establish a regular squash game and a growing friendship. They spent several evenings drinking together in the club's lounge. It was on one of those evenings when Harold asked him if he could look into someone from his company, as he'd suspected they had been stealing from him. After he figured out that Harold's VP had been embezzling, Harold offered him a position with the company.

Allen had only planned on playing the role of the private investigator until he had gathered enough evidence on Alec regarding Eddy's disappearance. But after a few months, he found himself really enjoying the job and decided to stay and work for his new friend. He had not found anything on Alec and was not able to go back into Canada anyway, so the decision to stay was an easy one. After sneaking into Alec's office and home on several occasions, he was never able to find anything that would help prove his innocence. Later he gave up, realizing he would probably never be able to prove his innocence and started to enjoy his new life in San Francisco as Tom Neale.

For the first time in a long time, he saw a future for himself. Until one day he had heard from one of his sources that a detective in Russell had been looking into the death of his ex-wife. His source, a young man who worked at the cemetery back in Saskatchewan where his ex-wife had been laid to rest, informed him that a detective had come by asking questions. He also overheard the detective mention he may plan to exhume her body. That was when he approached Harold about getting help crossing the border into Canada to move her body.

He had already done several illegal activities for Woodward Financial that would have put both he and Harold behind bars, so he was certain he would help. He never told him that he had escaped from prison, rather that he had only fulfilled his ex-wife's wishes and was worried because the local authorities were looking into her cause of death. Harold was reluctant to help at first, but after suggesting he could expose Woodward Financial for its illegal activities, he became less reluctant.

Harold Rhodes had obtained many connections over the years and Allen took full advantage, using a couple of them to get him in and out of Canada without being detected. So, the two men made their way into Canada, then to the graveyard before removing Rosa's body. They placed her bones in a garbage bag, then used duct tape to secure it before moving her out of province, where Allen figured she'd never be found, beneath the shed on the outskirts of Russell. After his escape from prison, Allen had hidden in that same shed for a few days and knew it would be a good place to hide her body, especially after they buried it beneath concrete.

"That's quite the story Tom. Sorry, I guess I should call you Allen," Alec said, now feeling a bit more at ease.

"Call me whatever you'd like," Allen replied.

"So, what did you have on Harold?"

"I think you know me well enough to know I'd never tell you that."

"So, why have you been following me around town? And what were you doing with Jenny? I'm assuming her hitting on me was part of your plan?"

"When I found out you were going to Russell, I wanted to keep a close eye on you. I thought you might go somewhere or do something that may help me prove my innocence." He sighed and continued, "And yes, I gave that waitress some money to dig around in your hotel room, but she came up with nothing."

"Was drugging me your idea or hers?"

"That was all hers. Listen Alec, all I ever wanted was for the truth to come out, so I can live out the rest of my years without having to look over my shoulder. I'm sure if you came forward and told the truth about what really happened, you wouldn't spend a day behind bars."

Alec was not sure about that but knew he had to come forward regardless. All the years he had kept it inside had been destroying him internally. Maybe after he came forward, his life would make a turn for the better, even if that meant doing some prison time.

"Listen Tom," Alec said, before letting out a large sigh. "I know I should call you Allen, but it just seems weird."

"It's fine, just call me Tom."

"Ok, Tom. I don't know if there are any words that I can say to show you how sorry I am for what we did to you. You're right, it is time for all of this to end. I promise you; I'm going to do what I should've done forty years ago and finally tell the truth. I'm just so sorry I ruined your life."

Allen put his hand on Alec's shoulder and replied, "It's ok Alec, that was a lifetime ago and you were a scared little boy. You've got your demons and I've got mine. My soul died the day my Rosa died." He glanced over at his ex-wife's remains, then continued, "I never should have moved her. I was selfish and didn't want to get caught and now look at what I've done to her. That's not a resting place for a wild animal, never mind a beautiful soul like Rosa." Allen's compassion for his ex-wife had Alec thinking of his own feelings for Sarah, and he suddenly felt unsure that Allen could have killed her.

318

"So why get Sarah involved? And where is she now?" Alec asked eagerly.

"Sarah?"

"Yes, my girlfriend, the woman you took, after you trashed her house."

"Alec, I have no idea who you're talking about. I didn't trash anyone's house, nor did I take anyone named Sarah."

"You met her at the cemetery. She was the one with me when we chased you by that marsh."

"Cemetery? Marsh? Alec, I'm totally confused here."

"Are you telling me you're not the one who has been following me? Weren't you the one in the overcoat?"

"Hey man, I was keeping an eye on you, but that wasn't me. I would not be running around in an overcoat. Sure, I've worn some disguises before, but do you think I'd wear an overcoat? I'd stand out like a sore thumb!"

"Yeah, I guess you're right. Now that you mention it, I couldn't see you doing that," Alec conceded.

"So, someone else has been following you?"

"Yes."

"Any idea who?"

"Well, up until now I had assumed it was you, so no idea" Alec replied.

"Well if it helps, I didn't notice anyone else following you while I'd been following you," Allen said, causing both men to laugh. "Hmm …"

"What is it?"

"There is something you should know. With all this digging I've been doing into Eddy's case, I did come across some new information. Information which leads me to believe he may actually be alive."

"Information? What information?" Alec asked skeptically.

"Well, are you sure he was dead when you put him on that train?"

"What information?"

"Just trust me, I'm fairly certain that he's alive. I also believe Grayson did not kill himself and that Eddy may have had something to do with his death."

"Why? How?"

"Think back to when you guys put him on that train. Is it possible he was still alive?"

"Well, I guess it's possible, but highly unlikely. I mean, there was blood everywhere and I didn't feel a pulse. He was so mangled; I don't see how he would've lived through that."

Alec sat slumped over, trying to remember Eddy's face when he had helped carry him over to the train, but could not recall what it looked like. Just the possibility of the eight-year-old mangled boy being placed in that train while still being alive

320

made Alec want to vomit again. He was envisioning lifting Eddy's crumpled body onto the train, when suddenly, shouting came from outside the shed.

"Who the fuck is that?" Allen shrieked, while Alec remained in a daze. "Fuck, it's the police!" Allen gasped, peering out the gap in the front doors of the shed.

The sound of screaming sirens approaching in the distance and grabbed Alec's attention before he quickly rose to his feet.

"Come out with your hands high in the air!" shouted a police officer.

With the large hole in the ground and the skeletal remains exposed, the two men inside the shed froze while several police officers could be heard rustling around outside.

"It's ok Tom. It's all going to be fine now. I'll tell them what happened, then you'll be in the clear."

"Thanks Alec, but what about Rosa? How do I explain this?" He asked, motioning to her remains on the floor behind them. "I cannot go back to prison again."

More shouting came from outside, one from a voice Alec recognized. He glanced out the crack of the door to see Detective Cole standing with a loudspeaker in his hand. Two police dogs pulled on their leashes while drool flung out of their mouths, in anticipation of rushing them.

"We'll figure it out Tom. Trust me, after I talk to them everything will be straightened out."

"You don't know that for certain," Allen murmured, looking defeated.

Alec looked back at him before slowly pulling back the door. "We're coming out, please don't shoot," he shouted, poking his head through the crack in the doors. He looked back at Allen again and pleaded for him to follow. "Tom, come on let's go. It'll be ok."

"You go Alec, I'll be right out."

"I don't believe you. I'm not going without you."

"It's ok Alec, trust me. I'll be right behind you. I just need to say goodbye to my Rosa."

Alec gave him a look of disapproval but could tell by the look he received in return, there was no point in arguing. Alec stood at the door with his hands exposed through the doorway, before looking back one last time. He thought about asking once more but was suddenly pulled through from the other side of the door. The door swung open and Detective Cole rushed in with his gun drawn, yelling at Allen.

"Bishop, get down on the ground, now!"

With an officer pinning him to the ground, Alec shouted, "Listen to the detective Tom!" Time seemed to stand still as he watched Allen staring back at him before mumbling something he could not understand. After looking back towards the detective Allen reached around to the back of his pants.

"Don't do it Bishop! Don't do it!" Detective Cole shouted.

"No! Tom don't …" Alec started shouting, but before he could finish, a loud bang echoed throughout the shed. Instantly, the bullet from the detective's gun drove through Allen Bishop's forehead, dropping him to the ground. Radiant red and blue lights poured through the front doors to the shed, as Alec sobbed. Tears rushed down his face, watching the police officers gather around Bishop. His large, lifeless, body smothered the bag containing his ex-wife's remains.

CHAPTER 22

Anyone looking into the interrogation room would have assumed the disheveled man being questioned was homeless. With his hair and clothes covered in dust, a very distraught Alec Jenkins had been waiting alone in the interrogation room for more than three hours. On the table in front of him sat a folder with Allen Bishop's name on it. Upon opening it, he found it to be the same one he had seen previously. When the officer standing outside the door was not looking, Alec grabbed one of the more recent photos of Allen Bishop and tucked it into the front of his pants before placing his shirt overtop. A few seconds later, Detective Cole entered the room.

"Good evening Alec. My apologies for keeping you waiting."

"No problem," Alec replied.

"Looks like we've got lots to talk about here," Detective Cole said, looking through a folder containing a stack of papers. "Maybe we should start with what you were doing in that shed with Allen Bishop."

"Well, like I told you before, I knew him to be Tom Neale, and I thought he'd been the one who had taken Sarah. So, when I saw him get into a truck with Jenny outside the Marby Hotel ..."

"Jenny?" the detective interrupted.

"Yeah, she's a waitress at the hotel."

"And you know this waitress?"

"Well, I know who she is, but I don't know her well. Anyway, I followed them to that shed. I waited outside until they left and then went in and looked around. I heard that a long time ago, Tom had buried his ex-wife's body in a shed exactly like that one."

"And where did you hear that?"

"From my old boss at Woodward Financial."

"Right ... Woodward Financial," he muttered, pulling out a pen and notepad. "So, let me get this straight, you're saying Allen Bishop had been going under the alias of Tom Neale while working at Woodward Financial. And at some point, your old boss in San Francisco told you that the man's ex-wife's remains were buried under a shed in Russell, Manitoba?"

"Yes, that's correct," Alec replied.

"Ok, so then what happened?" The detective asked, scribbling notes on his pad.

"After Tom and Jenny left, I dug her up, but before I was done Tom came back."

"With Jenny?"

"I don't think so, at least I never saw her come back."

"Ok, go on."

"I thought he was going to kill me, but instead he told me the story about his ex-wife. He said she was very sick and that he had helped her to die because that was what she wanted. He said he then moved her body because he had heard that police were looking into her death again."

"That's true," the detective said, continuing to take notes. "Then what happened?"

"Nothing really. He just asked me if I was going to tell the police."

"And were you?"

"Going to tell the police? Yes, of course," Alec replied.

The truth was, he was not going to tell the police about Bishop's ex-wife. Instead, he was going to confess as to what he and Grayson had done to the eight-year-old boy. Allen Bishop had suffered too much for Alec's mistakes and he was finally planning on doing what was right. But that was before Bishop was executed. While waiting three hours in the interrogation room, he had decided that there was now no reason to come forward. After all, Allen and Grayson were both now dead so there was no point in putting himself at risk for imprisonment.

"Ok, so after you told him you were going to tell the police, what happened?"

"You showed up and shot him."

"That's it?"

"Yup."

"And that's your full statement Alec?" the detective asked skeptically.

"Yes."

Detective Cole sat back in the chair across from Alec and leafed through his note pad while reviewing his complete statement. The room was cold and sterile just like the other times he had been there. He wanted to leave, but the detective looked like he was settling in for a few more hours of questioning.

"Just looking over my notes here and you said earlier that you'd never seen Allen Bishop before and the man who was killed today you only knew of as Tom Neale."

"You mean the man you shot and killed today," Alec snarled.

"Yes," Detective Cold replied, with a cold stare. "And this Tom Neale, he worked for you at Woodward Financial. A place where you're saying you held the title of President for the past several years. Does that all sound correct?"

"Yes."

"And this Woodward Financial is in San Francisco, correct?"

"Yes."

"You know after our first meeting, I looked into Woodward Financial, and you know what I found?" he asked, before Alec shrugged his shoulders. "I found absolutely nothing. There is not a single record of any Woodward Financial in San Francisco. I also found no record of any Tom Neale living in San Francisco or anywhere close to San Francisco." He glared at Alec, hoping for some reaction but received nothing. "So how do you explain that?"

The truth was Alec could not explain it. He also could not find any trace of Woodward Financial and he had spent the past twenty plus years working there. His life in San Francisco seemed to have just vanished.

"Listen Detective Cole, I'm assuming there's no record of a Tom Neale because Allen Bishop didn't want there to be any record of Tom Neale. And I don't know why there would be no record of Woodward Financial, but I can tell you with certainty, that's where I've worked for the past twenty plus years. Why don't you check my bank records? I'm sure you'll see where my paychecks have been coming from?"

"Oh, don't you worry Alec, I already have and there's not one deposit from a company called Woodward Financial. You know why? Because the company simply does not exist. So why don't you tell me the real story of your relationship with Allen Bishop?"

Alec sat back in his chair and came to the realization that he could not explain it any other way. He could not make sense of what was happening, so explaining it to the detective was an impossible task.

"Am I under arrest?"

The detective sat back in his chair and smiled at him before crossing his arms. Alec abruptly got to his feet, before making his way to the door of the interrogation room, with no resistance from the detective.

"I wouldn't get too comfortable out there Alec. It's just a matter of time before I figure out your involvement in all of this!" Detective Cole shouted at Alec, as he left the room.

Each time he left that building, he hoped he would never have to return, but he had a feeling this visit would not be his last. After all, the detective made it clear that he was going to keep pursuing him, and he assumed it would just be a matter of time before the detective figured out his involvement in Eddy's disappearance.

Alec wanted to find out if there was any validity to what Allen had said about Eddy still being alive, but he could not involve the detective as it would surely put more unwanted attention on him.

His focus turned solely to finding Sarah and the man who had been following him. If Allen was telling the truth about not being the one in the overcoat and that Eddy was still alive, there was a good chance it was Eddy following him around. And if that was the case, Eddy had also probably been the one who had taken Sarah.

After hustling back to the hotel, Alec approached the desk where Edgar was on the telephone. After Alec slapped down the photo, he had taken from the interrogation room of Allen Bishop, Edgar hung up the phone.

"What's this?" Edgar asked.

"Is this the man who was asking about me?"

"No," he replied, examining the photo. "Isn't that Allen Bishop?"

"Yes, it is. So, he wasn't the one that threatened you?"

"No, that guy was much younger than Bishop."

"How much younger?" Alec asked, as the hotel's phone began to ring.

"I'm not good with ages, but I'd say around your age," he replied, before turning to answer the phone.

"Ok thanks Edgar. Do me a favor. If you see him again, let me know."

"Will do, Mr. Jenkins," Edgar replied with the phone in his hand. Alec turned to walk away before Edgar said, "Oh by the way Mr. Jenkins, Sarah is here."

"What did you just say?"

"Sarah's here," he repeated.

"What do you mean, she's here?"

"She's in your room," Edgar replied, while holding his hand over the receiver. Alec stared blankly at him before Edgar continued, "Sorry, I didn't think you'd mind if I gave her a key to your room."

"No, not at all. Thanks Edgar!" The relief was like nothing he had ever felt before. Excitement quickly followed in anticipation of seeing her again. He turned and dashed towards the elevator.

"Mr. Jenkins, you forgot your photo!" Edgar shouted, before scooting over and handing it to him.

"Thanks Edgar," Alec replied, anxiously awaiting the elevator doors to open.

"Oh, and one last thing," Edgar said, turning back. "He had the strangest eyes."

"Eyes? Who?"

"The guy that came looking for you. He had really weird looking eyes." The elevator doors barged open before several people piled out into the lobby.

"What was so weird about them?" Alec asked, pressing his hand against the elevator door to hold it open.

"Well this may sound a little strange, but they kind of looked like eyes you'd see on a leopard."

In all his fifty years he had only ever seen one person with eyes like that and they were on an eight-year-old boy. An eight-year-old who Alec had stuffed into a box in a train. Could it be, that after all these years, Eddy was still alive?

After Edgar was summoned to the front desk, Alec rode the elevator to the sixth floor, thinking back to all the encounters he'd had with the stranger in the overcoat. He wondered if it could have been Eddy all along. He also thought back to his encounter with Mrs. Spencer and wondered if Eddy had actually been sleeping at her house like she had said. Maybe she was not as crazy as he had thought. Either way, he would be sure to pay her another visit to ask her some questions about her nephew, when he got the chance.

As the doors opened to the top floor, his mind quickly shifted back to Sarah. He was so preoccupied on the way up that he paid no attention to the elevator's other passenger. As he stepped off the elevator, he heard the woman behind him mutter something. He turned back to see a woman wearing a large sunhat and sunglasses which covered most of her face. She was reaching for him while shouting something inaudible, but before he could respond the doors to the elevator closed between them. He hesitated for a moment before turning and running to his hotel room. After swiping his key, he pushed through the door and was startled to see a teenager, sitting at the foot of his bed.

Beads of sweat ran down the young man's wispy beard. It was not until he rose from the bed that Alec realized the teenager was in full body armor. His legs were equipped with two handguns and several knives. A bulletproof vest and protective gear covered most of his chest and arms, while on his feet, he wore a pair of heavy combat boots.

"Who the hell are you?" Alec asked.

"Were you expecting someone else? Perhaps a cute redhead?" The teen replied, before letting out an awkward laugh.

"What did you do to her?" Alec barked, taking a step toward the gunman. He quickly stopped and took a step back once he saw the teen stand up and raise his pistol in the air. "Wait a minute, I know you."

"Yes, of course you do. It's been a long time, Alec."

"Grayson?" Alec gasped in disbelief.

"You got it buddy," he replied, before lifting and pointing his gun at him.

"This isn't possible. You don't look a day over twenty."

"I'm eighteen, actually."

"So, you're a ghost?" Alec asked.

"Something like that," he replied, then let out another awkward cackle. "Let's just say, I'm here to finish something that was left unfinished back in school."

"What was left unfinished?" A sudden loud knock at the door startled Alec, but Grayson appeared unfazed. He looked at the armed teenager for direction.

"Open it," he demanded, still pointing his gun at him.

Alec turned and placed his sweaty palm on the doorknob, turning it before slowly pulling it open. Standing on the other side of the door was the woman from the elevator. After removing her large sunhat and sunglasses she looked up at him and smiled. It took a couple of seconds for Alec to recognize her. The woman appeared to look identical to the last time he had seen her, nearly forty years earlier.

"Mrs. Sutton?" he asked in disbelief.

"Hello son."

"Son?"

"Give me a hug my boy," she said, reaching out to him.

"You're not my mother. Your Eddy's ..." and before he could finish, he caught a glimpse of his own reflection in the mirror beside the door. The eyes looking back at him were not the eyes of a normal fifty-year-old man, nor were the eyes he had grown accustomed to seeing his whole life. They were the eyes of a leopard. They were Eddy Sutton's eyes.

"Come on son, it's time to come home," Mrs. Sutton said, pulling him in and wrapping her arms around him.

"Not if I have anything to do about it," barked Grayson, again laughing tauntingly.

"No Grayson! Please don't do it!" Mrs. Sutton pleaded, while attempting to shield Alec in her arms.

The loud blast from the revolver echoed down the hallway as the two embracing figures fell to the floor. His ears ached from the high pitch ringing and for a moment the ringing was the only thing Alec could hear as he looked over at the body of Mrs.

334

Sutton, on the floor beside him. The bright light was starting to fill the room as he grabbed at his chest and stomach to feel for the gunshot wound but there was nothing there. He looked at Mrs. Sutton to see if she had been hit, but he could not tell as she just smiled back at him, while stroking his hair. As his eyes rolled back into his head, he heard voices directly above him.

"Eddy, can you hear me?" the first voice asked. "Come on baby, open your eyes. Please honey, open your eyes for mom! Did you see that? His eyes opened! His eyes opened!"

"Ok everyone, move back and give the boy some room," said a second voice. "Come on son, everyone's waiting for you to open your eyes."

CHAPTER 23

For almost eight years, the hospital room at Russell Health Center sat mostly stagnant. The voices coming from the small television in the corner of the room competed with the beeping monitors surrounding the unconscious patient.

There had not been much hope for Eddy Sutton since he had arrived by ambulance, nearly eight years earlier. The doctors informed Mrs. Sutton that the likelihood of her son waking from his coma was less likely with each year that passed. However, she never gave up hope and fought with everything in her power with the administrators to keep her child hooked up on all types of life support.

The hallway outside the room was quiet, as the morning shift were just settling in after relieving the evening staff. Like every other morning, there had been no change to Eddy's condition; that was until 6:20 that Sunday morning when one squeeze of the hand changed everything.

The boy's mother screamed hysterically after Eddy squeezed her hand, and the room filled with doctors and nurses. Some family members that were on their way out of the hospital after making their monthly appearance, had also returned to the room. Mrs. Sutton's screams had everyone in a frenzy. They all stood watching anxiously as the head neurologist, Doctor Cole, combed over the data spewing from the bedside monitors. Mrs. Sutton's excitement could not be contained as she continued pleading for him to wake.

"Eddy, can you hear me? Come on baby, open your eyes. Please, honey, open your eyes for mom!" Eddy's eyelids fluttered, before squeezing his mother's hand for a second time. "Did you see that?" she shrieked. "His eyes opened! His eyes opened!"

More people funneled into the room, including some of the night staff that had not yet left their shift. Doctor Cole maneuvered his way through the crowd of people, while frantically scanning over the data on the monitors.

"Ok everyone, move back and give the boy some room," Doctor Cole said, hardly able to contain his excitement. Placing his hand on the boy's head, he said quietly, "Come on son, everyone's waiting for you to open your eyes." The room fell silent as the crowd held their breath in anticipation. Loud gunshots echoed across the room causing everyone to jump. "Somebody turn that damn television down!" demanded the neurologist.

A few more flutters and then Eddy Sutton briefly opened his eyes for the first time in eight years, before closing them once again. The room erupted in cheers as he blinked incessantly. He groaned and furrowed his eyebrows while struggling to open them again, but the blazing light was too intense.

"Something's wrong!" Mrs. Sutton shrieked.

"No, no, it's ok. Can someone kill the florescent lights?" Doctor Cole asked the crowd.

After someone flicked the light switch off, Eddy slowly opened his eyes. While squinting, he first noticed the two doctors standing at the foot of his bed. Everything appeared a little blurry at first and his eyes were painfully dry, but he could make out the white coats and stethoscopes hanging around their necks. As the blurriness faded, he could see their mouths hanging open and their eyes bulging while staring back at him. Behind them were three nurses cheering and embracing each other. Looking to his left, he saw a woman he recognized squeezing his hand. He tried to say something to her but felt like something was stuck in his throat.

"He's trying to tell me something, doctor!"

"Give me a second, Mrs. Sutton," the doctor said, making his way around to her side of the bed. "Now Eddy, I'm going to pull this ventilator out of your mouth, so you can try to speak, ok?" Wide-eyed, he nodded, before the doctor grabbed hold of the ventilator. "Ok after I pull this out, it might take a few moments for your body to remember how to breathe, so try not to panic."

A nurse appeared on the other side of the bed ready to assist. She placed her left-hand underneath Eddy's head while raising it up off the pillow. Eddy stared at her while a tear rolled down the side of his face.

"It's ok dearie, I'm only here to get you sorted. Everything will be grand," she said smiling, in a thick Scottish accent.

"This is going to be very uncomfortable for a minute, but just hang in there, ok buddy?" Doctor Cole said, squeezing on the tube. "Here we go."

After pulling out the tube, the monitor's alarm screamed, before the nurse was able to shut it off. Eddy gagged and coughed, while he continued staring at the nurse still holding his head in her hand. His eyes widened, as he thrusted his chest in the air and struggled to breathe. The nurse, while still holding his head, with her other arm reached for the bag valve mask, but Doctor Cole stopped her by moving it out of range.

"It's ok son, no need to panic," Doctor Cole said, frowning at the nurse. "We have the BVM unit here to help you breathe if needed, but I think you can do it on your own." The boy thrusted his chest up in the air again before the nurse gave the doctor a stern look. "It's ok, he's got this," the doctor said calmly. While Eddy continued to struggle, some of the crowd began to voice their concern. The doctor shushed the room before leaning back over top of his patient. "You can do this son! Just relax and let your lungs take in the air. Nice and easy, son."

"Cyonatic lips ... O2 sats droppin' ... doctor give me the bleedin' mask!" demanded the nurse.

Suddenly the boy gasped, before his back lowered down to the table as his lungs filled with air. Two more big breaths and the room let out a big sigh of relief. Doctor Cole smiled, then snuck a sigh of relief. He and the nurse exchanged a smile and as she was about to say something, seemingly apologetic, to the doctor, Eddy interjected.

"Ellen?" he sputtered.

"Jesus, Mary and Joseph!" Ellen hollered, crossing herself.

"Ellen, is that you?" Eddy stammered, not taking his eyes off the befuddled Scottish nurse.

"Eddy, my son!" Mrs. Sutton shouted, before kissing his hand repeatedly.

With the room still a buzz, Doctor Cole patted the boy's mother on the back and said, "Well, Eddy, you gave us all quite the scare."

"Eddy?" the boy murmured, with a look of confusion. Mrs. Sutton looked at the doctor for a reaction, but he continued to focus on his patient.

"Eddy, I'm Doctor Cole. I know things are probably a little confusing for you now, but they won't be for too long. You are at the Russell Health Center. You had an accident and have been in a coma for quite some time now."

"Detective Cole?" Eddy muttered, trying to clear his throat.

"No, Doctor Cole," chuckled the doctor.

"Doctor? So, you're a detective and a doctor?" Eddy asked, just clear enough for the others to understand.

"Did he say he thinks you're a detective? What's happening?" the boy's mother asked.

"It's ok, Mrs. Sutton. He's going to be a little out of sorts for a while," replied the doctor. "I'm actually amazed at how well he's speaking already. I would have suspected it would have taken days or even weeks before he could speak this clearly. Eddy you can call me Detective Cole if you would like; I've always wanted to be one!" he said laughing. "Now can you tell me how many fingers I'm holding up?"

"Three."

"And how about now?"

"Four."

"Amazing, you're doing great!" The doctor scribbled some notes on a clipboard, then continued, "Can you tell me how old you are?"

"Fifty," he garbled.

"It sounded like he said fifty," Mrs. Sutton said nervously, as the rest of the room looked on.

"Yes, I'm fifty," Eddy said more clearly.

"What do you mean ..." Mrs. Sutton said, before Doctor Cole quickly interjected.

"It's very normal for there to be some confusion after waking from a coma, especially after such a long time. Just give him some time and he will come around. Now Eddy, do you know where you are right now?"

"Yeah, you just told me, Russell Health Center," he replied, with a smirk.

The room chuckled, as the doctor passed him a cup of water. "Here, drink some water. Your mouth is probably very dry. Ok smarty pants, where is the last place you remember being before this place?"

Eddy sipped on the water and appeared to be deep in thought. "I think I was in my hotel room," he said, again trying to clear his throat.

"Hotel room? What hotel room?" Mrs. Sutton asked.

"Mrs. Sutton, please ...", Doctor Cole replied before Eddy interjected.

"At the Marby Hotel."

The doctor smiled, then tapped Mrs. Sutton on the back, while motioning to the family members. "Ok folks, we're going to need to ask all the family to wait outside. Let's give Eddy and his mother some space and let our staff do their work. There will be plenty of time to talk with him later."

Eddy watched in silence as the room began to clear and the doctor gave direction to the other hospital staff in the room. Tears continued to roll down Mrs. Sutton's cheeks, as she continued squeezing her son's hand.

"Mrs. Sutton, may I speak with you outside for a moment?" Doctor Cole asked. After no acknowledgement, he asked again. "Mrs. Sutton? It'll just take a moment ma'am."

The doctor and mother smiled at each other then she kissed her son on the forehead before following Doctor Cole out the door. Eddy watched through the window as the two talked. Left inside the room were only a few of the hospital staff, including a couple of doctors and the three nurses he had seen when he first woke. Their emotions still appeared to be high as they stood in a circle talking. Eddy scoured the group looking for the smaller, elderly nurse who had held his head up while he struggled to breathe, until he found her nestled in between the two larger doctors.

"Ellen?" he blurted. The group stopped abruptly then turned to look at him.

"Yes, dearie?" replied the small, elderly nurse.

"How does he know your name?" asked the younger male nurse.

"Of course, I know her name Jason," Eddy replied, shifting his attention over to him. "She's been my secretary for over twenty years." The three nurses looked at each other with confusion.

"Twenty years?" chuckled the young male nurse, before continuing, "How did you know my name was Jason?"

"Why wouldn't I know your name? We went to the Giants game the other night. You bitched about Buster Posey the whole time."

"Who the blazes is Buster Posey?" Ellen asked.

"Do you know who I am?" Asked the third much older male nurse, after covering his name badge.

"Yes of course, Harold," Eddy replied, with a look of confusion before continuing, "Harold Rhodes ... but that can't be possible."

"Yeah, you're right," he responded, uncovering his name badge that read Harold. Turning his attention to his coworkers, he continued, "Maybe he saw my badge earlier, but how did he know my last name is Rhodes?"

"Because you were my boss. But you died a long time ago," Eddy muttered.

Ellen leaned in towards the boy and asked, "Do you know what your name is, dearie?"

"Yes, of course, its Alec," he replied, then watched as she furrowed her brow. "Why is the doctor and Mrs. Sutton calling me Eddy? He's dead."

Ellen made her way over to the side of the bed, placing her hand on his head. "Your name is Eddy, not Alec, darlin'," she said softly. "And you didn't die, love, you were in a mad, scary wreck. It's sure to be all quite confusin' for you really." The creases in her crow's feet grew as she smiled. He looked into her soft brown eyes, while she rubbed the top of his hand. "You're going to be grand soon enough, I promise."

"I don't understand," he replied, looking around the room at everyone gawking at him. "Why is everyone calling me Eddy? My name is Alec, Alec Jenkins."

CHAPTER 24

A few hours had passed since Eddy's awakening, but the hospital staff was still a buzz. It was not every day one of their patients would wake after being in a coma for several years. Other patients and their families were now aware of what had happened and conversations about the awakening could be heard throughout the entire hospital. Inside the room, Eddy and his mother had been left alone so they could talk.

Doctor Cole and an entourage of nurses entered the room. He smiled, looking over at Mrs. Sutton as she had fallen asleep sitting up in her chair, not letting go of her son's hand. Eddy stared off at the television in the corner of the room.

"She may never let go," Doctor Cole chuckled quietly.

"She fell asleep mid-sentence," Eddy whispered, turning his attention over to the doctor.

"With all the excitement she must be pooped. I see your speech has gotten much better already!"

"Yeah, we've been talking quite a lot since you left."

"Glad to hear," the doctor said, as Mrs. Sutton opened her eyes.

"How are you feeling son?" she asked, rubbing her sore neck.

"I'm a little tired."

"How's your vision," Doctor Cole asked. "Still a bit blurry?"

"Much better now, but my head hurts a little. I can't seem to move my left arm and neither of my legs," he replied with concern.

"It's going to take your body some time to bounce back, but I'm sure you'll be fine. You will not have much energy until you're able to eat and drink some more though, so try to drink as much as you can. I know your throat is tender but try to eat some of the soup they're bringing you. Everything is probably still pretty confusing to you, I bet, huh?"

"Yeah very," Eddy replied, glancing over to his mother.

She smiled and said, "I told him some things that had happened, but it just kind of seemed to make things more confusing."

"Well, there is another doctor that is going to come in here in a few minutes and ask you some questions, Eddy," replied Doctor Cole. The nurses behind the doctor gawked at Eddy, while whispering to one another. "Guys, do you mind?" Doctor Cole barked. Turning back to Eddy, he continued, "This doctor is a specialist who has worked with lots of other people like you. She's going to help you remember things … if that's ok with you?"

"Yes, ok," Eddy replied, turning his attention over to the television tucked away in the back corner. An episode of Cheers was just beginning, and he sang along quietly with the show's opening theme song. "Making your way in the world today takes everything you got." The nurses continued eyeballing him as he continued, "Taking a break from all your worries, it sure would help a lot."

Mrs. Sutton gave the doctor a look of concern, grabbing her son's hand. "I'm just so happy you're back, my boy."

The doctor scribbled something down on his clipboard. "Ok Eddy, so you can move your right arm, but your left arm and legs aren't cooperating? How about your toes?"

"I can't feel my legs or my toes. Am I paralyzed?"

After placing his clipboard on the bed stand, the doctor ran his finger up the bottom of Eddy's foot. "Can you feel this?"

"Yes, a little."

"And how about now?" he asked, doing the same to his other foot.

"Yes, I can," he said, letting out a sigh of relief.

"Well that's a good sign. I think you're just lacking some muscle memory, but that will come back in time."

"How long do you think that will take?" Mrs. Sutton asked.

"There's really no way to tell, but I wouldn't be too concerned. His speech is remarkably clear though, so that's very promising."

"How long have I been in this hospital bed, doctor?"

Doctor Cole glanced over at the boy's mother before reaching for his clipboard. While taking a seat at the foot of the bed, he placed his hand on top of Eddy's leg and replied, "It's been nearly eight years, Eddy."

"Eight years?" Eddy gasped, looking over to his mother. She smiled and nodded, confirming what the doctor had said before she wiped her tears away. "What year is it?" Eddy asked, looking at the doctor, then over to his mother.

"It's 1986," she replied, blowing her nose into a tissue. "We just celebrated your sixteenth birthday last month."

"Sixteenth?" Eddy gulped.

"You have an amazing mother, here Eddy," Doctor Cole said, patting him on the leg. "She's basically lived in this hospital room since the day you got here." He glanced over at Eddy's mother and smiled, as the door swung open and another doctor entered. "Ah there she is," Doctor Cole cheered. "Here's the doctor I was telling you about, Eddy. She's going to help you out with your memory."

Eddy stared at her as it was the same doctor he had first seen upon waking. He watched her intently as her long thick red hair, tied back in a tight ponytail, swung side to side, as she approached.

"Sarah?"

"Well hello, Eddy," she said with a smile, pulling up a chair beside him.

"Sarah, is that really you?"

"My name is Doctor Edwards, but you can call me Carol if you'd like," she replied.

"That's amazing, you just look so much like her," Eddy mumbled, not taking his eyes off the doctor.

"My daughter's name is Sarah," she replied, pulling out a note pad from her coat pocket. "People do say we look a lot alike," she said chuckling while searching for a pen in her other pocket. "Maybe one day you'll get to meet her. She's actually the same age as you."

"I've already met her Doctor Edwards," he replied. The three nurses standing at the foot of the bed looked on.

"Well that's not possible, Eddy," she replied with a chuckle, picking up Doctor Cole's clipboard. "We only moved here about five years ago and ..." she hesitated, scanning the clipboard. After finding what she was looking for she continued, "Well, you would've been celebrating your third anniversary in this room when that happened." Over her shoulder Eddy noticed Ellen whispering something into Doctor Cole's ear.

"Eddy, do you recognize Doctor Edwards?" asked Doctor Cole.

"Well her daughter and I ..." Eddy began to say, before noticing the nurses eagerly awaiting his response as his mother unknowingly squeezed the life from his hand. He glanced over at her and could see the stress written all over her face. Trying to reduce her stress, Eddy let out a sigh and continued, "No, I guess not. I think my brain is still a little messed. It would be nice to meet your daughter, Doctor Edwards."

His mother's grip loosened and her face relaxed. Doctor Edwards smiled while scribbling something onto her notepad. Ellen, Jason and Harold continued to eye Eddy as he turned his attention back to the television.

"I'm sure she'd like that too," she replied. "Eddy, do you mind if I ask you some questions which may help you remember things more clearly?" Eddy, seemingly oblivious to a question being asked, did not respond, but instead continued staring at the three nurses.

"Doctor Edwards is a psychiatrist," Mrs. Sutton said quietly, tapping him on the back of his hand. "Son, she can help you with your memory."

"Yes ok," he said, turning his attention to the doctor. "Sorry Doctor Edwards, this is just all so confusing. I don't really understand what's happening here."

"No need to apologize. I know everything is probably very confusing to you Eddy, but that's to be expected," she replied. "Just try to relax. Now, what is the last thing you remember before waking up in this hospital?"

Eddy remained stoic, examining the room.

"Eddy, the doctor asked you a question," Mrs. Sutton chimed in intensely.

"Give him a minute ma'am," interjected Doctor Edwards.

"Can I have a mirror?" Eddy asked.

"Of course," replied Doctor Edwards, looking over at the nurses. "Can one of you find a mirror?"

"I'll find one," Ellen said. The room sat in silence until she returned moments later holding a compact mirror. "Had one in my bleedin' purse," she said, nearly out of breath, handing it over to Doctor Edwards.

The doctor opened it, then passed it over to Eddy. He took it and rested it on his stomach. After letting out a deep breath, he slowly moved it up to his face, studying his reflection along the way.

His mother had kept his thick black bangs trimmed evenly across the top of his forehead. The sparse hairs on his chin accentuated his pointy jaw, while the dark circles under his eyes contrasted the sheer white backdrop of his skin. Upon seeing his drooping cleft lip and flat nasal bridge, he placed the mirror down on his chest to take a moment to gather himself once again.

"What is it son?"

"Give him a second," replied Doctor Edwards.

After taking another deep breath, he lifted the compact mirror off his chest and lifted it until it met the unsettling eyes looking back at him. The pupil in his left eye was not a regular black circle, instead it resembled a sperm cell as its dark black pupil appeared to be leaking a tale into its sharp orange iris background. His right eye looked much like something you would see in Michael Jackson's Thriller video; with its oddly thin oval black pupil floating amongst a radiant yellow bulbous iris.

"My god," Eddy gasped. "I really am him." After noticing everyone eyeing him, he gazed back into the mirror. "I really am Eddy."

"Of course," replied Mrs. Sutton, as a tear rolled down her cheek. "You're my baby," she said, squeezing his hand in hers. She smiled at Eddy, but he remained stoic, appearing to be still in shock.

"Let's take a break for now," Doctor Edwards said, rising to her feet. "I'll let you guys catch up and come back later. Doctor Cole, I think we should give these two some more time alone."

"Of course," he replied. "Let's clear the room everyone. It's been a crazy morning!"

The room emptied, with exception to Eddy and his mother, who sat in near silence for a few moments. She put her head on his chest while the voices of Sam Malone and Diane Chambers spewed from the television.

"I'm sorry I put you through this mom. It must've been terrible for you all these years," Eddy said, running his hands through her hair.

CHAPTER 25

Eddy and his mother had fallen asleep but were woken when Doctor Cole entered the room, mid conversation, with Doctor Edwards at his side.

"Oh, sorry you two, I didn't realize you were sleeping," he said, approaching the foot of the bed.

"It's ok, I think I've slept long enough," Eddy smirked.

"Somebody's got his sense of humor back," chuckled Doctor Edwards, looking over at the boy's mother.

"How are you feeling, Eddy?" Doctor Cole asked.

"A little better, my headache is gone."

"Do you mind if I ask you some more questions, Eddy?" Dr. Edwards asked, pulling up a chair beside him.

"He's ready," said Mrs. Sutton, smiling at her son. Eddy smiled in return before nodding.

"Yes, I'm ready now."

"Terrific! Now, where were we? Oh yes, let's start with what was the last thing you remember doing before waking up here today?" Doctor Edwards asked, readying her pen and notepad.

"The last thing I kind of remember is my mom and I pulling up to my cousin Grayson's house," Eddy said, as the doctors listened intently. "I remember my mom going inside, and I stayed outside to watch Grayson and his friend, Alec, playing hockey."

"Great! What next?"

"We went to the marsh. I remember trying to catch something in the water, a frog I think, but it kept getting away," Eddy said before taking a long sip of water.

"Ok, then what happened?"

Eddy looked over at his mother, then looked back towards the doctor, then replied, "Umm, that's about it. That's the last thing I remember."

"You're sure that's all you remember, Eddy?" Doctor Edwards asked.

He glanced over at his mother again, then replied, "Yes, I'm sorry but that's the last thing I remember."

"That's ok, you're doing great," she replied. "You've already made tremendous progress." She smiled, then lightly brushed her hand across Eddy's forehead, pushing his bangs off to one side. "Doctor Cole and Mrs. Sutton, would you mind if I spoke with Eddy alone for a few minutes?"

"No, not at all," replied Doctor Cole.

"Ok," replied Mrs. Sutton, before following Doctor Cole to the door.

Upon seeing the door was closed, Doctor Edwards continued. "Eddy, I wanted the others to leave so you could be open and honest with me ok?"

"Ok," he replied, remaining fixated on the door.

"Just know that whatever you say to me will be kept between us," she said, looking back at the door. "I won't tell anyone anything you say, including your mom."

"Ok."

"Do you remember if you and your cousin were close? I mean to say, did you see Grayson often?"

"Yeah, because our moms hung out. We'd usually go to their place."

"And what would you do at their place?"

"Play in the yard. Sometimes we'd catch frogs."

"With Grayson?"

"Yeah, and Alec too."

"And who's Alec?"

"He's Grayson's friend. He lives across the street."

"Were those boys nice to you?" She watched as he recoiled. "It's ok, remember what we discuss is just between you and I."

"Not really."

"So, they were mean to you?

"Yeah, they'd call me names and stuff," Eddy replied before the doctor scribbled on her notepad.

"What kind of names?"

"Oh, you know, things like Whiskers and Tigger. Just like all of the other kids say."

"Well, that's not very nice," muttered the doctor.

"It's because of my eyes and the disorder I have."

"The Cat Eye Syndrome?" asked the doctor, looking at her notepad.

"Yeah, but we just call it CES."

"Your mom and you?"

"Yes."

"And what is it like having CES?"

"I don't like it. The doctors told us it is a chromosomal disorder. My mom says I'm lucky to have it because it gives me these cool looking eyes, but I wish I didn't have it."

"Is that because kids at school tease you about it?"

"Yeah, I guess so. It's ok though. I got used to it after a while," Eddy replied, fighting back tears.

"Well let me tell you something Eddy, I like your eyes and I think they're cool," she said with a big smile and he returned the smiled. "So, you said the last thing you remember is you and the other boys going to the marsh. Do you remember going to the railroad tracks?

Eddy became quiet as she eagerly awaited his response. He glanced off at the television for a few moments before turning his attention back to her. "I'm sorry doctor, I don't remember anything about the tracks."

"That's ok Eddy. It may or may not come back to you, but if it does, you let me know. At this point the only thing that matters is that you're ok," she replied. The two sat in silence for a moment while Eddy gazed over at the television. The doctor wrote some notes down before joining him in watching the television. "Not this movie again," she groaned, rising from her chair before heading over to change the channel.

"Wait, turn it back!" Eddy barked after she had turned the station. "This is a good one!"

"You know this movie?"

"Yes, it's A Soldier's Story. It's one of Denzel's first movies," he replied, after she had returned to the channel.

"Denzel?"

"Yeah, Denzel Washington. You don't know who he is?"

"No sorry, I can't say I do," she replied, seeing Doctor Cole standing in the doorway.

"Doctor Edwards, can I speak with you for a moment?"

"Yes of course. Eddy, I'll be right back!"

The doctors spoke outside the door for a few minutes, while Eddy continued to watch the movie. He glanced over and noticed through the door's window that the three nurses had joined them. Moments later, Doctor Edwards came back into the room.

"Ok Eddy, where were we?" she asked, taking her position in the chair beside him.

"We talked about my CES, trains, and Denzel Washington."

"Oh yes, I see your short-term memory is much better than mine!" she chuckled, then picked up her pen and notepad.

"Eddy, sometimes people will have vivid dreams while in a coma. Do you remember any of your dreams?"

"Yes, I guess so. But they don't seem like dreams."

She smiled, then scribbled something before replying, "Sometimes these dreams are so vivid they can feel real for days or even weeks afterwards. Sometimes people will hear things around them while they're sleeping that will then show up in the dreams. Do you think this may have happened with you and your dreams?"

"Maybe," Eddy replied, thinking back. "But Doctor Edwards, you and your daughter were in my dreams too, and you said yourself that your daughter has never been here."

"That is a bit strange. Perhaps you just heard me talking about Sarah and she entered your dreams that way."

"Maybe, I guess that would make sense," Eddy replied reluctantly.

After a loud knock, the door swung open and two burly men appeared. They both wore dress shirts and jeans. They looked nearly identical, but one man wore a red necktie and the other, a blue one. Both wore a badge on their hip.

Eddy's mother appeared immediately behind the men and quickly stepped past them. "Doctor Edwards, these detectives are insisting they speak with my son."

"Would that be ok with you?" Doctor Edwards asked, turning to Eddy. He did not reply, only stared at the men instead. "What is it Eddy?"

"They were in my dream too," he whispered.

"Really? Are you sure?" Doctor Edwards whispered back.

"I'm positive. What do they want?"

"Doctor Cole mentioned they'd be coming by just to ask you some questions about what happened to you the day you got injured. Are you ok with that? If not, just say the word and I'll tell them to come back another day."

"Questions about what?"

"I think they're trying to find out who did this to you," said Doctor Edwards, placing her hand on his.

"Did what to me?" he asked, glancing over at the two detectives who looked on anxiously.

"Eddy, that day you mentioned being at the marsh, that was the day you went missing."

"Missing?"

"Yes, you were gone for days and nobody knew where you were. You were found in a crate on one of those trains that came from the marsh." She waited for a reaction but only saw Eddy staring blankly over at the two detectives. "The detectives want to find out who put you in that crate because they're pretty sure you didn't go in it on your own." Again, she waited for a reaction and when she did not get one, she continued, "Are you

360

going to be ok to answer a few of their questions?" He did not answer, only continued to stare at the detectives. "Eddy?"

"Yes sorry," he replied, before the doctor turned and nodded at the men nearly hovering over them now.

The detectives moved even closer to the bed, as Doctor Edwards reluctantly moved her chair over a few feet, where she sat and watched as they asked their questions.

"I'm sorry Doctor Edwards, but we really need to ask him some questions alone. Do you mind?" asked the detective with the blue tie.

"Yes, I do mind actually. I'd prefer to stay in the room," she said defensively.

"Fine by us. The boy's mother has to be here for the questioning so you may be as well," replied the detective in the red tie.

Doctor Edwards took a seat while the two men edged up to the side of the bed. Eddy's mother took a seat in the other open chair in the back corner, in front of the television.

The detective sporting the red tie spoke first, "Eddy, we're detectives from Winnipeg. I'm Tom and this is my brother Allen."

"You're brothers?" Eddy muttered, still gawking at them.

"Yes," Allen replied.

"Identical twins," Eddy chuckled.

"Yes, that's right," the brothers replied in unison.

"We've been working on your case since the day you went missing. We wanted to ..." Tom began, before Eddy interjected.

"Tom Neale."

"What's that?" asked Tom.

"You're Tom Neale," Eddy repeated.

The two detectives looked at each other, then back at Eddy. "It's Neale-Bishop actually," they both replied simultaneously. Their response made it apparent it was not the first time they had to explain their hyphenated last name.

After another shared look of confusion, then Tom continued, "We just have a few questions about the day you were injured."

"So, you are Tom Neale-Bishop ... and you're Allen Neale-Bishop?" Eddy interjected again.

"Yes, that's right," replied Tom. The detectives and the doctor exchanged a look of bewilderment. Tom then continued, "What can you tell us about the day of your disappearance Eddy?"

"Well, as I told the doctor here, I don't remember anything about the train. All I remember is going to my cousin's house, then playing with Grayson and Alec by the ..."

"What is it Eddy? Do you remember something else?" Doctor Edwards pressed. Mrs. Sutton turned her attention away from the television to hear what he had to say.

"I do remember the train. Those guys threw rocks at me, so I hid in one of the trains to get away," he said, then coughed and

362

reached for the glass of water sitting just out of reach. Allen picked up the glass and handed it to him. "Thanks."

"No problem. Please go on," Tom said anxiously, after taking back the empty glass.

"I don't remember much else except ... just that look in his eye."

"Who?"

"Grayson. He had this real evil look in his eye. Kind of like ... it was the same look he had in my dreams at the Marby Hotel."

The two detectives looked at each other appearing to be confused before asking in unison, "The Marby Hotel?"

"He's been recalling some visions he had while in the coma," Doctor Edwards intervened. Turning to Eddy, she continued, "So Grayson was in your dreams as well?"

"Yes. I think he showed up at my hotel and shot me. Only it wasn't me he shot; it was Alec. If that makes any sense."

"Alec ... as in Alec Jenkins?" Tom asked.

"Yes. I know it sounds strange, and it's hard to explain, but in my dreams, I was Alec Jenkins at the age of fifty."

The detectives glanced at one another before Allen asked, "Doctor Edwards, has anyone mentioned anything to Eddy about Alec?"

"No, not that I'm aware. We'd only just begun to scratch the surface when you walked in," she replied.

"What about Alec?" Eddy asked the brothers who appeared reluctant to answer. "What is it?" Eddy asked again, this time directing his question to Allen. The detective looked back at his brother again, then over at the doctor and she nodded, giving her approval.

"A few months after we found you, Alec Jenkins went missing."

"Missing?" Eddy asked.

"Yes missing," Allen replied. "We never did find him. He's most likely dead, as it's been almost eight years. His poor parents have been through hell and back."

"I can't even imagine what they must be going through," said Doctor Edwards.

"He actually would've graduated this week," Allen continued. "His parents told us they're going to go to the ceremony, so we figured we'd go as well."

"He was supposed to graduate this week?" Eddy asked.

"Yes, that's right," Tom replied.

"Wait, what's the date today?" Eddy demanded.

"It's June 20th, why?" Allen asked.

"June 20th," Eddy replied, mulling over the information. "That would be the six month and twentieth day, six twenty …"

"What is it Eddy?" asked Doctor Edwards.

"There's going to be a shooting today, at the high school!" Eddy shouted.

"Shooting?" Doctor Edwards asked.

"Yes. It's Grayson, he's the one who's going to do it!"

"Slow down son, what you are you talking about?" Allen asked.

"Detectives, there's no time to explain, but you need to find Grayson Spencer right now. He's the shooter! Today is six twenty and it is the day it all happens! It all makes sense now."

"Ok son, just relax," Tom said, looking over at the doctor who looked just as confused as he did.

"I'm not going to slow down. You guys need to go now and find him. I'm telling you; he's going to do it today!"

"Eddy, you need to calm down," Doctor Edwards said, placing a hand on his chest. "Is this coming from one of your dreams?" she asked, sounding skeptical.

"If he's telling you something is about to happen, I'd listen to what he's saying," his mother barked, turning her attention away from the television.

"Listen Eddy, it has been quite the morning and I think you're just a little confused," Doctor Edwards said, patting his chest. "All of these questions have got you riled up, but these detectives can't arrest someone because of something you saw in your dreams."

The room sat in silence while waiting for a response from Eddy. He stared back at the detectives, then over to the doctor.

As it was apparent that they were not going to listen to him he turned to his side, facing away from them.

"You guys are going to be sorry," he muttered.

"We'll come back later," Allen said quietly to the doctor, before the brothers made their way to the door.

"Hey detectives, do you know who Denzel Washington is?" Eddy asked, with his back towards them.

"Never heard of him," they blurted in unison, before leaving the room.

"Well, that was a waste of time," he heard Tom say from the hallway.

"Don't worry about them Eddy," Doctor Edwards sighed. "They were hopeful you'd have something for them and they're just a little frustrated." After getting to her feet she continued, "I'll come tomorrow, in the meantime, get some rest."

"Tomorrow is going to be too late," Eddy persisted, grabbing her by the arm, exposing her wrist band, one only a patient would wear. She pulled her hand away before heading towards the door. "Did you get your results back yet?"

"Results?" Dr. Edwards asked, glancing down at her wrist.

"Yes, from your mammogram?"

"How did you …"

"Breast cancer, right?" Eddy interjected.

"Yes, but I just found out two days ago so how could you have known that I …" she trailed off, staring at him.

366

"Sarah told me," he replied. "In what you keep referring to as my dreams."

Taken aback she stood and stared at him for a moment. "Ok, what else did Sarah tell you?"

"She told me lots about you. She told me that you'd never let her get a tattoo because you always regretted getting yours." Doctor Edwards looked at him inquisitively. "The bird cage on your lower back," he said without hesitation. "She told me you got it in your twenties after your parakeet died."

"Oh my ..." she gasped. "There's no way you could have known that!" She took a seat on the edge of the bed, trying to collect her thoughts, and Eddy lay silent. "It's such a bad tattoo," she conceded chuckling. "I was young, and it was the first pet I'd ever lost."

Mrs. Sutton, who had been sitting quietly in the back of the room, made her way over to the bed and patted the doctor on the shoulder, before saying, "I'd say it's time to get those detectives to grab Grayson before it's too late, wouldn't you?"

CHAPTER 26

The front page of the Russell newspaper on June 21st, 1986 featured a photo of several police cars out front of the local high school with the heading:

'LOCAL BOY WAKES FROM COMA TO SAVE FELLOW CLASSMATES.'

Also, on the front cover was a photo of Tom Neale-Bishop and Allen Neale-Bishop sitting on the hood of a police car, grinning ear to ear. The caption below read 'The Neale-Bishop detectives say surviving victim saved several lives.'

The Russell Health Center had become a complete zoo. Several police patrolled the front of the hospital while two guards stood outside of Eddy Sutton's hospital room. The boy was a hero and news reporters from across the country wanted an interview, but Doctor Edwards and Doctor Cole were not letting anyone in to see him. With all the chaos happening outside, Eddy Sutton and his mother remained alone inside, within the quiet sanity of the hospital room. Eddy had been asleep for most of the morning and early afternoon but was woken up after hearing a nurse and his mother talking at the door.

"Sorry son, I didn't mean to wake you," she said, placing a bouquet of roses on the television stand amongst a virtual garden of other bouquets.

"That's ok mom," Eddy said yawning. "More flowers?" he asked, watching his mother tuck a rolled up newspaper behind the television.

"Yes, can you believe it? The nurses just keep bringing them. I think the whole town has sent you some at this point! Looks like your left arm is coming around, hey?"

"Yeah I guess so," Eddy replied. "I just wish my legs would start working."

"It'll come son, just try to be patient," she said, making her way over to him. "Doctor Cole said you'll probably need to do some physio, but it will just be a matter of time before you're up and at it." She smiled then kissed him on the forehead. "I got you some chicken noodle soup and iced tea while you were sleeping. The doctor said you should try to keep to soft foods for a while because of that tube that was down your throat."

"What does it say?" Eddy asked.

"What?"

"The newspaper. I saw you trying to hide it.".

"Sorry son, I just wasn't sure if you'd be up for it yet," she replied, retrieving it. "It's on the front cover!"

"Oh, big story I see," Eddy said. "Can you read the article to me?"

"Are you sure you're up for it, son?"

"I'm not a child anymore, mother," Eddy protested.

"Ok fine. It says: 'local boy wakes from coma and saves students. At approximately 2:15 yesterday afternoon a tip from an unnamed source led police to the arrest of a seventeen-year-old male student who, credible sources say, had intended on executing a mass shooting at the Russell High School. Several guns, protective armor, and a suicide note were all found in the student's locker. Although police would not reveal where they received the tip, reliable sources said the two arresting detectives were reportedly visiting a sixteen-year-old male who had recently awoken from a coma at the Russell Health Center. More details to follow in the coming days as we receive more information on this case.' You're a true hero, my boy."

"Thanks mom," Eddy replied, as Doctor Edwards entered. Mrs. Sutton took a seat in the chair in front of the television.

"How's our hero feeling?" Doctor Edwards asked, perching at the end of his bed.

"I'm good thanks," Eddy replied. "Did you see what they wrote in the newspaper?"

"Yes, and now thanks to them it's chaotic around here today." She looked over to see Eddy's mother eating a sandwich with one hand while changing the channels on the other. "Anything good on?"

"Oprah," she replied with a mouthful of ham and cheese.

"Boy, does she ever like that show," she chuckled before turning her attention back to her patient. "Eddy, the two detectives are in the hall and they wondered if they could speak with you again. Would that be ok?"

"Yes, sure."

After the doctor gave a thumbs up to the officers peering through the window, the door swung open and the twin detectives entered.

"How's our hero doing?" Tom asked, peaking his head around the door with a bouquet of flowers in his hand.

"He's doing great," said Mrs. Sutton, reaching for the flowers. "Here, I'll take those from you. Thank you, that's very kind and thoughtful of you detective." Eddy watched his mother as she placed the flowers with the others. "These are just beautiful," she said before taking a seat back in front of the television.

"Let me guess, Oprah?" Allen chuckled.

"You know it," Doctor Edwards replied.

"Listen Eddy, we just wanted to thank you for everything you did yesterday," started Tom. "You truly saved a lot of lives by being so persistent. That kid had a mission to hurt as many people as he could, and you stopped him just in time."

"What did Grayson's suicide note say?" Eddy asked.

Tom looked at his brother, slowly shaking his head before replying, "I'm sorry son, but we're not at liberty to say."

"Come on now!" Mrs. Sutton snapped. "You wouldn't listen to him yesterday when he told you this was going to happen, and now you're telling him you won't tell him what the letter said? And because of what, police protocol? You guys would've had a lot of young dead people's blood on your hands if Eddy wasn't so persistent. I think it's the least you can do."

"Fine," Allen growled. "But you cannot let anyone else know of this information. If these reporters get a hold of this, we will probably lose our jobs."

"We're not talking to any reporters, so you don't have anything to worry about," Eddy assured.

"His letter was pretty messed up," Allen continued. "He had planned on killing specific teachers and any students that got in the way. There was some nonsense explaining why, but I'll spare you the details as the kid was just evil and full of hatred. None of it made much sense."

"He mentioned you in his letter, Eddy," Tom added.

"He did?" Eddy gulped

"Yes," Tom replied. "He admitted to sticking you in the crate on the train. We always suspected his involvement but were never able to find sufficient evidence."

"Is she going to be ok hearing this Doctor Edwards?" Allen asked quietly, motioning over to Eddy's mother.

"I'll be fine, just continue," Mrs. Sutton sighed.

372

"Are you sure?" Allen asked. "I mean, this is your nephew we're talking about."

"I'm sure, please continue," she insisted.

Tom glanced over at Doctor Edwards and after she nodded, he continued. "There was one other thing in the letter Eddy. Nobody knows about this so, again we're asking you, your mother, and you Doctor Edwards, to keep this quiet." All three nodded before he continued. "We now know from Grayson's letter that he also had something to do with the disappearance of Alec Jenkins."

"Is Alec dead?" Eddy asked.

"Yes, I'm afraid so Eddy. There's now no question in our minds that Grayson killed him." Allen said solemnly. "Probably to keep what he had done to you a secret. We can't prove it yet, but without getting into detail we're fairly certain that Alec was going to come forward days after your disappearance, before Grayson stopped him."

"There's one problem with nailing him to Alec's death though," Tom added.

"What's that?" Eddy asked.

"We don't have his body," the brothers replied in unison. Allen continued, "And without the body, it makes things a heck of a lot more difficult."

"You don't think Grayson's letter would be enough?" Eddy asked.

"Possibly," Tom replied. "But juries don't like to convict juveniles unless they're absolutely positive. If we could find Alec's body, there would be no doubt."

"And you're hoping I can help you find Alec's body?"

"Bingo," Allen replied enthusiastically. "With what you were able to do yesterday with those dreams of yours, or whatever they were, we hoped you could help us again. I know it's a long shot, but is there anything you can think of that happened in your dreams that could lead us to his body?"

"Not really. I mean I can't even remember most of those dreams anymore," he replied, lifting a spoonful of soup to his lips.

"Ah, we knew it was a long shot, but thought we'd at least ask," said Tom.

"Sorry guys. I wish I could've helped out."

"I think you've helped enough," Allen replied. "We should get going. Can we get you anything before we go, Eddy?"

"No, I'm ok thanks. My mom has been taking good care of me!"

"How's the soup?" his mother shouted from in front of the television.

"Very good, thanks mom," he replied, glancing over at her.

"Hey where did those flowers come from?" he asked, holding a spoon full of soup up to his lips.

374

"They're from the detectives. Aren't they beautiful? I love the bright orange color," Mrs. Sutton replied.

"Guy at the flower shop said they're tiger lilies," Tom said.

"Said they smelled the nicest," added Allen.

"You're certainly right about that," Eddy said with a big smile. "Hey detectives, I think I know where you'll find Alec's body."

"Really? Where?" the detectives asked in unison.

"At the Marby Hotel."

"Where he worked?" Allen asked.

"He worked at the Marby?" Eddy asked.

"Yeah, he mentioned doing some yard work there," replied Tom, before looking over, wide-eyed, at Allen.

"Check behind the hotel in the garden ... that's where he buried him."

"Are you sure?" asked Tom.

"As sure as I was yesterday," he replied. "I would start looking beneath the orange tiger lilies."

"Thanks Eddy, we will!" Tom exclaimed. "Come on Allen, let's go!"

As the detectives exited the room, Doctor Edwards rose to her feet while saying, "Well this is all very exciting! I need to get going. Do you need anything Eddy?"

"No thanks, doctor," he replied, staring at the orange lilies. As the doctor reached for the door handle, he shouted, "Oh hey, Doctor Edwards!"

"Yes Eddy?"

"Do you think I could see Sarah soon?"

"Yes, she's actually coming by here today. She said she wanted to see you," Doctor Edwards replied with a big smile, before exiting.

He smiled, thinking of seeing Sarah again and wondered if she would be as beautiful as he had remembered.

"What's happening on Oprah, mom?" Eddy shouted, taking another sip of his soup.

"Not much. Kind of a boring episode. She's got some bigwig businessman on talking about running for President."

"Oh yeah?"

"Yeah, some guy named Trump. Seems like a real know-it-all. There's no way this guy would ever win if he ran for President."

"Oh, I wouldn't be so sure of that," Eddy muttered.

Manufactured by Amazon.ca
Bolton, ON

16500871R00222